Heart and Soul

by Fred L. Helms

ISBN 978-1-938467-97-4

This is a work of fiction. All the characters in this book are fictitious, and any resemblance to actual persons, living or dead, is purely coincidental. The names, incidents, dialogue, and opinions expressed are products of the author's imagination and are not to be construed as real.

Published by

◤ köehlerbooks ™

210 60th Street
Virginia Beach, VA 23451
212-574-7939
www.koehlerbooks.com

Publisher
John Köehler

Executive Editor
Joe Coccaro

Dedication

This book is dedicated to those who have saved lives through donating organs or tissue and to the many families who have graciously allowed donation from a loved one, even in their grief and sorrow over the loss. Organ donation is truly a wonderful gift.

It is dedicated to the people who make transplantation work: the nurses, doctors, coordinators, and other professionals in hospitals who help families with the donation decision, as well as those who work with donation agencies and with transplant programs.

Finally, this book is dedicated to the memory of the doctors, coordinators, flight crews, and other professionals who have lost their lives as they worked to save others through organ donation and transplantation.

Heart
AND
S❤ul

A medical suspense novel

Fred L. Helms

VIRGINIA BEACH
CAPE CHARLES

"On a long flight, after periods of crisis and many hours of
fatigue, mind and body may become disunited until at times
they seem completely different elements,
as though the body were only a home with which
the mind has been associated but by no means bound."

CHARLES A. LINDBERGH
The Spirit of St. Louis

1

Counting the Beats

THE GIRL'S MIND raced with excitement, anticipating tomorrow's events. She thought about what she would wear, about how she would fix her hair, about her friends, about her routine. In her mind she rehearsed the dance, step by step, move by move, almost hearing the whir of the silver baton as it flew, spinning through the air.

Even though the house around her was silent, her excitement was palpable, and she struggled to settle down, to sleep. She had to calm down. It was going to be a long day tomorrow.

She deliberately forced her body and mind to still, concentrating on the quietness.

In the stillness, she could hear the old house creaking and the wind rustle in the branches. She nestled deeper under the covers, closing her eyes and trying to relax. It was warm and quiet in her bed. Quiet. She lay still.

Gradually, the girl became aware of her own heartbeat. She could hear a gentle pounding in her ears. The beat seemed faster than usual.

She moved her hand to her chest and counted the beats, watching the seconds flash on the digital clock sitting on the bedside table. She used the flashing dots as a timer: ninety. She remembered her health teacher saying that the average was seventy to eighty. She knew hers was normally slower than that—the rate of a runner. Her track coach said his resting heart rate was 55.

She slowed her breathing, taking long, deep breaths and exhaling with the rhythm of her heart. Four beats in... four beats out... deep, diaphragmatic breaths like her choir director had taught her. She continued the deep breaths, and listened in the darkness.

Her heart began to slow, just a little at first, but then more noticeably. She smiled, happy that she could have such control.

As she concentrated on her heartbeat, now tuned in to her body, she felt her pulse. It was in her right arm, just above her elbow, that she felt it first. Her arm was pressed down on the bed under her pillow. She could feel the strong *swish, swish* that correlated perfectly with her heartbeat. How odd to feel it so strong.

Curious now, she tried to see how many places she could feel her pulse. She felt it on the inside of her left foot, then in her temple, right where her head touched the pillow. Strong in her neck, softer on the inside of her knee... *swish swish, swish swish*... it was as steady as the clock.

She rolled over to get more comfortable, and there was an immediate increase in her heart rate. But, as she listened, it began to slow. She smiled again.

It was as if her heart was talking to her. She puzzled over this for a moment, her mind attuned to her heart.

It was a soothing sound. As if it were saying, "All is well."

Though she couldn't remember it, she had heard this sound since she was in her mother's womb. Her heart had been beating before she could hear or even be aware. Before she had developed into the being that she was now, before the knot of protoplasm that would become her brain had begun to form. For her, so far, it was a forever sound.

Closing her eyes, she turned and curled into a fetal position, snuggling into the soft mattress and cozy covers of her bed.

Gradually, her breathing became deep and regular on its own, and her mind and body calm, serene. But the beat of her heart continued in her ears, still just as strong, but now slower, peaceful.

As she drifted off to sleep, she smiled, comforted by the sound, knowing it would continue. It would always be with her.

The girl slept the sleep of the innocent, dreaming of singing, dancing, and light.

2

Gift of Life

WITH A HEAVY heart, David McAllister, or Dr. Mac as his patients and co-workers called him, pushed his thoughts aside and leaned over with the ten blade to open up the donor's chest.

He had begun the case as he always did, reviewing the chart, the donor's name, how and when death was declared, and the blood type. He had already learned the patient's history and her cause of death when the first call came to him earlier that day. It was a sad case. A young, healthy girl had been killed in a car accident. Her family was a wreck. Even in their grief, though, they had made the decision to donate, to give a wonderful gift to people they didn't even know. He knew lives would be saved as a result, but their raw grief made his heart ache.

At times like this, he envied the kidney guys. They were lucky. At least a lot of their donors were alive. Not so with heart transplants. *All* of his donors were dead.

David gently reached into the donor's chest and began to inspect the beating heart. It was a good heart. He was relieved. On the flight down, he had been worried. Even though the donor was young, car accidents can easily damage the heart. The girl had chest injuries and even a chest tube to re-inflate her left lung. Thank God there was no damage to the heart. This was probably Martha's last shot.

He looked up, turned his head slightly, ordering Lisa Kelly, the donation coordinator, to call Birmingham and tell his assistant to get Martha Lake ready for the OR.

Dr. Carver York, the liver and kidney surgeon, stood next to David and quickly did his assessment. "The liver is okay, but there is an anomaly that may keep us from using the pancreas. We may have to call about islet cells," York said.

Lisa was writing in the chart with one hand and holding a phone with the other, making arrangements with the coordinator in Birmingham. Things were about to get hectic. Fast. Organ procurement cases are not an everyday occurrence in most operating rooms. Many local hospitals, like this one, may only do three or four a year. This hospital, a three-hundred-and-fifty-bed regional in a city of only ninety thousand, had its share of donors, but this particular staff, except for the scrub tech, had never done one.

David could tell the surgical staff was tense. Organ donation had a completely different dynamic than other surgeries. They weren't used to dealing with death like this. It was unusual for any of their patients to die in surgery, but this was different. Organ donors, like this one, were dead *before* the surgery.

And this donor was just so young. He glanced again back up at the girl's face and was struck by how the spattering of freckles across the bridge of her nose made her look like a mere child.

Feeling the sudden heavy silence that filled the OR, David knew the surgical staff was having a difficult time. Yes, they supported organ donation. But that didn't change their uneasiness.

"Okay, guys, look alive," David barked. "Things are about to move quickly."

Tossing a glance to the nervous third year resident in the corner, he asked, "Newton, why are things about to move quickly?"

Startled at being addressed, the resident stuttered, "Because you're about to cross-clamp the aorta."

"And...?" prodded David patiently.

The resident flushed, "Oh, uhm... as soon as you cross-clamp the aorta, the clock starts ticking for ischemic time."

"Which is...?" David began bending back over his work.

"The ischemic time is the time from when the heart no longer gets oxygenated blood, usually when the donor's heart stops, to when blood flow is returned as the heart is restarted in the recipient," the resident hurriedly recited. "This is important because organ function after transplant is dependent on ischemic time. Too long an ischemic time and the heart won't function at all."

Not receiving an immediate pat on the back for his recitation, the resident pointed to the nearby coolers, and continued nervously.

"Cold ischemic time is preferable to warm, so the organ is cooled down and placed in a cooler on ice while being transported to the recipient. Even cold, though, there is a finite amount of time before organ function will be compromised. So... um... things have to go fast from here on out."

"Right you are," muttered David as he completed his final inspection of the heart muscle. He smiled. This was a good heart.

He nodded to all the waiting surgeons around him, and leaned in closer to begin the cross-clamp.

Lisa's face broke into a relieved smile as she reported the good news to the transplant coordinator up in Birmingham. "Clarissa, the heart is good. No problems with it. They just started to cross-clamp and Dr. Mac will be headed your way in no time."

She clipped her Motorola shut, closed her eyes and breathed steady breaths... *one... two... three...* She loved her job. She did. And knowing that someone was about to receive a life-saving transplant made all her work worthwhile. But she was tired. Exhausted. At this point, she'd been working straight on this case for over thirty hours. Her pager had gone off at a few minutes after seven the evening before, and that was *after* she had only been home from work for less than two hours. All she'd wanted to do was kick up her heels and eat a pint of Ben & Jerry's Chocolate Fudge Brownie.

Groaning a little, she took off her watch and stuffed it in her pocket. She didn't want to be tempted to clock watch. She needed these next few hours to go by as fast as possible, and right now, the minutes on her rose gold watch seemed to be taunting her.

As the regional organ donation coordinator, she was the first-line soldier in the organ transplant battle, a battle against time, grief, death, and circumstances. She was responsible for getting to the hospital quickly after a referral and evaluating whether donation was even possible.

Last night, her job had been hard. If donation was possible, it was her responsibility to discuss donation with the family of the deceased to get consent for donation. Imagine having to approach a grieving family, having to confirm their nightmare is true that their loved one is dead, then having to ask if they will consent to donate their loved one's organs. No matter how many times she did it, the rawness of families' grief seeped into her heart.

And last night? Last night had hurt more than usual. True, it was always a lot harder when the donor was young. But this had felt different. More somehow. More shock... more pain... more grief...

3

Rachel

RACHEL WOKE UP before her alarm went off.

Light was just beginning to filter through the blinds, casting even, horizontal shadows on the wall, like a ladder to the sky.

She lay in bed a moment, warm and snug, listening again, gradually becoming aware of the sounds outside her window. It was fall, and she could hear the rustle of the wind in the live oak trees that stood in a ring around her house. Far off, she heard the sound of an outboard motor starting up at the boat landing. *Someone going out early to see if they could catch some shellcrackers,* she thought.

Then she heard the mockingbird that lived outside her window. She'd nicknamed him Max about a year ago. She smiled contentedly as she bathed in his first song of the morning. It trilled from low to high, three notes down and three notes up: one and two—three and four, one and two—three and four. Then he would pause to listen.

Listening to Max, she heard another familiar sound outside, and smiled again. It was her little horse, Quando, trotting around the pasture by her house. She heard a soft whinny, followed by a little snort. He was saying good morning.

Sitting up in bed and stretching, now fully awake, she felt a tingle go up her spine. This was the day that she had been waiting for! It was finally here! She caught her breath in anticipation.

First of all, it was the Friday of the big game, the biggest football game of the year. And this year, it was homecoming. Jackson County was their archrival, and everyone at Marianna High couldn't wait to trample them.

She was a junior at Marianna High. She ran track, sang in the choir, and played clarinet in the band. But, during football season *she* was a majorette. Excitement, nervousness, and pride fluttered through her. She was the *only* junior majorette.

It'd actually been a dare at first. Rachel and her best friend, Susan, had a long-running tradition of daring each other to do outlandish stuff, and back in August, Susan had dared her to try out for the majorettes. It was stupid, really. It was meant to be a joke. Only seniors were majorettes.

She didn't understand completely why Beverly, the head majorette, went against years of tradition. Yes, her tryout had been great and she was athletic, with long legs and flowing blond hair, but she was a *junior*. And she'd *made* it!

Rachel went to the window and opened the blinds, swooping them up so swiftly that the mockingbird just outside flew over to another tree. It had rained the night before, and there were still puddles, reflecting the bright morning sun.

Going into her bathroom, she shook the tangles out of her long hair and started brushing her teeth. She looked in the mirror, and could see the excitement already sparkling in her dark blue eyes. She leaned forward, checking her smile.

Suddenly, she noticed a little rainbow on her face, and was puzzled for a second. Someone had put a tattoo on her cheek! She gasped and stared at it.

Weird, she thought. It was a perfect little rainbow, vivid red to deep violet, shimmering on her cheek. She shook her head a little. It sparkled, moving across her cheek to her chin. She laughed at herself. It was just the sun reflecting off the beveled edge of the mirror, spangling the colors onto her face. She put her finger up to see if the rainbow would show on it. Then she stood still, gazing into the mirror at the vibrant colors on her cheek.

She smiled, her cheek dimpling through the colors.

She loved rainbows. Always had. There was a big poster of

a rainbow on her bedroom wall, taken during a storm in the mountains, that had *Follow Your Heart* across the bottom. She'd always been a sucker for rainbows. But, her favorite was a beautiful blown glass heart her grandmother had given her. It was a deep blue and had a colorful rainbow embedded inside the glass that sparkled and shone when the light hit it. She kept it safe, right on her night table beside her bed.

After one more glance at the rainbow on her cheek, she turned and stepped to her closet, still smiling at the unexpected, thinking again what a wonderful day this would be.

She hurriedly pulled on her favorite shirt. She was a hard-core Florida fan, and this shirt had been her undershirt every day since football season began, and she would wear it every day until the last game—hopefully, a bowl championship game. Her mother hated it, constantly reminded her it was filthy—even when it wasn't—and made her wash it every other day. She was actually pretty surprised her mother hadn't slipped in her room one night and kidnapped the hated tee.

Despite her mother's protests, this shirt was her favorite. It was already soft and slightly faded, the orange more than the blue. It was short, sometimes leaving her belly button in view, fit snugly, and had a low neckline. Most days no one could tell she had it on, particularly as the days grew cooler and she started wearing sweatshirts and sweaters to school.

She stepped into her jeans and slid on a baggy sweatshirt. After one more glance in the mirror, she went to get her shoes and bag.

Rachel could hear sounds coming from the kitchen and knew her mother was up. Her father was home, so her mother would be up earlier, and would probably make breakfast. She liked it when her father was home. His job on an oil rig kept him away a lot. Another good thing when he was home—they had two cars.

She pulled the new driver's license out of her purse, just to look at it again. It really wasn't a bad picture, though they had told her not to smile. It had her full name and address, her birth date, and her height and weight: *Rachel Alexandria Raines, 5' 9", 125 lbs., Sex: F, Eyes: blue, Hair: Blond*. She had already memorized her license number: *3285113*. There was also a little red heart under her picture with *donor* printed on it.

Susan had made a face when the lady asked if she wanted to be a donor, but Rachel had quickly piped, "Sure. If I can help someone else after I die, that would be cool."

She just got the permanent license in the mail the previous day. She gave the plastic a little kiss, did a little victory dance, and slid the license back into her purse.

Her mother called out.

"Breakfast is ready."

With a smile and a quick step, Rachel headed to the kitchen. She opened a cabinet and got out a packet of oatmeal. Her mom had already set out a little jar of Tupelo honey and had some hot water ready to go on the stove. Rachel had oatmeal and honey every morning. Tupelo was her favorite.

The side door to the kitchen clanged open as her dad tromped in.

"Good morning, babe," he said, and ruffled her hair.

Her dad was a bear of a man, very muscular, face and arms always tan from working in the sun. His hair was longer than usual. He hadn't a chance to get a haircut, so it was tied in a small ponytail behind his head.

She beamed at her dad.

"You look like a surfer dude," she said, smirking.

Her dad reached back and tugged on the ponytail, giving her a wink and a smile.

Her mom stood in the kitchen, pouring two glasses of orange juice. Her mom was a lot like her: tall, slim, pretty. Her hair was also in a ponytail, and reached down her back. People in town often mistook her and her mom for sisters.

As in most families, her parents had divided roles. Her mom was home most of the time, and she'd dubbed herself the disciplinarian. Her dad was twice her size and commanded a gang of stevedores at work, but he was the soft touch. He smiled contentedly as he watched his wife and daughter sit down with him at the table. He was immensely proud of his only daughter, and everyone knew it.

As they ate, Rachel chattered about her upcoming day. School would let out early at two, she had to be at the band room at five, and the game started at seven. There would be a homecoming dance after the game. Rachel's excitement bubbled over, and infected both her parents.

"I won't have much time after school to get ready for everything," she said, smiling at her dad. "Can I use the car?"

Her mom chimed in, looking at her husband. "It'll have to be yours, I have a lot to do."

"I got my *real* license, it came in the mail yesterday," squealed Rachel. She pulled it out of her bag with dramatic flourish to proudly show her dad. He took it and gave it a look, knowing the importance that this little piece of plastic held for his daughter.

He smiled and nodded as he passed the card back to her. "Okay, but just to school and back, and no passengers for a while."

"But *Dad*," Rachel pleaded, her eyes widening, "Can't Susan come, too? I promise I'll be careful."

"Just Susan?" asked the dad, looking over at the mom. Her mom gave a slight nod, graciously allowing her dad some control.

"Yes, sir," Rachel smiled, happiness twinkling in her dark blue eyes.

She shot up, gave her mom and dad a quick hug, grabbed an apple from a bowl on the counter, and ran out to check on Quando.

The little horse met her at the gate, nuzzling at her, but she kept the apple hidden behind her back. She laughed as he sniffed under her arm. "We can't go for a ride today, Quando, but tomorrow is Saturday and we'll ride all the way to the creek, I promise." Quando pranced, shaking his head up and down as if he understood, and she gave him the apple. She loved the little horse, and they had spent many hours racing down the trails to the creek and in the fields around her house.

The horse nudged her with his head, not enough to knock her off balance, but enough to make her wrap her arm around his neck. She laughed again. It was his way of giving her a hug. She squeezed his neck and gave his ears one last scratch, then turned and ran back inside the house to wash up and brush her teeth. Her mom and dad were still at the table, drinking coffee and talking in low tones.

Five minutes later, she breezed through the kitchen, backpack in hand, grabbed the keys to her dad's car from the hook as if she had been doing this for years, and ran outside.

Her mom looked at her dad and shook her head, the beginning of tears welling up in her eyes.

"Our little girl is all grown up," she said, her words clipped.

Her dad stood and walked over to the window, watching as Rachel almost skipped across the yard. He wanted to keep his face away from his wife, so she wouldn't see that he had tears in his eyes as well.

The mockingbird also watched as Rachel walked up to the father's car, pride in her step. He would usually dive-bomb her when she was this close to the nest, but this time he just watched, turning his head sideways to see her better.

She opened the door on the big Lincoln, and slid into the driver's seat. It took her a minute to get the wide front seat forward so that she could reach the steering wheel. She took the time to adjust the mirrors, just like she had learned in Driver's Ed. The steering wheel seemed to be higher than normal. Rachel was used to her mom's Honda Accord and didn't realize that the steering wheel on the Lincoln was adjustable.

She dutifully buckled her seat belt, slid forward, and then started the big V-8. She had to sit up high to see. She pulled the shifter down into drive and started out the gravel driveway. When she stopped at the road, the big car jerked to a halt with a jolt, rocking back and forth. The brakes were much more sensitive than on the Honda. So was the accelerator. She started out into the street, peering over the big steering wheel.

· · ·

It was only a few blocks to the school, but by the time she got there, Rachel already felt more comfortable with the car. She had to park in the student area, looking around as she drove in.

Ricky Thomas was just getting out of his red Ford pick-up when she parked.

"Look at you!" he said.

She grinned as she closed the door.

"It's my dad's car."

"Nice," said Ricky. He wasn't talking about the car. But she didn't notice.

Rachel took her backpack from the back seat, slammed the big door, and walked across the lot with Ricky. He was a *senior*.

Classes were a blur to Rachel. At lunch she and Susan planned their whole afternoon and evening. They would meet at her dad's car as soon as school let out. She'd take Susan to her house, then go home to get ready for the game. Then, she'd pick Susan up and head to the game. As soon as the game was over, they'd head to Rachel's house to get ready for the dance there. They would have to have their clothes ready to change into quickly, and since Susan lived several miles away, this seemed like the best plan.

Everyone was talking about the dance, so Rachel and Susan stopped by the gym on their way back to class. The junior class always decorated for the dance, as a gift for the seniors. When Rachel and Susan stepped into the gym, they were awed. It looked beautiful. Several of the junior girls on the decorating committee and their mothers were still working on the stage. Rachel and Susan laughed as they walked back to the classroom together. So far, it was shaping up to be a great day.

When the bell rang, Susan rushed to the student parking area. She found the Lincoln, and was leaning on the hood when Rachel walked up with Ricky alongside.

"See you tonight, Ricky," Rachel threw over her shoulder as she and Susan got in the car. After she closed the door, she turned to Susan with glee in her eyes.

"He said he wanted to dance with me tonight! Can you believe it?"

"Whoooa," breathed Susan, "that's awesome."

As the girl drove out of the school parking lot, she shivered with excitement.

It was about three miles to Susan's house, out in the country on a dirt road. The road was called River Road because it followed the river. It was older than the town, older even than the state of Florida. It had been a Seminole Indian trail long before the white settlers came.

Susan's house was less than a mile beyond the curve. After she dropped her off, Rachel rushed home to get ready herself. No one was home, and she went into her room, quickly getting her majorette stuff together. Her outfit consisted of dark tights, red satin shorts, and a black satin top with a sequined red "M" emblazoned across the front. Rachel quickly shed her jeans and sweatshirt, but not her Florida undershirt.

She put on the majorette outfit, and started to get her dress ready for the dance. It was a simple blue dress. She loved it. The top part had little half sleeves, and the bottom was a broad flowing skirt, longer in the back than the front. The fabric was thin and silky. The color really set off her blue eyes and blond hair.

As she was getting the dress ready, she noticed some sort of stain or mark that she had not seen before. She raced to the laundry room and got a cloth and some laundry soap. It only took a minute to wash the mark away, but then she had to hang the dress up for the spot to dry.

It was nearly four thirty and Rachel started to feel rushed. Flustered, she ran to the bathroom to fix her hair and do her makeup. She needed to hurry.

Rachel grabbed her baton and dress and ran outside.

• • •

The live oak tree had stood at the curve in the road since the time of the Indians. It had been planted by floodwaters from the river in some century long before. Whether the Indian trail or the tree came first, no one alive knew.

It had seen Indian travelers camped in its shade.

It was fully grown when Ponce de Leon, the Spanish explorer, followed this same path in search of the Fountain of Youth.

It was standing in this very spot when Thomas Jefferson and Ben Franklin signed the Declaration of Independence.

It was there before its surrounding land had even been settled by migrating Florida natives.

It was one of the largest trees in the state, spanning nearly 200 feet, with its shade covering more than three quarters of an acre.

It had a scar on one of its big limbs where someone in a bygone era had hung a tire swing. There were some sets of lovers' initials carved and scrawled on the trunk, some so old that the bark had almost grown back over them, the love now sealed forever in the gnarly wood.

The trunk of the tree was seemingly impenetrable, broad in diameter, a massive monolith, nearly twelve feet in width. Thick and gnarly, it looked as if several trunks had fused together as one.

The tree's shade was so dense that nothing could grow under it. The ground around it was sandy and smooth, as if it had been swept clean by some old lady with a broom.

One massive limb grew straight towards the road, as if the tree was longing to take the path that it had for so long stood rooted beside. The big limb was like an arm with an elbow that touched the ground about a third of the way out, and then bent upward and climbed at almost a forty degree angle towards the sky. It ended in a forked branch that had been broken off in some summer storm, and the branch looked for all the world like an emaciated finger pointing to the heavens.

· · ·

Rachel slid to a stop in Susan's dirt driveway. The car rocked back and forth again, dust flying all around. She still wasn't used to the brakes.

Susan jumped in, all dressed in her band uniform, the clarinet case in one hand and her hang-up bag in the other. She threw the case and bag in the back seat and slammed the door, forgetting to buckle her seat belt. Rachel stomped down on the accelerator and the big V-8 roared as they left the house.

They chattered about the coming dance, deciding to keep Susan's clothes in the car and go straight to school. Rachel looked over at Susan as they neared the curve, her foot still pressing down on the accelerator.

"Watch out for the curve!" squealed Susan, seeing the tree coming at them.

Rachel slammed on the brakes hard and the big car swayed violently, sliding and fishtailing as they went through the curve, the big oak flashing past on the left, and then she floored it again.

They grinned at each other as the car straightened out on the other side.

They both knew that the band director would give them

detention if they were late.

Rachel got them there in record time. Thankfully, there was a spot right in front of the band room.

Everything took longer that night.

The band had to play at the beginning of the game as the homecoming queen and her court came into the stadium. Rachel stood at attention with the other majorettes and the flag corps, forming a double line with a path for the troop of young ladies and their escorts.

The principal did a little speech and crowned the Homecoming Queen. The band played the school's alma mater. Then everyone stood as it played the national anthem. Rachel stood at attention, her baton at her side, her right hand over her heart. She could see Ricky on the sideline, and their eyes met for a moment. She blushed and jerked her head back up to the flag. She thought she felt her heart skip a beat.

After the song ended, and everyone in the stands sat back down, the homecoming court and the band marched off the field.

Then the football teams took the field.

Halftime came and it was her chance to show off her twirling skills. She did not drop her baton, even when she threw it, whirling like a silver pinwheel high in the air.

In the second half, Ricky Thomas scored the winning touchdown with only minutes to go. Everyone was on their feet and Rachel felt her heart rise in pride as she watched him cross the goal line.

As soon as the game was over, the band and most of the fans ran onto the field and she ran up to Ricky and gave him a hug. He had on the pads and other paraphernalia of football, so she couldn't even get her arms around him. His white jersey and pants were stained with mud and grass. She wrinkled her nose at the smell of stale sweat and fresh grass.

He grinned at her and winked.

"See you at the dance?" he asked.

"I'll be there," she yelled over the noise of the crowd.

She watched as the football players gathered up their gear and trundled off to the locker room, patting each other on the back. Susan had found her and they laughed together as they walked to the band room to put away their things.

After celebrating for a while with the other band members, she and Susan jumped in the car to go home and change. When they walked into her house, Rachel's parents were still gone, probably out with friends. Rachel tied up her hair and jumped into the shower for a quick rinse-off. When she came out of the bathroom, she already had on her nylons and the little Florida shirt.

"Seriously?! Please tell me you are *not* wearing that!" wailed Susan.

"Yes I am," Rachel said resolutely. "It's my lucky shirt!"

Seeing the look on Susan's face, Rachel tried to reassure her, "It's okay. The dress is loose. I already tried it on under the dress and it doesn't show."

Susan laughed at her.

"You're *so* weird," she muttered.

They helped each other dress up for the dance, then got their things together and walked to the car.

When the girls pulled up to the gymnasium, the local rock band was already playing. Kids were standing around outside, talking and laughing. Everyone was excited at the win.

Rachel and Susan walked inside. It was even more beautiful now, with overhead lights low and the stage lit with colored spotlights. The floor was full of dancing teenagers, all under the watchful eyes of several teachers lined up along the back wall. There were tables on each side, and Susan spotted a group of band people at one table towards the back. A professional photographer had set up by the door, and they took their turns getting a portrait made.

They eventually made their way through the crowd to the table. One of the trombone players eyed Rachel up and down, whistled sharply, and said, "Wow, you really look great!"

And she did. The flowing blue dress was sort of short and sassy, and her blond hair was up in a neat braid that Susan had done for her. The trombone guy asked Rachel to dance. She nodded, grabbed his hand and happily dragged him to the dance floor. She didn't seem to sit down the rest of the night.

Ricky Thomas even kept his promise, and danced with her, twice. One was a sort of swing dance, where he whirled her around and around, and she was breathless after it was over, her heart racing.

The next dance was a slow one, and Ricky wouldn't let her sit down. She could feel his warmth as he held her close, and her heart continued to race. She could hear the swish of her pulse as she laid her head on his shoulder. It seemed as if they were the only ones on the dance floor and time were standing still.

"I'd like to see you again," he said, as he took her back to her table.

"That'd be great," she said with a smile as she sat down, still breathless.

Rachel's curfew was twelve and it was already past eleven. As she drove Susan home, they giggled over how fun the night had been. Rachel turned on the radio, and they sang along with a popular love song.

When they stopped in Susan's driveway, Rachel announced dramatically, "This has officially been the best day ever."

Susan laughed as they walked into the house. They both changed quickly and then sat on her bed. They had reminisced for a while before Rachel even thought to look at her watch.

"EEKS! Crap! It's already five after twelve!" she yelped as she jumped up. "I've got to go!"

Giving Susan a quick bear hug and grabbing her blue dress, she sprinted out to the Lincoln, quickly sliding in under the steering wheel and tossing the dress into the back seat. She turned the key with her right hand as she buckled up with her left.

She started the engine and jumped a little bit as the radio began blaring. She rolled down the windows, pulled the shifter into reverse and quickly backed out of the driveway. The car rocked again as she stopped. She jerked the shift lever down into drive and stepped on the gas like she had earlier. The big car leapt forward with a roar.

The powerful engine quickly had the car up to fifty, and she was still accelerating. Rachel was sitting up on the front edge of the seat, a smile on her face and her long blonde hair blowing in the wind. She sped down the dirt road, now driving with her left hand and reaching over to change the channel on the radio. Not able to find the knob in the dark, she glanced down and to the right, just for a moment. The radio controls were not the same as on the Honda, and she fiddled with the knob, trying to find the right station.

Distracted, traveling nearly sixty miles an hour, she glanced back up, and was already at the curve.

Surprised, she steered to the right, took her foot off the accelerator and hit the brakes hard... too hard.

The touchy brakes locked up and the deceleration thrust Rachel forward, increasing pressure on the brake pedal. The front tires began to slide, and the rear tires also lost their grip on the sandy dirt of the road. The rear of the car started to skid around. She pulled down hard on the right side of the wheel, trying to get the car to come around.

The five-thousand-pound behemoth was completely out of her control.

The car continued sideways, directly towards the tree. It slid under the huge, long, slanting limb that pointed up the road. The bottom of the limb contacted the roof of the car just above the driver's door. The frame deformed downward, shattering the window as the roof above her began to buckle.

The limb weighed more than a ton, and the angle was such that it effectively pinned the car between itself and the ground. In a cloud of leaves and dust and with a squeal of tortured metal, the huge limb crushed the Lincoln and instantly stopped its momentum. Rachel's body continued sideways, and she slammed hard into the door. Mercifully, she never felt anything after the blow to her head.

The accident was over in just a few seconds.

4

The Curve

PARAMEDIC JAMES HALL had just arrived home. He had been working the homecoming game with the Marianna Fire Department that evening.

He was tired. Like most firemen, he worked twenty-four-hour shifts. His had been on since seven in the morning the day before and still had about six hours to go. James had stopped by his house on the way back to the fire department. He had wanted to grab a clean shirt since his had been splashed by blood from a slightly wounded football player. He had just stepped back outside when he heard the crash and then a car horn blowing in the distance. He checked his radio. His house was less than a mile from *the curve*. He jumped into his truck and headed that way.

As he drove up on the scene, he saw clearly where the car had skidded, jumped the ditch, and gone through the fence. He shifted his pickup into four-wheel drive and drove over the ditch and through the broken fence, stopping with the car and the tree in the stark glare of his headlights.

At first glance, the crash didn't look too bad. The car seemed to be upright and whole. The lights were still on and the windows on the passenger side were intact. The horn was still blowing.

It was only when he got out and approached the scene, with

his Maglite in hand, that he saw the true severity of the wreck. The limb had completely crushed the roof of the car above the driver's seat.

That's the Raines' car! Oh, God, let them be okay.

Hall had seen his share of auto accidents, and this treacherous bend in the road had hosted several.

He jerked open the passenger door of the Lincoln. He quickly played his light over the car, initially looking for Tom and Leslie Raines. As soon as he caught a glimpse of long blond hair his heart sank. *Oh, God, no. It's Rachel!*

He quickly ran his light over the seats in the car. Thankfully, there were no passengers, just a crumpled blue dress in the back. He slid sideways into the area in front of the seat, facing Rachel. As he examined her, he could see blood in her hair and on the seat under her head. But she was breathing.

James grabbed the radio on his belt and called for help.

Again, as chance would have it, the truck and crew that James had left had just pulled out of the stadium. They activated their lights and siren and sped to the scene. They were there in about five minutes.

When the crew arrived, James was still in the car, face to face with Rachel. He asked for and then placed a C-collar around her neck. Her breathing was becoming labored, so he asked for an oxygen mask. Another crewman tried to get to the driver's side of the car. The heavy limb had crushed the roof and she was pinned under its weight. James could reach back along Rachel's side, but couldn't move her. He got out and they tried to move the limb by brute force, four men lifting at once, but it would not budge.

A crewman grabbed a chainsaw, and James told him to cut the limb off out beyond the car to shed some of the weight.

As James looked at Rachel's seemingly lifeless body, he began running through in his mind the quickest way to get her help. *We need to call in MAST.* MAST, the Military Assistance to Safety and Traffic had a unit in his area at Fort Rucker. The local MAST system used air evacuation helicopters. The crews had been trained in rescue operations and responded to military crashes. They were also available for civilian rescues. The closest neurosurgeon to the accident was in Dothan, Alabama at South

Alabama Regional Hospital. James called South Alabama Regional and described the nature of Rachel's injuries. The emergency department at the hospital communicated with the MAST commander and the emergency evacuation helicopter and crew were dispatched to the accident scene. The flight was approximately forty miles, but would be the quickest way to get Rachel to the appropriate facility, far quicker than an ambulance on the two-lane back roads.

James could barely get his hand between Rachel and the roof, and her legs were wedged under the steering wheel. A wrecker had been called by police dispatch and arrived after only ten minutes.

James got out of the Lincoln and had the wrecker driver attach his lift cable to the end of the limb pressing down on the car. He got back in the car and placed a special jack on the floor of the car to lift the roof. Under supervision by one of the firemen, the driver started to slowly raise the limb off of the car. James simultaneously used the jack inside the car.

James was afraid that when the pressure of the limb was removed from Rachel there would be a change in her vital signs. He was right.

As Rachel's legs were freed from the pressure of the limb, she suddenly stopped breathing. Hurriedly but gently, knowing she may have sustained a spinal injury, James and another medic slid her out of the passenger side of the car and laid her on a backboard on the ground. They swiftly reattached the mask and an ambu bag and gave her several breaths.

To James' immense relief, she started to breathe again, but slowly and erratically. *That isn't good. But at least she still has a good pulse*, noted James, trying to convince himself that Rachel would be fine. Her only other injuries were a broken ankle and a contusion on her left ribcage.

James placed his stethoscope and listened to her heart, smiling grimly when he saw the orange gator shirt. Her heartbeat was strong and steady, but tachycardiac. He placed a blood pressure cuff and checked her pressure. *Too low. We can't lose her! Where is that damn helicopter?* Just then he heard its *thump thump* in the distance.

By this time, bystanders had begun to arrive. Rachel's

parents, Tom and Leslie, came running up. James stood, blocking Rachel's body from them. Both stood shocked, gasping for air, crying.

The big Huey helicopter flew low over the site, red lights flashing, its bright spotlight lighting up the scene below. The pilot was looking for obstacles and power lines, but the only obstacle was the tree. The chopper was so loud that no one could hear. It wheeled in the air like a great bird of prey, and then leaned back to land on the dirt road. The leaves of the live oak tree trembled in the rotor wash as the big machine sat down.

A crewman jumped out, a duffle over his shoulder. Right behind him was a flight nurse, medic kit in hand.

Ducking low to avoid the still turning rotor, they ran over to where James had the girl on the backboard. They both wore green Nomex flight suits, and James noticed captain's bars on the shoulders of the man.

"I'm Doctor Powell," yelled the captain over the whirl of the helicopter blades. "Tell me what you've got."

It was unusual for a doctor to be on the MAST helicopter, but the flight surgeon had made a point of being on call one night a week, and this was his night.

"Hey, Doc," shouted James over the declining whine of the helicopter. "I'm James Hall, EMT. We have a single passenger MVA, car versus tree, sixteen-year-old female, unresponsive. Injury to the left side of her head, looks like she hit hard. She was pinned in the vehicle. She also has a left ankle fracture, left chest contusion, no other injuries as far as we can tell. Heart rate one hundred ten, B/P ninety-five over forty-six. No cardiac arrest, but her breathing is very labored. I think she's gonna need intubation soon."

The captain was examining the girl, his stethoscope to his ears.

"Let's do that now," he said. "I don't want to attempt an intubation in the aircraft."

He looked up. "She's got diminished breath sounds on the left side, too."

The flight nurse quickly opened the toolbox and laid a tray on a sheet next to Rachel. She drew up a medication into a syringe and handed it to the doctor. He quickly injected it into Rachel's arm. Removing the oxygen mask from her face, he got into position above her head. The nurse held a light and the doctor quickly and deftly inserted the ET tube into Rachel's trachea. He re-attached the ambu bag to the tube and hooked up an O_2 tank he had in the duffle. The nurse began to squeeze the bag, delivering oxygen to Rachel at a steady rate.

She was intubated in less than thirty seconds. James was amazed at how smooth and quick the captain was, in the field and in the dark.

"Let's start some dopamine," directed the doctor, as he took the ambu bag from the nurse and continued to squeeze it rhythmically. "How much does she weigh?"

"Looks about one hundred twenty pounds," said James.

"Figure fifty kilos and start dopamine at ten mics," the doctor called over to the flight nurse.

The nurse was already taking out an IV set-up.

"Hang a liter of normal saline, too."

The nurse quickly started the IV.

"Let's get her in the aircraft," said the captain. "Are her parents here?"

The mother and father stepped up.

"I'm sorry," spoke the captain, seeing them for the first time.

"One of you should go with her," he said, "But there is only room for one. We are going to South Alabama Regional in Dothan."

Tom looked at his wife.

"You go," he said. "I'll be there as soon as I can get there."

"I'll take you, Tom," James said. "We can get to Dothan in less than an hour."

James helped the other paramedics and the captain carry the stretcher to the helicopter, the nurse running alongside with the IV. They ducked under the blades of the dark green machine, and slid the stretcher into the back. Rachel's mother was buckled into the jump seat beside the stretcher, and the doctor sat beside her. The nurse was across from them, hanging the IV and then taking the ambu bag from the captain. Hall watched the door slide shut and then he moved away from the aircraft, turning to watch it take off.

The turbine began its noisy rise and the blades began to whirl, slowly at first, then faster and faster, now beating the air with a steady throb. He could see the pilot looking up and around, sizing up the distance from the old tree. Then the ungainly flying machine slowly lifted and turned, and James watched as it rose awkwardly, pivoting sideways, over the live oak tree.

Suddenly, a chill ran up his spine.

As the helicopter turned toward him, James clearly saw Rachel's face in the windshield.

It was her, larger than life, blond hair blowing in the wind, a smile on her face. It looked like she even moved and tilted her head, like she was looking out at him.

He stared at the image, watching her as the big helicopter slowly turned.

Then, startled by the vision, he blinked his eyes, and she was gone. Now it was just the windshield again, and he could still see the pilot's green helmet through the plexiglass.

It had lasted only an instant, but the image would be forever etched in his mind. Rachel's face, unmistakable, and she was smiling at him, moving and alive. It was like a picture on a movie screen, but real.

He turned, thinking that maybe it had been a reflection of the arc lights, but they all faced down, towards the car and the trunk of the tree. He looked back, but the helicopter had turned, and the image was no longer there.

At that moment, he realized that Rachel wasn't going make it. He shook his head and closed his eyes.

"Damn it," he cursed, exhaling with a sigh.

With a heavy heart James watched as the tree waved its limbs in the rotor wash from the hovering helicopter. In the surreal light cast by the moon, the fire truck, and the spotlights, it struck him, oddly, that it looked like a wretched old lady wringing her arms in anguish.

Shaking his head and wiping tears from his eyes, James watched as the helicopter turned north, nosed over slightly, and sped away, covering everyone with noise and wind.

As it climbed into the night sky, its rotor thumping deliberately, he noticed four bright stars beyond, forming a huge square, like a door in the darkness. The helicopter was headed directly for the center.

He kept watching as the machine's flashing red lights slowly receded, perfectly framed by the Great Square of Pegasus, the constellation believed by the ancients to mark the doorway to heaven.

5

Pupils Fixed

CATHY COX HAD been a critical care nurse for more than fifteen years. She was the one the doctors requested when a case was difficult. Cathy had seen it all. This did not make it easier, though, when she came to work and was faced with young people who had been in tragic accidents.

Cathy had two children of her own, a seventeen-year-old daughter and a fifteen-year-old son. They were the center of her life, and she could not imagine how she would feel if one of them was hurt. She really had a heart for her work, and for her patients and their families.

Cathy was respected by her peers, often serving as preceptor for new nurses coming to work at the hospital. She knew critical care medicine better than some of the doctors that she worked with, but was a consummate diplomat when it came to working with them.

The unit Cathy worked in, the Surgical Intensive Care Unit, was the place the most severely injured patients were sent. They received the motor vehicle accident (MVA) cases, the homicide and suicide cases. All of the cases involving head trauma and strokes were in her unit. The two neurosurgeons in town alternated call, and one of them was always available.

As Cathy rode the elevator to the fourth floor, she wondered what would be facing her that day. When she left the day before, there had been only three patients in the SICU, and she knew one would be going home. She hoped she didn't get the patient in bed four, a teenage boy who had been on a motorcycle. An elderly lady had turned left in front of him and he had slid under her car. The lady continued to drive for several feet before she stopped, and the boy was badly injured. They had had to amputate one of his legs and he had been in a coma on the ventilator for two months.

When Cathy stepped off the elevator on the fourth floor, the hall outside the unit was lined with teenage kids. They were sitting on the floor, in the ledges of the windows, and all of the chairs in the waiting room were full. Cathy smiled grimly at the adults as she walked by, knowing there must be a young person in the unit.

When she walked in the door, the unit manager briefed her. "It's a sixteen-year-old female, MVA, closed head injury. She came in around one-thirty this morning. Her pupils are fixed. She's unresponsive, no cough or gag. She has been posturing a little, but that's going away. The CT shows massive injury to her brain. Dr. Yunis took her to surgery and then just closed back up. He has told the family there is nothing he can do. That they'll just have to wait and see if there is any improvement."

Cathy sighed and shook her head. She looked over towards room 8, the last one on the right. She could see the patient, head partially shaven, intracranial pressure monitor protruding from her skull. She could see someone sitting in a chair beside the bed, with her face down in the sheet, and knew it was the girl's mother. As she stepped closer, she could see the girl's long blond hair laying out on the pillow, and the ETT and NG tubes going into the girl's mouth and nose. The girl's hair had been brushed with care. Cathy sighed again.

Laura Jones entered the room seconds after Cathy. "Sorry you have to come in on this," she said.

Cathy just nodded to her.

Laura continued, laying an IV bag on the counter. "Dr. Yunis said to be ready with some Nipride. Her ICP has been high. Did you see his note?"

Cathy shook her head, picked up the girl's medical chart

and flipped to the doctor's progress notes. There was a detailed handwritten synopsis of the girl's accident and admission course. Cathy had no trouble deciphering Yunis' chopped script: she had seen it many times before. He had written that the CT showed a massive intracranial bleed with shift. Then there was a surgical note where he wrote that he had opened the skull and grey matter had come out under pressure. He had closed without being able to do anything surgically. He wrote that he had spoken to the girl's family and told them the prognosis was grim. "Damn it," said Cathy, under her breath.

Why? Why do these things happen?

Then she thought, *This could be my child.*

She flipped through the rest of the chart, looking at the labs and x-ray reports. The girl also had a collapsed lung when she arrived at the hospital, and a surgeon had placed a chest tube to re-inflate the lung. She had a fractured left fibula, at the ankle, and a couple of cracked ribs on the left side.

An orthopedic surgeon had wrapped the ankle, and wrote that he would follow up later. The CT report showed a massive intracranial bleed, and Cathy knew that this one injury would most likely be fatal. Tears welled up in her eyes.

She knew in her heart that the orthopedic guy wouldn't have to come back.

Normally, a nurse in the SICU was responsible for two or three patients. In this case however, the nurse manager had assigned Cathy to just one, the girl. And this one would probably require all of her energy, all night.

Cathy continued to review the girl's chart, as Laura told her what had gone on so far in the girl's care, and what the doctors had said. Laura went over all of the meds that the girl was on, and had been on, and the treatment plan.

Laura looked at her, a worried look in her eyes. "I haven't seen any spontaneous breaths since about nine and the posturing has stopped."

Cathy shook her head at this, another bad sign. "Who's on for pulmonary?"

"It's Dr. Lipps, and she said she would be back by at five. She wants a blood gas at four thirty. Dr. Yunis said he would be back by six. I hope he's in a better mood than he was this morning.

He yelled at me when I called him about the b/p at four thirty."
Laura was tired—it had been a long night.

"He's always this way when it's a young person," said Cathy,
shaking her head.

She and Laura continued to go over the girl's care. Cathy
asked for the girl's mother and father's name, and how they were
doing so far.

"The father's a basket case, but I guess I would be, too. He's
in the waiting room, says he can't stand to see her like this. Her
mother is a little better, has been in the room most of the time.
She seems to understand what's going on."

"The kids from her school want to come in, but I've only
allowed a few at visiting hours, and only the ones the mother
okays. There's about a hundred of them, seems like. One of the
girls was taken down to the ER; she was sobbing so much she
couldn't get her breath." Laura looked down with a sigh.

"The Florida highway patrol has been by, and they want you
to call them with any updates. The investigator's card is taped to
the front of the chart."

They both walked into the girl's room, and Laura introduced
Cathy to the girl's mother. The mother looked up as Laura said
to her, "This is Cathy, she will be taking care of your daughter
now. I'm about to go home, but I'll keep you guys in my prayers."

"Hello, Ms. Raines, I'm Cathy, I'll be here for a while now,
and I promise I'll take good care of your daughter. If there is
anything you need, please let me know."

The mother smiled a brief smile and nodded at Cathy, then
looked at them and asked, "Is the doctor going to come by?"

"Doctor Yunis is supposed to come by later this evening,"
said Cathy. "And he should be able to talk to you then."

"Can I get you anything? Maybe some coffee or juice?"

"No, thank you," said the mother. "Laura brought me some."

She gestured to a cup of juice on the small bedside table. It
was untouched.

"We need to look at a few things here if that's okay," smiled
Cathy.

"Can I stay in the room?" asked the mother.

"Yes, that's fine," said Cathy, smiling.

Laura showed Cathy all of the IV lines that the girl had, and an arterial line that the surgeon had put in. This allowed the doctors and nurses to monitor the girl's blood pressure and heart rate. Her pressure was hovering around 100/50, and her heart rate was 98. Her oxygen saturation was 96.

"She's getting eighty cc an hour of ringers, and is still on ten mics of dopamine. She was on dopamine and neo, but we were able to come off on the neo. It's still hanging, though, if you need it," said Laura.

They walked back to the nurse's station, and Laura sat down with a sigh.

"I just feel for her mom and dad. I don't have a good feeling about this. The girl hasn't done anything since she got here. And her mother hasn't touched the juice, and hasn't eaten all day. She doesn't want to leave the room, even for a minute. She told me her daughter was a wonderful girl, all about her being in the band and chorus, and doing well in school."

Tears were welling up in Laura's eyes. "Why does it always seem to be the good kids that this happens to? And look at her, she was a beautiful girl. I just don't know if I can handle this anymore." She sniffed and wiped her nose.

Cathy knew Laura was at the end of her rope. She was glad she had come in a few minutes early.

"I'm gonna finish charting and go home," said Laura. "I just want to sit down with my kids and hug them close."

Cathy smiled and shook her head slightly. She knew how Laura felt. Laura had four boys, ages four to ten.

Laura sat down with the chart to finish her nursing notes.

Cathy walked back into the girl's room.

That's when she noticed the bird.

A bird? Cathy did a double-take. It was a mockingbird, sitting just outside the partially opened jalousie window, sitting there, singing a song.

That's odd, thought Cathy.

The hospital sat in the middle of a huge parking lot, with doctor's offices all around. The SICU was on the fourth floor, and beside them there was only the flat roof of the adjoining three story office building. She could see the roof, outside the window, with its big air conditioning and heating systems festooned like mushrooms. But there weren't any trees or plants for birds.

The bird was on the ledge of the girl's window.

Right there.

Cathy walked slowly toward the mockingbird. It looked sideways at her and hopped away, jumping off the window ledge to the roof beyond. When she turned around, it fluttered back to its place. It looked at Cathy, and then it turned its head, as if it were looking down at the girl, whose long blond hair was carefully laid out on her pillow. It started to sing again, a plaintive love song. It would sing a minute, then stop and look down towards the girl.

Cathy went back out and sat down with Laura.

"Did you see that bird?" she asked, softly.

Laura glanced up at her. "Yeah, it's been there all afternoon. It's weird. It sits there and sings, and just moves away a little when you go over there. I think it must have a nest out there somewhere."

Cathy looked back in the girl's room. She could see the bird on the window ledge. It was singing and looking in the window, for all the world like it was watching the girl. Cathy looked down to see chill bumps pop up on her arms.

And I thought I'd seen it all.

She shook her head slowly, then turned back to her notes.

After Laura had left, and things had settled down a little, Cathy went in the room to do her regular patient check-up. The girl's pressure was trending down, and Cathy wished she had that crit. She was sure the girl needed more volume, but couldn't increase the IV rate because she didn't want to increase the intracranial pressure.

Just then, the lab tech walked in. Cathy smiled and said, "She has an art line on the right side. I'll help you. And I need these, stat."

Cathy gently lifted the girl's right arm to get access to the line. The lab tech drew a syringe of blood from the port in the line. She filled several blood tubes, spun them between her fingers, and then labeled them with stickers from the girl's chart.

After the tech left, Cathy took a minute to straighten up the sheets, laying the girl's long hair back out like it had been. She noticed the mother watching her. "She has beautiful hair, so long and thick."

The girl's mother said, "She never wanted to cut it. When she was little it went all the way down her back. But then she decided to keep it a little shorter. It's going to take a while for the other side to grow back out."

She was talking about the part that had been shaven for surgery. "But her hair always grows fast, so maybe it won't take too long."

Cathy smiled at the mom. "Is she a junior or a senior?'

"She's a junior, at Marianna High. We moved there from Pensacola. My husband's family is from the area, and we wanted a smaller town atmosphere for her. She's in the band and runs track. An honor student... " The mother's voice trailed off.

"You must be proud of her," said Cathy, looking up to see Dr. Zeid Yunis come into the unit, trailed by his P.A., Sarah Perkins.

"Excuse me a minute," said Cathy.

"Hello, Cathy," said Dr. Yunis, as he picked up the chart. "Any change?"

"No, sir," said Cathy, shaking her head.

"Would you ask her mother to go out for a minute?"

"Yes, sir."

Cathy went back into the girl's room. The mother had her head down on the side of the bed, and Cathy could see her shoulders shaking. Cathy walked over and gently placed her hand on the mother's shoulder. "The doctor is here and wants to do an assessment. Can you come back in a minute, please?"

The girl's mother looked up, her face red and her eyes puffy. "Can I talk to him?"

"After he sees her, I think you can."

"Thank you," said the mother as she went out of the room.

Dr. Yunis and Sarah walked in after the mother had left. Dr. Yunis began his exam. "Has she been responding at all? Breathing over the vent?"

"No sir. I haven't been able to get any response. And her blood pressure is trending down, even with the dopamine."

"You can go up on the dopamine as needed, but keep the Nipride handy."

Dr. Yunis shook the girl and called her name, loudly. He got down close and called her name again. There was no response. Then he took a small penlight out of his pocket and checked the girl's eyes. He was looking for any response to the bright light, but her pupils stayed fixed and dilated. He moved her head back and forth, but her eyes did not react. He did several other tests, but could get no response to any stimuli.

"The posturing has gone away, too," he said. He shook his head. "Has pulmonary been by?"

"No sir, not yet," said Cathy, "but I expect them soon."

"Have Dr. Lipps do an apnea test, but I'm writing a note that she meets the clinical criteria for brain death. Would you ask her mother and father to come back?"

"I will," said Cathy, and went out to the waiting area. She asked the girl's parents to come back into the small conference room just outside the unit door. Their pastor was there and they asked if he could come in as well.

"Of course," said Cathy.

Dr. Yunis had finished writing in the chart when she went to get him. She took him in to the family, and stood in the doorway listening as Dr. Yunis explained brain death to the mother and father. He told them that he had asked the pulmonologist to do another test for brain death, and explained how it worked. Dr. Yunis then gave them the option of one more test, a blood flow study.

"Cathy, we need you," called out the unit manager.

Cathy hurried back into the room.

"Her pressure has shot up to the one-eighties, and her heart rate is one-fifteen," said the manager.

"She's herniating," said Cathy, turning off the dopamine pump. "Help me hang the Nipride." They both worked quickly to get the new IV bag hung and perfusing.

Blood was rushing into Rachel's brain, causing it to swell. But, because the brain is encased in the skull, the swelling had no place to go, no place except where the spinal cord exits at the brain's base. If the pressure is too great, the narrow passage can be blocked, stopping blood flow to the brain and killing the patient.

Cathy and Pam worked quickly to get the IV bag spiked and hung. While they were working, the girl's blood pressure went over 200, then 220. It took a couple of minutes for the Nipride to start working, but even then the girl's pressure was in the one-eighties.

Dr. Yunis walked back into the room.

He shook his head. "Be ready to restart the dopamine. Her pressure will come down just as quickly as it went up."

Cathy nodded.

Yunis continued, "They want to do a blood flow study. That's fine; maybe it will help them understand. I'll write an order in the chart, and you need to go ahead and call radiology. I'll tell Amanda to consult Dr. Lipps for an apnea test as well."

At that moment, Dr. Lipps, the pulmonologist, walked into the unit.

"Hello, Ellen," said Yunis.

"Hello Zeid. Any change?" asked Dr. Lipps.

"She meets the clinical criteria, but the family wants a cerebral blood flow study. Can you do an apnea test?"

"Yes. We'll do it now," said Dr. Lipps, shaking her head. She looked over at Cathy. "Cathy, would you page respiratory, please?"

Yunis walked back over to the nurse's station. He looked at the unit secretary. His words came out short and clipped.

"Amanda, call radiology. We need a blood flow study done on room eight. See who is down there to read it and ask them to do it stat. And then page Lisa Kelly and tell her to come in."

Dr. Yunis walked into the nurse's lounge and closed the door. Cathy had walked out of the room to page respiratory for Dr. Lipps. She knew Dr. Yunis was upset. Cathy looked at Amanda, her lips a tight line. She drew in a deep breath, then let it out in a sigh.

"You need to call Lisa," she said to Amanda.

"I know. Dr. Yunis already said."

6

Family First

LISA KELLY WAS expecting a page. She had been in her small office at the hospital that morning and had been called by one of the ICU nurses about a young girl had been admitted the night before after an auto accident. The nurse had told her that the girl had a closed head injury and had a GCS of 3.

"Not good," Lisa thought.

The Glasgow coma scale is a measure of brain function, measuring three types of response: eye-opening response, verbal response, and response to pain. The sixteen-year-old patient was non-responsive to all of the tests.

It was hospital policy to notify the organ donation agency in cases such as this, even though they had not yet declared the patient dead. Cases like this quickly shift from medical evaluation into the legal realm. Lisa knew she would be called in to help the family navigate this stressful, emotional stage.

Late in the afternoon, Lisa's pager went off with the number for the intensive care unit. When she called she was told that the neurosurgeon had declared the girl brain-dead and had ordered a blood flow study to confirm it. Once that was done, hospital gears shifted. Lisa would check to see if the patient had *donor* on her driver's license or had signed a donor card. Then, if donation was a possibility, and when it was appropriate, she would talk to the girl's family.

Lisa got to the hospital within about thirty minutes of the page. She stopped for a minute at the elevator on the first floor, pausing to compose herself before pushing the up button. In this hospital, the intensive care unit was on the fourth floor. The elevator opened at the end of the hall, and across the hall from the elevator was the door to the unit. The unit was small and semicircular, with ten patient beds arranged around a central nurse's station. This particular unit was specific to neurosurgical patients. The family waiting area was next to the ICU door, and the area around the unit door and the family room door was open. Lisa knew that many times family members would be standing outside the unit door, either waiting for visiting hours, or talking to friends and relatives.

She took a minute to say a prayer for the family and for the young girl, and to calm and focus herself on the task she was about to begin. She hoped she would be able to go into the unit without encountering the patient's family first, so that she could review the patient's status with the nurse. As she paused, she also reflected on the fact that the girl was almost the same age as her own daughter, and prayed that she herself could emotionally deal with that and continue to do her job.

Lisa always tried to treat every family with respect and love, and for the next several hours, if they donated, she would be a source of comfort and help to them. Her focus would be on them. She sometimes got flak from her coworkers in the main office because she often, at least at the beginning, spent more time with the family than in managing the donor situation. Lisa told them that if it wasn't for the family, there would not be a donor, and that she was going to take care of them as well. The organ procurement agency, after seeing her success with families and her high consent rate, had now begun to hire people as family services coordinators, whose only job was to work with donor families. Other coordinators were sent in to manage the donor cases while these family coordinators continued to help the donor families. Unfortunately, Lisa's area was too small to allow hiring another coordinator to work with her, so she still had to do both jobs.

Most of the time this was okay with Lisa, since she was very zealous about her job, and did not want someone less motivated to come in to work with her. She had seen how people who were less caring or who had a poor bedside manner could scuttle the chances for donation. She had had cases torpedoed by zealous nurses asking too soon, and by doctors who would not allow her to talk to families at all because it might add to their grief. If anything, in most cases it actually helped the family in their grief to know that others had been helped.

Lisa hoped she could help this family.

When the elevator doors opened, Lisa was startled from her reverie by Dr. Zeid Yunis, the neurosurgeon. He gave Lisa a cursory nod, barely glancing in her direction.

This was a tough situation for all involved. Dr. Yunis cared about his patients as well, and to see Lisa was to admit that he was not successful in his efforts to save the teen's life. Dr. Yunis actually liked Lisa and certainly respected her. But he had probably just spent all night and most of the morning working on the same patient that would now become hers. Neurosurgeons are famous for their egos, and Dr. Zeid Yunis wasn't what you'd call atypical in that department.

As the elevator doors opened on the fourth floor, Lisa took a deep breath and looked out in the hall outside the intensive care unit. There was a huge crowd of young people, high school aged, milling around outside the unit door. She sighed as she made her way down the hall, and was glad that there is a staff entrance close to the elevator. She did not want to confront or approach the patient's family before she had had time to review the chart and talk to the unit nurses about the situation.

When Lisa entered the unit, she greeted each nurse. She had worked with each on occasion and felt comfortable with them. In this situation, though, she was glad that the call came from Cathy, one of the most experienced nurses. Cathy was taking care of the patient.

Cathy was sitting at the desk writing a nursing note when Lisa walked in. She looked up and smiled.

"Hi, Lisa, how are you?"

"I'm fine. How are you?"

"I've been better."

Dr. Lipps was at the other end of the long desk, writing in

the chart.

"She's in room eight," said Cathy.

Lisa looked down that way, seeing the patient in the bed and someone else in the room. She could see blonde hair.

Cathy shook her head, "Sixteen year old female, car versus tree. Closed head injury. Dr. Yunis did a clinical exam and Dr. Lipps just finished an apnea test. She didn't breathe. She has two death notes, but we are going to radiology for a flow study."

"How is her family," asked Lisa.

"Taking it hard, like anybody would. Her father can't even go in the room. Her mother stays in there all the time, mostly crying. They are the only family, she's an only child. There are tons of high school kids, but we only let a few in at visiting hours. They line up at the door and troop in two by two. They have a minister here, and the principal and band director are here, too. Her track coach was here most of the day."

"I saw the crowd in the hall," said Lisa. "Are her mom and dad accepting things?"

"I think they know, but we are doing the flow study for them. I think she's been clinically dead since she got here."

"Did Dr. Yunis say anything about donation?"

"No, and he won't come back. Dr. Lipps will tell them the results of the blood flow study. I will mention it then."

"What do you think?"

"I don't know, but I think they will talk to you. I will call you back when she comes up from radiology."

"Is she stable?" Lisa asked.

"She is now. Her crit came back low and Dr. Yunis let me hang a couple units of blood. She had a herniation episode just about forty-five minutes ago. Pressure shot up, then back down. Things have settled down now. She's on twelve mics of dopamine now. Pressure is around one ten."

"How long before radiology comes?"

"They should be here shortly."

Lisa sighed. "What a terrible tragedy." She shook her head and looked down, thinking about how the girl's mother and father must feel. She sighed again, shaking her head.

Then she said, "Do you think it will take about an hour for the study?"

Cathy nodded.

"Then I am going to run home and change. I've been in these clothes all day and I need to be ready to stay the night. Just page me when you are ready for me to come back."

7

Life and Death

DR. MCALLISTER WAS looking through Martha Lake's chart. Martha was sitting in a chair beside the bed, her husband, Alan, on the small sofa beside her.

Glancing up, David could not help but marvel at the difference. Just a few days ago, she had been almost comatose, barely responding when he would check on her. Her O_2 saturation had been about as low as he had ever seen. Her skin had been pale and her nail beds blue, her heart barely able to keep her alive.

Now she seemed to light up the room with her smile. Martha's face and hair were perfect, her skin glowed with health, her fingernail beds were pink, and her eyes were bright and clear.

"Hi, Dr. Mac," she chirped.

"Well, hello yourself," he laughed, "you are really looking good."

"And feeling good, too," she smiled.

Martha had been healthy until about three months ago. Already the mother of a four-year-old girl, she had become pregnant again. But early in the pregnancy she had had some unusual complications, becoming very weak and short of breath, almost unable to get out of bed. When she went to see her obstetrician/gynecologist, the doctor had been very concerned and had sent her to see a local cardiologist. She had done an echo and discovered that Martha's heart was enlarged and beginning to fail. The doctor told her she had peripartum cardiomyopathy. Martha's heart function was only about twenty percent of normal.

Some peripartum cardiomyopathy patients can recover or stabilize with medical intervention, but Martha continued to worsen. She miscarried. Her heart continued to decline and the cardiologist recommended a consult with Dr. McAllister. When David first saw her, her ejection fraction, a measure of heart function, was down to fifteen percent. She was immediately admitted to the transplant hospital.

The transplant committee agreed that Martha was a candidate for heart transplantation. After a long discussion with Martha and her husband she was placed on the national transplant waiting list. Although he never discussed this with his patients, Dr. McAllister didn't think Martha would live more than six weeks without a new heart.

As he got to know Martha over the next few days, he marveled at her spirit. She always greeted him with a smile, and would joke about all the tests, medicines, tubes, and other paraphernalia that had become part of her daily routine. David noticed that, even though she was very ill, her appearance and dress remained meticulous. She beamed with pride when her daughter was in the room, always bragging about her child's drawings or counting skills.

But, as the days passed, Martha Lake's heart weakened until she barely responded. She was moved to ICU.

Four weeks became six, then eight.

After Martha was placed in the unit, she was considered a Status One patient. This meant that the next available heart that was her blood type, and otherwise matching her, would be hers.

Martha's blood type was A, not rare, but as in all transplants, there was a huge element of chance. First, a type A heart donor had to be located, then the donor's heart had to be close to her size range, and it had to be in good enough shape to transplant. Hearts also have only a short time after donation to be transplanted, so the heart had to be nearby.

And of course, for Martha to get a heart, someone else had

to die.

This is a very real and emotional issue for most transplant patients, and for many, a heart-breaking one. When Martha had been better, she had discussed this with her family and with Dr. Mac. He had said, or course, that Martha was not the cause of another person dying, that people die every day. He had said they were just hoping that if someone did die, they could be a donor. Though she knew this was true, she still had problems with the fact that she was hoping for a transplant. In fact, Martha's family, others who loved her, her minister and the members of her church, the nurses in the unit, and even Dr. Mac, were praying for her. David was worried that she would soon be so sick that she would have to be taken off the transplant list.

Fortunately, Martha had cheated death. A donor had been found.

8

Calling

DR. MCALLISTER HAD seen the results of hundreds of heart transplants, but it never ceased to amaze him to see the miracle that occurred when someone who was so sick received a new heart. And Martha Lake was a walking, talking poster child, her quick recovery surprising everyone.

After writing a progress note in Martha's chart, David strolled down the hall to his office and dropped into his chair. Still smiling at how well Martha's new heart was doing, he glanced over towards a picture on the desk, a portrait of a pretty blond lady at the beach, and remembered the first heart transplant he had ever witnessed.

As a young medical school resident, he was assigned to the transplant service for one of his rotations. Up until then, he had been planning a career in general surgery, hoping to return to his hometown to practice with a local surgical group. One of the surgeons was the father of his best friend in high school, who had encouraged David's interests in medicine. David had even qualified for a local scholarship for medical students that had been set up by a retired physician. This doctor had started a small hospital in the town and it had grown to a medical center with more than two hundred beds and state-of-the-art care for local patients. David knew he had a nice job awaiting him, a good income and an established practice that he could move into. He had planned his life to this point around that goal, knowing he would be welcome and accepted back in his hometown, and able to be close to his family and old friends. He, too, would become a part of the comfortable, respected medical community, probably marry a local girl and start a family.

His first night on the transplant service changed that plan forever.

He still remembered the voice on the other end of the telephone after his pager had gone off.

"Dr. McAllister," the voice said, "This is Elsa, the transplant coordinator. Dr. Brighton said to page you and ask you to meet us at the organ transplant lab in one hour—at eleven. We are flying to Oklahoma City for a heart. Do you know where the lab is?"

David showered quickly, and started to shave. While he was looking in the mirror as he ran the electric razor across his day-old whiskers, he felt his heart racing, and could see that his pupils were dilated with excitement.

He'd soon be on a private jet and then scrubbing in with one of the most renowned cardiac surgeons in the country. They would remove a heart from someone who was dead and transplant it into someone who needed it.

• • •

When he arrived at the organ lab, Elsa, who had paged him, was getting together the various packs and coolers needed for the heart procurement.

"Can I help you?" she said as he walked in the door.

"I'm David McAllister," he said, looking down at all of the paraphernalia she had gathered up.

"Can I help *you*?" he smiled.

The OR supplies for the heart cases were in a large rolling duffle. Beside it sat two igloo coolers containing the saline and preservation solutions.

"I'm Elsa Benz. It's nice to meet you, Dr. McAllister." Elsa's voice was melodious with a German accent, even more memorable in person. So was Elsa herself.

"Please call me David," he stammered as he gazed into the bluest eyes and most perfect face he could ever remember seeing.

Elsa returned his gaze without a blink.

"Thank you. David, I have everything ready to go, but I will need your help to carry this down to the van and when we get to the hospital. Is this your first heart?"

"Yes," David replied, finally regaining his composure, trying to contain his excitement over this beautiful, slim blonde. Precisely at that moment, Dr. Brighton walked into the lab.

David McAllister had never been one for titles or even mildly concerned about social standing. He had grown up middle-class near a small city, where his father was a well-respected farmer and businessman, also on the school board. He had attended church and other civic functions along with doctors, lawyers, judges, even a congressman. These men and women had all been regular people, part of his family's social structure. He attended parties and such at their homes and they were often visitors in his. Even as a young man, David had been included, sitting with them at dinner and discussing everything from politics to football. These people had always treated him with respect and as an equal.

Albert Sheridan Brighton, on the other hand, was only one step down from God Himself. He was an M.D. and Ph.D. and made certain everyone knew it. At this University Medical School, and at this University Hospital, he *was* God. And when he walked into the room, he expected to be treated that way.

"Elsa, is the aircraft ready?" he asked, looking down at her.

"It will be ready when we get to the airport, sir," she said.

Brighton finally acknowledged David, turning and nodding to him.

"McAllister," he said, after glancing at the embroidered name on David's lab coat. "Pick up these coolers and let's get to the airport. I have a patient who needs this heart badly, and it's not going to be any good if we don't get there ASAP!"

Brighton was tall and stately, and dressed impeccably in a perfectly tailored black sport coat, an ivory dress shirt with a conservative striped tie, and grey dress pants. His dark eyes seemed to take in everything at once, and it only took him an instant to size anyone up. His hair had receded slightly, and he tilted his head back a bit as he spoke, like a greyhound sniffing the wind. He had an interesting way of speaking, almost with his teeth clenched together, and his words came in quick, short syllables. It was obvious that he was used to command.

David had met Dr. Brighton only once in person, on the day he interviewed for medical school. He had seen Brighton from a distance several times and had been told by the other residents to avoid him if possible, stay on his good side at all times, know thoroughly everything about the patient, and never question Brighton's diagnoses.

He and Elsa raced down the hall, carrying all of the equipment for the case, and barely able to keep up with Brighton, who carried only himself. The drive to the airport was a blur. David was in the back seat of the organ donor van while Elsa drove and Brighton rode shotgun, not saying a word.

The jet was waiting at the private gate, and they unloaded everything from the van, handing it up to the pilot, and then following Brighton up the narrow stairs into the plane.

The flight in the small jet was memorable, and not just because he got to sit across from Elsa. McAllister loved to fly: he even intended to become a pilot someday himself. He always asked for a window seat on airline flights, and would spend most of the flight looking out the window at the beauty of the sky, the clouds, and the earth below. He was awed by the sky, so vast and ever-changing, and by flying in general.

This night the flight was beyond beautiful.

The sky was absolutely clear, so clear that after they were aloft he was not able to tell where the stars ended and the lights on the ground began. After they left the area of the city, the flight took them over large open spaces with scattered farms and small towns. The random lights on the ground were spaced like the stars above, and there were so many stars. It seemed he could clearly make out the Milky Way. They were up so high that he could even see the lights of airliners below them. He wanted to keep looking out the window, but the view close in front of him was also awesome.

The jet had "club" seating. That is, the two seats on each side faced each other. David was facing forward, and Elsa was in front of him facing his way. She had her eyes closed, attempting to doze on the flight up to Oklahoma. He knew that he should be doing the same, but was too excited to even think about sleep.

Dr. Brighton was in the seat beside him, already stretched out and fast asleep. David had heard that Brighton could work rings around the other doctors, and that he had a reputation for needing very little sleep. This brought a smile to David's face. *Dr. Brighton does sleep. He's not a god after all,* David thought, grinning.

He turned his head to look out the window, and noticed in the reflection that Elsa was watching him, quizzically. He glanced over at Dr. Brighton and then at her, shook his head slightly and put his finger to his lips. "Shh," he said very quietly, with a wink, and folded his hands and bowed his head. She grinned at him and shook her head.

• • •

It was only about an hour and a half to Oklahoma City, and Dr. Brighton was awakened by the *thump* of the airplane's landing gear going down. He sat up, and began to reorient himself.

David sat upright, pretending not to notice that Dr. Brighton had been asleep. Brighton turned and said "You need to use every available chance like this to catch a little restructuring time for your mind. There will be times when it is the only bit of sleep that you get, and you need to discipline your body and mind to make do with this limited resource."

"Yes sir," David responded.

"Do not hesitate to take a quick catnap during the day if you get the chance," Brighton continued, "and do not plan late-night activities when you are on call. The very night that you stay up partying with friends you will be paged at two in the morning for an emergency case that will require every bit of skill, stamina, and smarts that you have. Your chosen profession requires uncommon discipline, and of course it requires this in life choices, as well."

David nodded and said a quick, "Yes, sir."

He smiled again as he noticed the only accoutrement Brighton had on his coat. It was a small silver lapel pin, depicting a black and white hounds-tooth hat.

By this time the jet had landed and was taxiing up to the general aviation ramp. David noticed through the window that there was an ambulance sitting next to the office, waiting to take them to the hospital.

Well, he thought, *first time in a jet and first time in an ambulance all in the same night.*

Elsa and Dr. Brighton got off the plane while David helped the pilot lift the duffle and the coolers out and into the waiting hands of the ambulance crew. Everything was placed unceremoniously in the back of the ambulance, and then Elsa, Dr. Brighton and David all climbed in the back as well. There was a cot in the middle with the coolers and equipment, and benches on each side.

This time Elsa sat beside David, and he was very aware of her closeness. He caught a whiff of her perfume. The ride to the hospital took only minutes at this time of night.

At the hospital emergency room, it was the same drill in reverse, and the ambulance crew was kind enough to load the equipment back on the cot and roll it through the hospital as they followed the local transplant coordinator to the surgery suite. Elsa left them to go to the female changing area. David and Brighton went into the surgeon's locker room. The OR charge nurse had given them hospital scrubs before they entered, and had also asked them their glove style and size.

The other transplant team waited, including the surgeon who was there for the liver and kidneys, Dr. Carver York. When they were introduced, David smiled in spite of himself at the name, and Dr. York looked at him and knew immediately why he smiled.

With a grin on his face, white teeth flashing, he said, "It's from my great uncle, George Washington Carver."

"Ahh," said David. He did not realize that this would be the beginning of a long friendship and productive professional relationship with Dr. York.

The donor was already on the operating table when the team entered, prepped and draped for surgery. The soft blue of the sterile drapes over the body contrasted slightly with the hard green of the walls and floor.

Although the room was large, it was crammed full of equipment and personnel. The group included David, Elsa, Dr. Brighton, the two other surgeons, a surgical assistant and an organ perfusionist, plus the local transplant coordinator, the scrub tech, two nurses, an orderly, and several others. David later found out that the several others included a surgeon who wanted to view the case and two nurses who had worked with the donor in the Intensive Care Unit before she died.

This donor was a thirty-seven-year-old female who had suffered a closed head injury in a car accident. She and her husband were on vacation and had been on the road all day. She had fallen asleep with her head against the car door. As they traveled, a man who was DUI ran a stop sign and crashed into her side of the car. She never regained consciousness. She had been taken almost immediately by ambulance to the hospital and had undergone emergency brain surgery, even though the neurosurgeon had stated that it was probably hopeless. She did not recover any brain function and was declared brain-dead after a flat EEG and various other tests on the second day. The organ donation agency had been called and had sent a coordinator to assess the situation and to talk to her family about donation if she were a candidate. She was, and her husband had graciously allowed donation, essentially following his wife's wish. She herself had been an intensive care unit nurse for most of her career, and the coordinator in the room related to the doctors how her husband had been insistent about donation.

He had stated, "Saving people's lives has been her life's work. It was her calling. Organ donation is just an extension of that. Of course we will do it."

As the doctors scrubbed for surgery at the sinks, David was struck by the circumstances of the donor's death and by the uncertainty of life. The story of how organ donation was a continuation of this lady's patient care brought tears to his eyes.

Dr. Brighton took his place and then the rest of the surgical team filled in around the operating table.

David, his gloves up to his chest, stepped sideways up to the table opposite Dr. Brighton. He was glad that he had spent a lot of time in a gown and gloves before this, and felt for the scrub nurse. She had her hands full with all of these surgeons. Four surgeons and one assistant were probably more than the lady had ever worked with at one time.

David had trained as a scrub tech to help pay his way during his college pre-med years. He had hundreds of hours doing just what the lady was doing. He had also worked as an orderly weekends and summers in high school. He was comfortable and relaxed in the OR as he stood across from Dr. Brighton, who, like a field colonel, would give the command when to start. When everyone was in place, and after a silent glance and nod to the other surgeons, Brighton looked up to make sure there was a sterile cover on the light handle, then reached up and adjusted the light. He glanced to his right, nodding to the scrub nurse.

"Scalpel!" demanded Brighton, and the case was begun.

He placed his gloved left hand on the donor's chest, feeling for the notch of the sternum, the landmark he would use as he started the incision.

With practiced ease, he cut through the skin and muscle over the sternum, a long, straight incision down to the bone, lifting the knife at the end almost with a flourish. He handed the used scalpel to the scrub nurse, who discarded it to the side.

Since this was a heart donor, a midline incision through the sternum had to be made. This required a saw to cut through the bone.

The Soren saw is like a small version of a carpenter's circular saw. David had never seen one used, but had heard that it was wise to stand back to keep from being splattered by blood. After the skin incision was made, Dr. Brighton showed David the landmark to look for in placing the saw. David leaned in as Dr. Brighton held the saw to the donor's chest at exactly the correct spot to start the cut.

"Clear!" he said sharply, to warn that the cut was about to begin.

"How do you keep from entering the pericardium?" David asked Brighton.

"You have to be careful how you hold the saw." The guard on the saw blade was designed to keep the saw from cutting too deep.

"Sometimes, we have to use a Lebsky knife and a hammer if a saw is not available. But if a hospital has a thoracic surgeon, they will have a Soren saw," he said as he placed bone wax on the edges of the exposed sternum.

Dr. Brighton stood back as Dr. York continued the incision straight down across the abdomen. They wrapped sterile towels over the exposed bone and placed the chest retractor to spread the ribcage to have good access to the heart.

David could now see the pericardium, the tough layer of tissue forming the sack that protects the heart. He could see the proximal side of each lung, and noticed the lungs had small dark spots.

"Did she smoke?" he asked.

"She had in the past," said Dr. Brighton, "But not for the last ten years. However, you will see some tar deposits in almost everyone's lungs. It's from smoke and pollution in the air. A smoker's lungs will have much more. I have seen lungs that are almost entirely blackened by the deposits."

David nodded, mentally kicking himself that he had not read the history and physical in the chart. He should have known that she had smoked.

Dr. McAllister and Dr. Brighton watched as the two other surgeons began the process of gaining access to the liver and kidneys. This involved dissecting away some of the adipose tissue in the abdomen and the connective tissue around the viscera and moving sections of the small and large intestine away from the liver. David could now see the liver clearly, and it looked healthy, with clean sharp edges, not congested or bloated with fat or fluid.

The surgeons would continue until they had complete access to all of the important vessels around the liver and kidneys. A cannula would be placed in the aorta and in the portal vein to perfuse the liver and kidneys with the cold preservation solution.

Dr. Brighton began to make a cut through the pericardium, the sack of connective tissue that protects the heart.

David had already seen a heart bypass procedure, but this was the first time he had seen a healthy heart so close. He held a retractor as Dr. Brighton continued to clear the cavity and to examine all aspects of the heart.

"This heart looks fine," announced Brighton. "Elsa, call Dr. Turner and tell him I have visual acceptance of the heart, it is normal, and to go ahead and call in the team."

He began the process of dissection of the tissue from around the heart and great vessels in preparation for removal. David was amazed at the smooth interior of the pericardium, designed to give a friction-free environment for the beating heart.

Dr. York and his assistant were still dissecting around the liver and its vessels, and gaining access to the kidneys.

David felt a soft hand on his shoulder blade and turned to see Elsa very close on his left, holding an IV pole.

"Would you let me hang the perfusion solution and hand the cannula off to you?" she asked.

She opened the sterile pack with the cannula for the heart, and held it out to David. He reached into the pack and removed the device. She then asked the scrub nurse to hand him the IV set for perfusing the heart, and told him how to hook the cannula to the end and then hand her the other end to hook to the bag of cold solution that she had ready to hang on the IV pole. Dr. Brighton clamped the tubing to the sterile towel next to the open chest, and after Elsa opened the port under the IV bag, he allowed some of the solution to run out into a basin to make sure that there were no bubbles of air in the line. Then he closed off the clamp, stopping the flow.

Elsa then began pouring icy cold saline solution into a basin on the back table, getting it ready to use for topically cooling the heart.

After this, when everyone was ready, the aorta was cross-clamped.

Dr. Brighton looked up at the bright red letters of the digital clock on the OR wall which read 03:12.

Dr. Brighton called out the cross-clamp time to Elsa and quickly began to flush the heart with the solution, and barked to the scrub tech, "Slush, please."

Elsa motioned to the full basins of slushy saline, and the CST handed one of them to Dr. Brighton. As David held the retractor to give good access, Dr. Brighton slowly poured the entire basin of cold saline into the open chest, around the heart. This, along with the ice cold perfusion solution now flowing through the heart itself, almost instantly cooled it down to the temperature of the solution, about four degrees Celsius.

The two other surgeons did the same with cold saline in the donor's abdominal cavity. This step was precisely timed so the organs would be cooled rapidly after cross-clamp. Any warm time without perfusion would be detrimental to the function of the transplants, and as David would later learn, especially detrimental to the heart.

Everyone waited a few minutes and watched to be sure that the perfusion solution from the IV bags was flowing correctly.

Then the surgeons began to work to actually remove the organs. Dr. Brighton showed David the correct landmarks for dissection of the vessels around the heart, careful to preserve plenty of length for making the anastomosis back to the transplant patient's vessels when the heart was implanted.

Brighton quickly finished, and reaching around the heart with both hands, brought it up and out of the donor's chest and held it closely to his own, protecting it against the front of his surgical gown as he walked carefully around the OR table to a sterile basin Elsa had set up on the back table. He gently laid the heart down in the container of solution, and examined it thoroughly, looking into the opening of the atrium and inside the other vessels. He showed David the inside of the heart. It was almost white, and very smooth.

"This is nature's Teflon," Dr. Brighton said with a smile.

As Elsa stood by with a bag of the cold solution ready to pour onto the heart, Brighton placed the heart in the center of the sterile bag and brought the sides up. He nodded to Elsa and she filled the bag almost completely full of solution, leaving just enough room for him to twist the top of the bag closed and then to knot it. They did the same with the next bag, and then with another, finally closing the container with a snap top. Dr. Brighton placed the container in another sterile bag and tied it closed.

Brighton then picked up the bag and carefully gave it to Elsa, who, after placing a label with *Heart,* the donor's medical record number, the blood type, and the cross-clamp time on the bag, lowered it gently into the cooler that had held the cold solution. This cooler had already been labeled with the information about the donor. She carefully covered the container completely with ice, placed a surgical towel on top of the ice, and closed the cooler.

By this time the other surgeons and their team had removed the other organs. Elsa began to quickly gather up all of the miscellaneous paraphernalia as the doctors went back to the OR table to sew the donor back up and reconstruct so that the body would look normal again. Dr. Brighton removed the chest retractor, showed David the running stitch used to close the chest and left him to finish. David carefully, almost reverently, closed the long incision, making sure that it was done properly and well. He knew that this person had loved ones, and wanted to be sure that everything was correct. He looked up as Elsa took the retractors to pack them up. She glanced at him with a pleased look, and he was surprised that it made him happy to have her approval for his work.

They finished in the OR and quickly stripped off the surgical gowns and gloves. They washed up at the scrub sinks. Picking up the duffel and other cooler, they left to go. Brighton was standing at the door of the surgical suite, holding the cooler with the heart. He had already changed clothes.

David and Elsa did not change out of their scrubs; they just grabbed their street clothes. They ran down the hall behind Brighton, David carrying the other cooler and Elsa dragging the duffle on its little wheels. She had already called the ambulance back, and was on the phone as they ran, breathlessly telling the pilot to be ready to leave as soon as they made it back to the airport.

The rest of the morning was just as amazing for David. There was a run to the ambulance for the rush to the airport, a quick ride to the jet for the flight back with Elsa and Dr. Brighton, a helicopter ride from the airport to the hospital, landing on the roof, and the run to surgery. He would scrub in again to assist Dr. Brighton in transplanting the heart.

This night and day would forever be etched in his mind.

The patient was in the OR when they returned with the heart. She was already asleep, and Dr. Turner, the transplant fellow, had the room set up completely for the case. David couldn't believe that this many people could fit in one OR. Not only was the regular staff of nurses, anesthesia personnel, and scrub staff in the room, there was also the perfusion staff with the heart bypass machine. The machine was huge, and took up most of the space on the left side of the bed. After he had scrubbed, gowned and gloved, he had a hard time staying sterile as he squeezed between the machine and the OR table, leaving the bulk of the space beside him for Dr. Brighton, who backed into the room, his hands dripping from the scrub he had just finished. He had on a pair of glasses with magnifying loupes, held securely in place by a bright red strap.

"Could we have some music, please?"

The circulator nodded and walked over to a small tape player mounted to the wall. Soon the sounds of a classical piano piece were flowing quietly through the room. Brighton smiled at her and nodded.

Now glancing over at the scrub nurse, his favorite, he smiled and said hello. With a silent glance and a nod to the other surgeon, he looked up to make sure there was a sterile cover on the light handle, then reached up and adjusted the light. He placed his gloved left hand on the patient's chest, feeling for the notch of the sternum, the landmark that he used as he started the incision.

Brighton, without looking up, opened his hand and commanded, "Scalpel!" The case began.

David watched as the same basic steps were followed in opening the chest as had been followed with the donor. When the sternum was retracted and the pericardium opened, David gasped. This had to be the ugliest heart that had ever continued to beat.

It was almost too large for the cavity, a dull gray, and covered with yellow scar tissue. It moved in an odd wriggle that could never be mistaken for a normal rhythm. That it was moving any blood at all was a miracle.

Dr. Brighton looked at him over the magnifying lenses. "Vicky has had several prior surgeries and has one of the worst cases of cardiomyopathy that I have ever seen. This heart looked bad on the chest X-ray, and worse on the echo, but I didn't know it was this bad. I don't see how she has made it this long."

He shook his head, then looked up at David and smiled.

"Well, we've got a new one for her, and it's going to work perfectly."

He quickly began the process of placing the tubes for the bypass and preparing the heart for excision. The patient was placed on bypass. Then, as David watched in awe, Dr. Brighton quickly cut through the heart vessels, reached in, and scooped out the diseased heart. It was so odd to look into the empty cavity, seeing only the pericardial wall posterior to where the heart had been. He could clearly see now how the inside of the pericardium was exquisitely smooth. Smooth to allow the least amount of friction for the beating heart. To David, it was another glimpse of the magic and miracle of the human body.

While Dr. Brighton removed the old heart, the assisting surgeon had stepped to the back table and opened the container that held the donor heart. He opened the bag and lifted out the new heart, examining the vessels and making sure the flaps of artery and vein were correct to make the anastomosis into the patient's arteries and veins. He cradled the heart against the front of his gown as he carefully brought it to the table for Dr. Brighton, who received it almost reverently. David watched as Brighton held the heart over the cavity, assuring himself that there was nothing left in there to interfere with the transplant, and carefully laid the new heart in place.

David nearly couldn't believe the contrast between this heart and the other. This one was pristine and healthy: the muscle tissue strong and vibrant, even in its present ice cold state. The other heart had looked like a piece of old rotting meat.

Dr. Brighton began the process of sewing in the new heart, careful to make the anastomosis perfectly, with stitches so small that David again felt awe, this time at the skill of this surgeon. David glanced at the clock on the wall. From the incision to this point had been only been about forty minutes. Again he was amazed. To open the chest, start bypass, remove the old heart, and now almost have the new one in in less than an hour was really fast, and the truly amazing thing was that Dr. Brighton had never appeared to rush his technique. He obviously had this down to a fine art, exactly the right steps at exactly the right time in exactly the right sequence. No wasted movement or effort at all.

David knew that the heart only had about four or five hours at the most of viability between the donor and the recipient, and the clock was ticking. It had been three hours and forty-two minutes since the aorta was cross-clamped in the heart procurement as Dr. Brighton finished the last vessel.

He was reminded of the his old Aikido instructor, a man whose every movement seemed planned, and who never seemed to waste a motion. This was the way it was with Dr. Brighton. Everything was perfectly planned and executed so that the case went as quickly and smoothly as possible. David realized that this was the only way a successful heart transplant was possible.

He watched as Dr. Brighton prepared to open the vessels so that blood could flow to the new heart. Throughout the procedure, one of David's jobs, along with holding the suction and keeping good access for Dr. Brighton with a retractor, had been to periodically place ice cold, sterile slush over the heart. If the heart had been allowed to warm to body temperature too early, it would have started to deteriorate, and might not have worked.

Now it was time to see if it would.

David watched as Dr. Brighton opened the vessel and allowed the blood into the heart. The color of the heart immediately began to darken to that of a healthy organ, and the heart began to warm. Dr. Brighton massaged the organ slightly to keep blood from pooling inside. David wasn't sure, but he thought he saw the heart begin to contract slightly. After a minute or two, Dr. Brighton carefully massaged the heart again. It slowly started beating, the rhythm irregular and somewhat disorganized at first. David looked on in amazement as the new heart took a few minutes to settle down to a regular rhythm. Dr. Brighton watched closely for any signs of weakness in any of the sutures, but there were none. The heart continued to beat happily, and David noticed that it was not like a sudden squeeze, but that you could see the muscle contract in a sequence that caused the blood to flow through in the most efficient way. He could actually see the *lub-dub* cadence take place, as each chamber contracted in its turn. Each part of the heart working to pump at exactly the right time. Just one more of the amazing characteristics of the human body, he thought. And, the difference between this heart and the one that had been there could not have been greater.

Dr. Brighton looked at the perfusionist.

"Off bypass," he directed.

A couple of minutes later, Dr. Brighton instructed David and the other assisting surgeon to close.

• • •

David looked back over at the picture of Elsa on his desk. It had been more than ten years since that night, the night that changed his life forever. He had fallen in love with Elsa. They were married and now had a son. He had done a heart transplant fellowship and was now back at the medical college as a professor and transplant surgeon himself. He smiled and shook his head, still remembering that first night.

9

Sensitives

AS HE WALKED into the clinic, McAllister was pleased to see Martha Lake's name on the patient list. She had an appointment at nine that morning.

Transplant patients normally spend the first few days after the procedure in the hospital. Then, for the next few weeks, they move into "the townhouse," a building on the same block as the hospital that at one time had been a hotel. The hospital board had purchased the building when the hotel closed, hoping to use the land someday for expansion. In the meantime, however, it was used by patients who needed to stay close to the hospital, but not in the hospital itself. It was perfect for transplant patients from out of town, both while they were awaiting a transplant and during the month or so afterwards, when they had to have regular follow-ups. At first these were daily, then every other day, then twice a week, and so on until the patient was released to go home.

Martha was several weeks out and had done exceptionally well after her heart transplant. David knew she would soon be ready to go home, perhaps the end of this week. As he stood at the door and glanced through her chart, he remembered the night that she received her new heart. He remembered how deathly ill she was, and how glad he was that the heart had been good.

The transplant had gone well. There had been no acute rejection process, and for this he was thankful. Acute rejection can occur immediately after transplant, and could be deadly. In that situation, the transplant patient's body immediately recognizes that the organ is foreign, and organizes a reaction to get rid of the foreign body. One of the reactions was to form antibodies against the organ. These so–called "killer cells" would target the organ and actually destroy it, just like the body would target a bacterial infection. This type of rejection was more difficult to control. Usually, however, the rejection reaction by the body would be slower, and could be controlled by antirejection medications. This reaction was monitored by various tests, and the patient's drug regimen would be tailored to control it. The medications for rejection had been improved tremendously over the years, and for most patients were now just a few pills each day.

As David knocked on the door and then walked into Martha's room, he was greeted by all three of the Lakes. Martha was sitting on the exam table, smiling. Alan was in a chair against the wall, as was Kristi, their daughter. Kristi was close to Nicholas' age. Alan stood and shook his hand, and David went over to check on Martha.

"Good morning, Dr. Mac," said Martha, with her characteristic big smile.

Martha had been a beauty queen at her high school, and then had done some modeling in college. Today, she looked wonderful. He could tell without an exam that she was doing well. Her complexion was healthy, her nail beds were pink, she looked ready to get up and run a mile.

David smiled back at her. These were the times that made his long hours so worthwhile. As he examined her incision, he saw it was healing well. When he listened to her heart, it sounded perfect. Martha described how she was feeling and everything seemed fine. He discussed her plan, that she could start thinking about going home soon, and then asked if she had any questions.

"I do," said Martha. "I want to talk to you about my donor."

She glanced over at Alan who picked up Kristi from her chair, and said hastily, "We'll wait in the lobby, honey," and nodded a goodbye to Dr. Mac.

After the door closed, David sat on the stool next to Martha, and spoke softly, "You know, Martha, I can't tell you a lot right now, but later on we may be able to talk more about that. It's up to the family of the donor."

"No, that's not what I mean."

Martha looked down.

"I know my donor was a girl in an accident, the nurses told me that much. It's something else, Dr. Mac."

She paused and drew in her breath, then looked up at David.

"I've been having a dream... She paused a moment, looking down. "It's coming from my heart."

"What kind of dream?" asked David, slowly.

"It's about her, Dr. Mac."

Martha looked down again, tears beginning to well up in her eyes. "She's in a helicopter. I can see her face in the windshield. She has light brown hair and dark eyes. She is smiling at me, a big happy smile... And she lets me feel a good feeling, like everything's okay... it's hard to describe."

Martha looked back up at him, her voice trembling.

"Has anyone else felt this way?"

"It's okay, Martha. People often have vivid dreams after a transplant. We think it may be the medicines, you know, the prednisone and the others."

"No, Dr. Mac, this is not that, I've had those, too. This is her, for real. The dream comes from my heart. I can feel it. She's not driving the helicopter. I just see her face, like in the glass. She is young and pretty, and she's smiling, like she's happy. Oh, and she is wearing an orange T-shirt with blue trim. I think it has a lizard or something on it. I can see it clearly... "

She shook her head, then looked directly at him. "Tell me the truth. Has this happened before, or am I the only one. Is it crazy?"

David paused, looking at Martha, then sighed, shaking his head.

"No, Martha, you're not crazy. It has happened before, and I can't explain it. But I do have someone who would like to talk to you about it. Would you be willing to tell someone else?"

"A shrink?" squeaked Martha worriedly.

"No, no." David laughed. "This is a lady who has a special interest in this. Her name is Dr. Sally Debardeleben. She is a psychologist, and also a nun, believe it or not. Look, I don't understand these dreams, but she can help you. Can I call her? Would you talk to her?"

"Yes, sir," Martha said excitedly.

"Is there anything else?" David asked.

"No, Dr. Mac, and thank you."

Martha looked into his eyes, her voice still trembling with emotion.

"I'm really not crazy?"

"No, you're not crazy, I think you are doing great."

David stood, looking down at her with a smile.

"I'll call Dr. Debardeleben. See you Friday."

David breezed out the door. He wrote a quick note in the chart, and then told Kim to call Dr. Debardeleben.

As he sat at the desk, Elsa came up behind him.

"What's wrong?" she asked.

"It's Martha Lake."

"Oh, no," said Elsa. "Is she okay?"

"She's doing great."

"Then what's wrong?"

"I think she's one of Dr. Debardeleben's *sensitives*."

"Really?" Elsa's eyes lit up with curiosity.

"Yeah, she's having dreams about her donor, and from what I remember, they seem pretty accurate."

"Sort of like Carolyn Jones?"

"Yeah, the same kind of thing. It gave me goosebumps when she described her donor. I remember that the girl was airlifted by helicopter to the hospital, and Martha is dreaming about a girl in a helicopter. She sees her face and everything. And just like Carolyn, she says, 'It comes from my heart.'"

"At least she's calling it *her* heart, and not *that person's* heart."

Kim came over and announced, "Dr. Debardeleben is on the phone, line one."

"Thanks, Kim," said David. He picked up the telephone and punched the button.

"Hi, Sally, how are you?"

"Fine, David, how are you?" came back a voice he enjoyed. Sally had the slightest south Alabama drawl in combination with a low pitch as smooth as molasses.

"I'm good, just busy as usual," said David.

"So, what's up, Doc?" He could hear the smile though the phone line.

"I think I have another of your sensitives," he said. "Female, recent heart transplant, doing well, but having dreams that seem to be pretty realistic. Are you still interested?"

"Absolutely, you know I am. When can I come by?"

David covered the phone mouthpiece and questioned Elsa, "Tomorrow morning?"

Elsa nodded.

"How does tomorrow morning look?" he said into the phone.

"I have an eight o'clock client, but then am open from nine to eleven."

David smiled at how psychologists had "clients" instead of patients.

"Good. Let's say nine-thirty."

"See you then," she said. "Tell Elsa hello for me."

"I will," said David, with a sparkle in his eyes. "Thanks."

He hung up the phone.

"She says hello."

He smiled down at Elsa.

"You knew she would jump at coming over here," said Elsa. "I'm just glad she's a nun."

David laughed. "You're one to talk."

Kim was looking at them strangely.

Elsa grinned at her. "He says I have a flock of guys following me around all the time."

"That's right," said David. "Let's see, there's that drug rep... no, two... then there's the bug man, and then there's Ken..."

"I know," said Elsa, with a sigh, "I just can't keep up with them all."

David laughed. "Sally is strictly a professional relationship."

"Suuuure," Elsa smiled back, "but I'm still glad she's a nun."

• • •

The next day David was sitting in his office when the receptionist called back that he had a visitor, Dr. Debardeleben.

"Tell her to come on back."

A few seconds later he heard a soft knock and stood to open the door.

"Good morning, David." Sally smiled up at him.

"Hello, Sally. It's good to see you."

Sally was in her early thirties. She had jet-black hair down to the middle of her back, and dark eyes. She was dressed in a smart black skirt and cream-colored satin blouse. And she was a stunning beauty.

David knew that she had Italian heritage. She had been born in Europe to a military man, but raised in Alabama. He had learned on previous visits that her father was a helicopter pilot and had settled in southeast Alabama after retiring from the military. He had had flight training at Fort Rucker, and fell in love with the South. Sally had gone to college in Alabama, but then completed a doctorate in psychology at Notre Dame. Her mother was a staunch Catholic, and Sally had participated in mission trips from the small Catholic parish that they attended in Dothan. She had fallen in love with ministry. She had become a sister before going to Notre Dame, and was now working at Saint Vincent's hospital in Birmingham. She also worked as a professor at the University.

David had met her when she came to see him about a client who was a heart recipient. The client was having trouble accepting the death of the donor, among other things, and had been referred to Sally by the client's parish priest. The client was also having dreams about her donor. Sally had asked for a consult with Dr. Mac to ask about the ins and outs of heart transplantation, and to discuss the client's past medical history. They had hit it off from the beginning.

David had had more than one heart recipient with these types of issues. He was interested in what was going on, but, with his research and transplant schedule, was not able to give it a lot of thought. He had asked other surgeons about the issue of dreams or other things at various meetings over the years, but most ignored it completely or said it was just the prednisone.

He would never forget the time he had asked an older

transplant surgeon, one of his mentors, about it.

"David, a heart is just a pump," the doctor had said, emphatically.

A few of the younger surgeons, though, had agreed with him, that it was happening and was an interesting issue. But David, well trained in research-based medicine, still wasn't sure it was real. He thought maybe patients had learned about their donor through the news or the hospital grapevine, and were elaborating on the story with their dreams.

David was glad to have a psychology type interested. Sally, for her part, was perfect for the job. She had done extensive research in thanatology, the study of death. She was an expert on grief reactions, both of patients faced with death and of families of patients who had died. She also had a strong interest in near-death experiences. End-of-life issues were important to her fellow Catholics, and she was becoming a recognized expert.

To know her, however, one would never guess this interest of hers. She was vivacious and positive. She liked teaching, and her classes were generally enjoyable for her students, the males especially. And her clients tended to do well, as she worked to get them to think beyond themselves.

Over the last few years, though, she had become intrigued by Dr. David McAllister and his transplant patients. She had read research from other transplant centers where patients were reporting similar experiences. It was interesting that most of the people who reported dreams or thoughts about their donor were heart transplant patients. It was less common in liver, lung, and kidney patients, although there were a few cases.

She herself had begun a study, with some funds from the church, of patients who had been transplanted here in Alabama. David had referred about twenty people to her over the years, and she had dozens more who had agreed to be interviewed several weeks, then several months, after their transplant. The transplant programs at Vanderbilt in Nashville and at Emory in Atlanta had agreed to let her interview some of their patients who had the dreams.

Dr. Debardeleben now had about forty-five heart patients who reported dreams or other signals from their donors. She also had a few liver recipients and several kidney recipients in her study who reported similar experiences.

By this time, she had interviewed hundreds of transplant recipients. Most had few or no strange or unusual effects from the transplant. But there was a group, about ten percent, who did report unusual memories or dreams. She called them *sensitives*. She had found that most were women, and most had certain characteristics. They were usually not type A personalities, but more nurturing types. Most of them also scored high on an intuition scale from an instrument that she had developed to assess these patients. Patients reported all sorts of phenomena, from dreams and visions to food cravings.

Sally, because of her duties at St. Vincent's Hospital, had often been involved in cases where patients had died and were donors. One of her jobs was to attend and support the family when patients were dying or being removed from life support. She was also on the donation committee, and was one of the hospital counselors who went into the room with the donation coordinator when they asked permission for organ donation. She was respected by the Organ Center staff as an advocate.

Sally had gotten permission from the organ bank to research the medical and social histories of donors for patients in her study. She had done meticulous research on the types of donors that seemed to evoke responses from recipients.

The organ donation center had special donor recognition services where families could meet recipients. There was also a large celebration each year called the Transplant Picnic, where patients came from all over celebrate their transplants. Donor families were invited to this as well, and this was often the first time that they got to meet transplant recipients. Sally attended all of these and gave families questionnaires to fill out about the donor.

She also interviewed donor families after donation and asked for information about the person and the circumstances of their death. This was all kept confidential, but she had seen time after time when the recipients knew things about the donor that were not public and had not been known by anyone except the donor's closest friends and family. She never told recipients if their information was true, but their dreams and intuition often matched the donor's situation to an unbelievable extent.

She impressed the director of the organ center with her interest and expertise, and was asked to be a consultant for them to help deal with families who had issues after donation. She made it a point to visit the families of donors from her hospital within a few days of the death, giving them information on grief and offering counseling help if they needed it. She found in her study of these families that donation was often therapeutic for the family of the donor.

Sally even researched accident reports in which donors were involved. She was particularly interested in those connected to her sensitives. After several years, she had compiled an impressive amount of data.

It was not unusual, in fact it was becoming very common, for patients to meet the family of their donor some time after the transplant, usually at one of the recognition services. Sally isolated reports from recipients prior to these meetings, knowing that later reports would be skewed by what patients learned about their donor.

This was why she was here today. She had asked David to call her immediately when a patient mentioned dreams or other phenomena about their donor.

"I appreciate you coming at such short notice," said David.

"The patient is a thirty-three-year-old female, married, one child. Her name is Martha Lake. She is a delightful person. She had a peripartum cardiomyopathy. I think it was probably something viral. She is less than a month out, but seems to be doing very well. Like usual, I want to wait until you talk with her before I tell you what I know about the donor."

"You still think they are picking up this information somewhere else, don't you, David."

"I know some can be from the hospital grapevine, news stories, and such," said David, "but some of them seem to go way beyond that. Martha's donor was over two hundred miles away, from Florida. I haven't seen any local news on the donor's accident, and Martha was in a coma at the time. She has described what the girl looked like, and what she was wearing the day of the accident."

Sally smiled at David's clinical manner, but was surprised by his next question.

"Where does this come from, Sally?"

"I don't know for sure, David. And yes, you are right, some of the information is learned from outside sources. But I have too many documented histories now of sensitives knowing things that they could not possibly know in normal ways."

She went on, her dark eyes shining.

"It almost always has something to do with the heart. There are a few patients with other transplants who have cravings and strange dreams. One who never liked oatmeal and now loves it— turns out the donor's favorite breakfast was oatmeal. Now, this may be attributed to prednisone or other medications—appetite is increased and so on."

"But I have heart recipients who know the donor's pet's name. One who was an artist drew a picture three weeks after transplant of a young Hispanic guy. She had no reason, she said that it just came to her. The picture captured her donor perfectly, hair style, eyes, right down to the mustache. He was from Chicago and she was in Nashville. I checked the local and national news for that day, and there was no story anywhere. The transplant surgeon who took the heart went on vacation the next day; his partner did her transplant."

She went on.

"I do not think these cases can be explained in a normal clinical manner. We know there is something beyond this life, and perhaps there is communication between that world and this one. Many of the dreams involve a visit by the donor, so that could explain them. But there seems to be something else going on in some of my cases."

David nodded, having expected a spiritual perspective from Sally, and even agreeing that this was possible.

Sally smiled at him, knowing what he was thinking.

She paused a moment then, as if debating with herself whether to go on. She glanced to her left.

Then, still smiling, she looked at David and continued.

"Another explanation is that the heart has some sort of memory, and *it* is communicating with the recipient."

David looked at her quizzically.

"What do you mean the heart has memory?"

"I don't know for sure," Sally said, "But it seems to happen so much more with hearts that I think there is some kind of special energy there."

David thought a minute.

"There is energy there," he conceded. "The heart has a lot more electrical energy than the brain, but it's different. It is not a thought process or memory system like the brain has."

"I know," said Sally, "But there is something else there, some kind of memory, a memory on the cellular level. I don't understand it at all, but I believe what these people are saying."

They talked some more, and then David gave her Martha's phone number. As she stood to go, she gave David a big smile.

"Thanks," she said, "You know that some of the other surgeons think this is crazy. I appreciate you working with me on this."

"This is interesting to me, as well."

He stood up.

"It's always good to see you, Sally. Let me know how this goes with Martha."

He watched her as she walked down the hall, thinking about what she said about the heart and its energy.

10

The Pump

DR. MCALLISTER AND others had often thought that if there was some way to sustain the heart out of the body, then transplants would be more successful. Transplant success almost always hinged on time. Even with the heart in ice, the maximum time between the donor and recipient was only about four or five hours. After that organs began to deteriorate, and would not work after being transplanted.

That short window made it imperative that donor and transplant recipients be within about eight hundred miles of each other. David and his wife, Elsa, wanted to figure out some way to overcome the time-distance quandary. Think of how much a donor base could be expanded if, for example, a matching donor heart in Los Angeles was available to a patient in Atlanta. Keeping organs viable for longer periods was not a new concept. Kidneys had been sustained in such a way for quite some time, the McAllisters observed. After removal from the donor, kidneys were often placed on "the pump," a perfusion machine that pumps a solution through the kidneys. This pump actually pulses, and has been shown to help kidneys function better as well as giving doctors an assessment of how well blood will flow through the kidney after transplant. In the case of the kidney perfusion machine, it is not blood that is pumped through, but a solution that has been developed to sustain the kidney. When the kidney is in this cold state, it does not need much oxygen to remain viable. The kidneys can be kept on the pump for two days if necessary.

The heart, on the other hand, is a muscle, and a prodigious user of oxygen. While a heart is in the cooler, it is not functioning— just cold and still. But during this time there is always going to be a breakdown of the cells and a certain loss of function at the cellular level. This is certainly much slower while the heart is cold than it would be if it were not.

A heart can take only a few minutes without oxygen in its normal state. This is illustrated when someone has a cardiac arrest and resuscitation is not immediately available. If more than just minutes pass, it will be impossible to restart the heart. Doctors have learned over the years that if a patient was cold, as happens in a drowning in cold water, and/or young, then the heart may be restarted after a longer time.

The first heart transplants were attempted without cooling the heart. These were not very successful. Only after brain-death protocols were established and hearts could be quickly cooled after they stopped did heart transplants become a true option.

The McAllisters wanted to go a step farther. They wanted to try a perfusion machine *for hearts.*

Could hearts be kept on a pump like kidneys? What would be the best method for such a system? Would the solution need to be cold or warm like blood?

As David McAllister experimented the same basic questions kept coming back to him. What if the heart was beating on its own in a warm, oxygen-rich and nutrient-rich solution that mimicked blood? Wouldn't it function better after transplant? Could a heart go longer ex-vivo before transplant if it was pumped?

McAllister had been working with a company that made artificial hearts for years. He was involved in clinical trials of some of the most advanced artificial hearts, and had several patients functioning well on these machines.

They had their limitations, though. One was the fact that the power supply had to be outside the body, while the artificial heart was of course implanted inside. He would never forget the sad case he had had of a patient who had one of the portable artificial hearts. The power supply was in a small suitcase, and there were leads going into an access port in the patient's chest. The device had functioned well in several patients, and some had even been allowed to live at home. Most were waiting for a transplant of a real heart, and this was just their life-sustaining bridge until a heart came available for them.

This patient had moved back home and was able to live a fairly normal life, going out to eat, to shop, or even to church with his machine in tow. Then one day he accidentally closed the car door on the leads from his heart machine. David would never forget the frantic call from the patient's wife, and the absolute powerlessness that he had felt. There was nothing anyone could do for the man.

That man was not just a patient, but had become a friend. Most of David's heart patients were like this, almost like family. David became even more convinced that human hearts need to be replaced with human hearts. He renewed his vow that day to do what he could to increase the transplant of real hearts for these people.

McAllister had approached the artificial heart machine company several years earlier about a heart perfusion machine. They were interested, and began a product development program, naming David their chief researcher. He had come up with a research protocol and submitted it to the National Institutes of Health for a grant. This had come about, and the funding had allowed him to start a perfusion lab. Through the artificial heart company, he got to work with some of the best biomedical engineers in the country. The research had been going on for a couple of years, but with mixed results.

Elsa McAllister actually ran the program, since David had so many responsibilities with his patients. She spent a couple of days a week in the lab, working on parameters for the pump and research protocols. David was only able to be present in the lab a few hours per week as things developed, but got busier as the machine actually came online. He was aided by a couple of transplant fellows, as well.

There were many issues and hurdles to be overcome in the development of the heart perfusion machine. A major one was the perfusion solution, and its temperature. Another issue was the oxygenation system. Of course the machine would have to be portable to facilitate transport of the heart from some outlying hospital.

The early studies used pig hearts attached to artificial vessels, which continued to pump, using a fluid to mimic blood. They had tried using normal body temperature fluid and very cold fluid. They had found that warm was better than cold, but there were problems with keeping the beating heart oxygenated and getting rid of waste byproducts. There was recent promise in the use of an artificial blood product invented by the Japanese. David had actually done a couple of the pig heart transplants using heparinized blood from the donor pig, and this worked to some degree, but not well.

The newest perfusion machine, designated the MT12, was a wonder of modern engineering. It incorporated a type of artificial lung capable of supplying sufficient oxygen to a functioning heart, as well as cleansing the carbon dioxide from the perfusion solution. The device required a tank to supply oxygen, but since it was just the heart muscle being oxygenated and not the whole body, the tank could be fairly small. There were two semi-permeable membranes in the machine, one so the perfusate could pick up the oxygen and one using a solution to remove the carbon dioxide. There was also a small pumping system to facilitate the heart if needed, but to the awe of the scientists and David McAllister the heart actually served to pump its own perfusate, just as it would in the body. There was even a small computer to record pressures, pulse rate, and oxygen saturation. A port took samples of the perfusion solution to monitor levels of electrolytes, hemoglobin and other components.

They had recently moved from pig hearts to human hearts donated for research. These hearts were from donors whose hearts could not be transplanted due to age or disease. Many times, when families give consent for donation, they also give consent for research. If research consent was given for a heart and it was viable enough for the pump program, McAllister would use it. The results were beginning to be positive, but had not moved far enough to actually use the pump for a human transplant. David had applied for research authority to attempt the human transplants, but this had not yet been approved.

David was in the process of publishing his research in the journal of the American Society of Transplant Surgeons.

Experiments with body temperature hearts were more promising: they would actually beat for several hours. However, oxygenation and nutrient systems did not seem adequate for the task, and the heart muscle was being damaged in the process.

David had struggled for months with how to limit damage to the heart while it was pumping, and to understand what the mechanism was that was causing the damage. So far, there had not been a resolution of the problem.

• • •

After working in the lab one afternoon, he came home for dinner. He looked forward to these family nights together. Sometimes Elsa would cook and sometimes he would. They might even order out if it had been a busy day for both. The main thing was that they were able to sit down as a family and have a meal, and discuss what was going on in their lives. Their eight-year-old son Nicholas would talk about school or they would talk about other issues. Sometimes they talked about the research.

This night, as they sat watching TV with their son, a program was on about Charles Lindbergh and his solo flight across the Atlantic. Nicholas liked airplanes, and had told his dad that someday he wanted to be a pilot. He was interested in Lindbergh, and they had seen that this show was scheduled on TV. Both David and Nicholas sat in rapt attention at the story of Lindbergh and how he made the flight from New York to Paris in a single engine plane.

When the program was almost over, David looked down at his son and asked, "Did you know that Charles Lindbergh also helped develop the first heart bypass machine?"

"Nope!" said Nicholas, looking up. "I just thought he was a pilot."

"Well, he was a great pilot, but he also was interested in medicine. One of his family members was sick with heart disease, and Lindbergh wondered why an operation could not be done. At that time there was no open-heart surgery and no bypass machine. He knew Dr. Alexis Carrel, a famous surgeon, and approached him about working together on an artificial heart machine."

"Like the artificial heart that you and mom are working on?"

"Sort of, but this one was to keep a person alive as surgery was being done on their own heart. It was the forerunner of the heart bypass machine that we use today."

"Maybe someday I can be a pilot and a doctor, too," said Nicholas.

"Maybe so, kiddo," said David, smiling as he leaned over and ruffled his son's hair.

The Lindbergh program had finished and the next show was about the bears in Alaska. It showed footage of bears catching salmon in the streams during the summer, and fighting with eagles over fish they had caught. The program discussed the bear's habitat and range. Of course Nicholas was interested in bears, so he and David sat and watched. Nicholas smiled and laughed at a clip of two grizzly cubs splashing in a stream, "learning" to fish.

Then a segment came on about the bears in winter, with an interview with a Denali National Park veterinarian discussing bear hibernation. The veterinarian stated, "The bear's heart rate slows down dramatically during hibernation, to about an average of ten beats per minute. The kidneys and other organs almost shut down completely and the metabolic rate drops by sixty to seventy percent. The bear's oxygen and calorie requirements go down significantly, but his body temperature only drops about fifteen percent."

David sat up with a start when he heard this. He looked over at Elsa, whose blue eyes were dancing with delight. She had heard it, too.

"That's it!" he cried, "That's what we need to do!!"

"What, daddy?" asked Nick, looking up confused.

"We need to put the hearts into hibernation!" exclaimed Elsa.

David jumped up, already excited at the thought, scratching his head and thinking about the problem from a whole new perspective.

He began rambling aloud as his jumbled thoughts poured

breathlessly out. "I know we can slow the heart but all of our experiments have been to cool them way down. Maybe if we can slow them and only cool them slightly, we could keep them viable."

He looked sideways at Elsa, and continued talking as he paced excitedly.

"That would still significantly lower the metabolism of the heart ex vivo, and the lower oxygen and nutrition requirement would lower the waste byproducts and limit the free radical damage."

He thought a minute, then continued, "We need to talk to someone who knows about bears. And I think I know the person who would know that someone."

He beamed at Elsa.

"Elsa, I've got to call Carver. Now."

When Dr. Carver York answered the phone, it took him a minute to realize who it was. "York, grizzly bears are the answer!!" was all he had heard.

After clearing up the confounding issue of the caller's identity, York was back on track. "What's got you so excited, David?"

"Bears!" said David.

York was lost again.

"You mean Chicago? Did they win?"

"No, not Chicago," David laughed. "Grizzlies!"

"Oookay," said Carver, "Let's start over again... "

David smiled at Elsa as he explained to Carver the program that they had watched that night. Carver had been involved in the heart research project from the start as a consultant. His expertise, of course, was in the kidney perfusion machine protocol, and he was a proponent of pumping kidneys. In fact, the transplant program at the University pumped every kidney. Because of this expertise, he had been a valuable resource in the heart project.

Now he understood why David was so excited.

"I think I know the person you need to talk to," he said excitedly to David. "Can I come over?"

"Absolutely," David replied, as he gave Elsa a big thumbs up.

Carver lived a couple of blocks away, in the same

neighborhood as David and Elsa. The area had been one of the first suburban developments in Birmingham, and most of the houses were older family homes. It had seen a time of decline, but in recent years young professionals who worked in the city had begun to buy the homes and remodel and restore them.

The street from Carver's house wound around the house behind them, and Elsa and David stood at the window watching for Carver. He came around the bend on his Segway. They laughed as they watched him lean into the curve of the road, small headlights ablaze.

The neighborhood had nice sidewalks, but York was in a hurry, and there was no other traffic, so he was in the street. Seconds later, he was at the carport door.

David laughed at Carver's gadget.

"When did you get that thing?"

"It came in last weekend." Carver said. "They have them at the bike shop."

Carver was an avid bicycler. He had two road bikes and a mountain bike, and it was nothing for him to do fifty miles on a Saturday. He and David had known each other since they first assisted Dr. Brighton years ago when David got his start in the transplant business.

Carver and David had since distinguished themselves in their respective fields and often stood side by side in procuring and replacing vital organs. David was the heart guy; Carver the kidney and liver specialist.

Elsa had started some hot chocolate for Nick, and offered the guys some. Both were on call.

David walked over and switched the TV to the weather, just to see the current temperature. As they sat together at the table in the family room, David explained a little more about what they had seen.

"When the bears go into hibernation, their heart slows and their oxygen use declines. They obviously go into a functional hypothermia, and it looks like all of their metabolic processes slow down as well. This is just what we need on the heart perfusion machine."

"I can't believe that we didn't think of this before," said Carver.

"It was like a Eureka moment," David said, and Elsa nodded.

"I actually got a tingle up my spine when the vet said the heart slowed down."

"Okay, I think I know the guy we need to talk to," said Carver. "He was a vet student when I was at Auburn, the best in his class."

"He wasn't that interested in normal vet medicine, though. Didn't want to treat dogs or cats or even horses. He was interested in predators. You know, lions... and tigers... and bears."

"Oh my!" said Nicholas, and everybody laughed. He and Elsa had watched *The Wizard of Oz* just two weekends ago.

"Anyway," said Carver, "Joseph is now a vet with the Park Service. The last I heard he was in Yellowstone, doing research on wolves and bears. I think he may be the one who can help us. If not, I'm sure he knows who to call."

"That's great!" David was grinning. "It may be just what we need keep the hearts viable longer."

"I remember a researcher at our last national transplant meeting talking about doing an echo on a bear. Was he from Minnesota? Elsa, do you remember that?"

Elsa nodded. "I think he was from Washington State."

David continued, "I remember a picture of him on the ground with a bear almost in his lap. He had shaved the bear's chest area and was doing an echocardiogram. The bear had to be asleep, but I can still see the guy in my mind reaching around the bear to do the echo. I wonder if he has any data about bears and hibernation."

Carver shook his head, "I was probably in a different session."

"Bears aren't the only animals that go into hibernation, Daddy," chimed in eight-year-old Nicholas. "I remember Nature Channel talking about frogs... and something else—hogs—no, groundhogs."

"Ground hog?" said Carver, laughing, "Isn't that what we eat for breakfast with biscuits."

He was always joking with Nicholas.

"No, you know, the one that sees its shadow on Groundhog Day. It's been on TV!"

David smiled. "You are right! I wonder if there are any studies on frog hibernation."

He paused a moment. "No, we probably need to stick with mammals, animals with a four-chambered heart like us."

"What's a chamber, Daddy?" Nicholas asked.

"Well, you see, son, the human heart is really two pumps in one. That's why when you listen to your heart you hear *lub-dub*. Two beats. There are four chambers. Each side has an atrium and a ventricle. The right side of the heart pumps blood through the lungs to release carbon dioxide and pick up oxygen. The left side pumps blood through the rest of the body."

David nodded at Nicholas.

"The heart is the most important organ in the body."

"It is not!" interjected Carver. "The kidneys and liver are just as important as the heart, and what about the brain? The heart is just a pump. You heart surgeons think you are the most important, but you're really just glorified plumbers. Just hook up the pipes right and fix the leaks, and you're fine. Anybody can transplant a heart! Nicholas, it takes real skill to do a kidney-pancreas transplant."

Everybody laughed. Nicholas was used to hearing Uncle Carver and his tirades.

"I've got to get back home, long day in the clinic tomorrow. I'll look up Joseph's number and see what he knows about hibernating bears."

David nodded at him. "And I'll try to get up with that guy in Washington, and see what he knows about bear hearts."

"Sounds like a plan," added Elsa as they walked Carver out to his new Segway.

"Thanks for the chocolate, lovely lady." He smiled at Elsa. "I still don't understand why you hang around with this plumber."

Elsa shook her head, smiling back.

"And I'll take you for a ride soon, Nicholas," he said, as he stepped aboard.

They were amazed at how the contraption kept its balance as Carver York spun it around.

"And I'll see you tomorrow, David." He whirred away.

"What a character!" Elsa was shaking her head.

"Yeah, but he's the best kidney-pancreas guy in the nation, probably in the world. Who would believe that we'd have him here in little ole Alabama?" David bragged.

"Daddy, I want to hear the lub-dub," declared Nick.

"Okay, son. Els, do you know where my old stethoscope is?"

"I know where it is, dad."

Nicholas ran to the drawer in the entry to get the stethoscope.

They sat down on the couch and David placed the earpieces of the stethoscope in his son's ears, and put the diaphragm onto Elsa's chest, over her heart.

"See if you can hear Mom's heart first."

"Yes, I can, but it sounds more like *k-bump, k-bump* to me."

"Now listen to yours." David held the device in place on Nicholas's chest.

Nicholas listened a minute. "I hear it—only it's faster,"

"Let me hear it," spoke David, and he listened to the sound of his son's heart.

"You're right. It is *k-bump, k-bump.*" He smiled and removed the stethoscope, then gave his son a hug.

"Now you need to go off to bed, its past time."

"Okay, dad," Nicholas said with a little bit of a pout. He obviously had no energy to fight his fate, though. He stood with a yawn, and sleepily muttered, "Come'n and kiss me goodn'ght, please."

David waited until Nicholas disappeared to his bedroom and then put the stethoscope back onto Elsa's chest.

"Now it's my turn," he said, and moved the scope around, making sure he touched the best parts.

"Hmmm, seems that the rate is rising a little, too."

He leaned over and kissed his wife.

"I think it's getting close to our bedtime, too," he whispered.

Elsa pulled him close, and continued the kiss. Then she smiled at him.

"Let me get Nicholas tucked in. Then you go say goodnight to him and I'll change into something more comfortable."

"Hmm, sounds good," said David, smiling at his wife.

• • •

The next day, in the middle of morning clinic, McAllister's nurse Kim Chou stopped him just before he entered a room for a patient exam.

"Dr. York is on line two for you," she said with a smile.

David picked up the phone and punched the line button.

"Hey, Carver."

Carver's crisp voice came over the line. "Hi, David. I've got some good news... about the bears. Believe it or not, my friend Joseph is in the middle of a study of grizzlies in Montana, and would be delighted to help us with any info that we need on hibernation. He can't come here, though. He suggests a trip to Montana. Do you think the Dean will okay it?"

"I think the Dean will okay it if Kardia will pay for it," said David. "Did you ask what would be a good time?"

"He said anytime in February or March. It's real cold there, though—minus ten."

"That's okay, maybe we can go skiing. Can you come by at lunch and compare our calendars? Elsa will be here then, too."

11

Visit

IT HAD BEEN just over two weeks since Rachel's fatal accident. Lisa Kelly had since received information about the organ transplant recipients and wanted to give the girl's family an update. She had been worried about Rachel's parents and called them to set up a time when she could visit. It would take Lisa about an hour to get to the family's home in Marianna.

Lisa knew that Cathy lived down in the edge of Florida, so she gave her a call to see if she might want to go along. Cathy was off that afternoon, and interested in going, so Lisa stopped by and picked her up. Lisa had already been by the unit a couple of times in the past week to follow up with the staff, but had not seen Cathy. The secretary said she had been working nights, and Lisa's schedule had prevented her from going by on the evenings Cathy was working.

It was a nice day, the sun was shining, and the weather was clear. There wasn't much traffic, so the drive went quickly. They talked about the case on the way down, and Lisa told Cathy about the patients. Cathy was glad the transplants had worked out, but was concerned about the girl's parents. They discussed some issues they had with their own children, and by then they were in Marianna.

It was not hard to find the girl's house: the father had given good directions and it was not far from town. As they drove up into the dirt driveway of the small house, they noticed how neat and tidy it was. The yard was well kept and it looked like the house had recently been painted. There were several live oaks surrounding the house, and a couple of citrus trees by the front door, already covered with oranges, shining in the bright sunshine. There were also several pots of live flowers on the front porch of the house, contrasting nicely with the brown clapboard siding.

"I can't get my oranges to do well; it gets too cold," said Cathy as they started to get out of the car.

Lisa looked over at her. "He has his on the south side, and I bet he covers them when it freezes. They sure are pretty."

As they walked up the steps, they noticed several vases of cut flowers through the front window, and some that were in wreaths. Lisa paused a minute before knocking on the door, and she and Cathy looked at each other.

Lisa took a deep breath and then knocked.

The girl's mother came to the door, and greeted them.

"Please come in," she said.

They walked into the living room of the house, noticing more flowers around the walls.

"So many people sent flowers," said the mom, "and we left most out on the gravesite. But I kept these here at home."

As Cathy and Lisa looked around the cozy family room, they noticed several pictures of the girl. A large portrait hung on the living room wall, and several smaller pictures of her were on the side tables and shelves. They chronicled the girl's growing up. In some, she was in her band uniform. There was one of her holding a trophy from some running competition.

"That's what she looks like," said the mom. "Isn't she beautiful?"

The portrait on the wall was professionally done, and looked fairly recent. Rachel was in a pretty blue dress, and her braided blond hair was to one side, hanging down in front. Her eyes matched the dress, and her smile was perfect.

"She is beautiful," said Lisa, and Cathy nodded.

The mom smiled at them. "You won't believe what we paid for that smile."

Just then, the father came walking in from the back. He greeted them, giving each a hug.

"I'm sorry, I had to take care of some business down at the cemetery."

He pointed out the window, and they could see a cemetery about a half-mile up the street, next to a little white church.

"She's out there."

His shoulders sagged noticeably, and he sighed as he motioned for them to sit down.

"Thanks for coming," he said, as he and his wife sat down on the sofa beside each other.

Lisa waited until they were seated and then said, "I want to tell you about the transplants. Is that okay?"

"Yes," said the mother quietly, leaning forward. "Could she help anyone?"

Lisa nodded, smiling at the mother.

"She saved several lives."

Lisa leaned forward toward the girl's mom and dad.

"We were able to do heart, liver, kidneys, and pancreas. And the eye bank did corneas."

The father took the mother's hand, looking at Lisa and nodding slightly.

Lisa continued. "Rachel's heart went to a thirty-three-year-old lady. She has a young child. She had just developed heart disease, and the doctors didn't expect her to live even another week. She is doing fine right now. Rachel's liver was transplanted into a twenty-three-year-old lady, and she is also doing well. Two people got kidney transplants. One was a young man about twenty-seven, and the other was a lady about thirty. She also got the pancreas transplant. They are both doing well, too. I don't know yet about the cornea transplant recipients: the eye bank will be in touch with you about that."

Lisa paused, letting the news sink in for a minute. Then she smiled again. "I will be sending you a letter in the next few days with this information, and we also have someone on our staff who works with families after donation. You will be hearing from her, as well."

"Can we meet these people?" asked the father.

Lisa looked at him. "That is a possibility. Many times the

recipients will want to get in touch with the family who gave. Sometimes they may not be able to. You have to give them some time, time to recover from the surgery, and heal. That's another thing that our family liaison will help you with. If she gets letters or information from the recipients, she will call you and let you know."

"We would like to meet them, someday," said the mother.

The father leaned forward.

"I want to show you something." He reached in his pocket and took out a small plastic card. It was the girl's driver's license. He handed it to Lisa.

"Look at it." He pointed to the little red heart. "She had 'donor' on her license. She had just got it, just before the accident. The kids at school said she showed it to everybody the day she got it, and told them they should be donors, too."

"She was just sixteen." He looked down, shaking his head.

"You should have seen her funeral," said the mother. "There were so many people there that they wouldn't all fit in the church."

Cathy looked at her.

"I heard about that. I know some of the kids who go to school with her."

"Thank you, Cathy, for taking such good care of our daughter," said the mother. "You will always be special to us."

"And thank you for helping us during such a bad time, Lisa. We know that's what she wanted, and it's nice to know that she helped those people."

Lisa looked at the picture on the wall again, and shook her head. "She is so beautiful."

Lisa and Cathy stood up, and hugged Rachel's mother and father.

"Wait," said the mother. "I want to show you something else."

She went into an adjoining room, and came out with something in her hand.

"Come over here," she said, as she put the object down on the table.

It was a beautiful glass heart, deep blue in color. It had a multicolored rainbow embedded in the glass.

"This was one or her favorite things," the mother said.

"Rachel loved rainbows," said the dad, smiling.

"Beauty after the rain," he said, almost to himself.

Then he looked at Lisa.

"Would you tell the lady that got her heart... tell her every time she sees a rainbow, to remember our daughter?"

"And tell her every time we see a rainbow we will say a prayer for her," said the mother, "And the others, too."

Cathy and Lisa stood with the mom and dad for a moment.

Lisa handed the father her card and said, "If there is anything I can do, or if you have any questions, please call me."

They said goodbye to the mother and father, hugging them both again.

• • •

"Whew," sighed Cathy, as they drove away.

"I don't see how you do this all the time."

Lisa looked over at her. "It's the best part of my job." She smiled, her eyes still moist with tears. "To let families know how they have helped other people, saved their lives. It's why I do what I do."

Cathy looked at her and smiled back.

"You're right," she said softly.

Lisa started the car and put it in drive. She glanced back over at Cathy.

"Do you want to stop by the cemetery?"

"Sure," said Cathy.

They drove down the street and turned in by the white cinder block church. The cemetery was behind it, and they drove down a narrow gravel path between the graves. Most of the gravestones were simple: gray or white granite, with the name of the deceased, the date of their birth and death, and maybe a line or two about them. Some were more elaborate, but all were basically the same, a memorial of the life and death of someone's loved one.

It was not hard to find the grave of the girl. It was the one covered in flowers.

They went by it slowly and Lisa stopped the car just beyond.

The cemetery was silent when they got out of the car, the silence broken only by the thud of the car doors. They stood by the car for a second, and then walked over closer to the fresh grave, their shoes crunching in the loose gravel. The grave was piled high with wilting flower arrangements from the funeral, and there was a little shrine beside it, evidently done by her high-school friends: pictures and mementos and a little cross. There was fresh dirt on the grass around the grave.

Lisa and Cathy stepped up closer, looking at the pictures.

Suddenly, surprising them both, a bird that had been sitting unnoticed in a tree next to the grave flew down towards them, flying really close, showing the colors in its wings. It flew so close to their heads that they could hear the swish of its wings in the still air, but it made no other sound. It wheeled and landed back in the tree and then looked at them, turning its head sideways to see them better. After a minute, when it recognized who they were, it started to sing. It was a plaintive love song: soft and sad, three notes down, three notes up. One and two, three and four, one and two, three and four. Then it would pause to listen.

Neither Lisa nor Cathy paid the bird any attention as they stood beside the grave. They stood in silence for several minutes, smelling the smell of the flowers. Then they crunched back through the gravel to the car.

"That's a lot of flowers," said Lisa.

Cathy nodded, tears in her eyes.

Then, as they were about to leave the cemetery, Cathy turned to Lisa.

"Do you want to try to find were the accident happened?"

"Okay," said Lisa.

"It was on the old river road, and that's just a little ways south," said Cathy. She pointed left as Lisa pulled out to the highway.

It only took a few minutes to get to the turn for the old dirt road, and they continued down it until they reached the curve.

It was easy to see where the accident had happened. The fence was still down, and the tracks from all the vehicles were still visible in the field beyond the fence. Lisa pulled over onto the side of the road and they both got out of the car. They could see the fresh cut on the tree, and the amputated limb on the ground to the side, where the wrecker driver had left it. The leaves on the limb had all curled up and turned brown.

Of course the Lincoln was gone, but they could tell where it had been. They walked across the trampled grass and up under the tree, into the space that had been opened up. Both stood there silently, listening to the soft sound of the breeze that moved through the leaves of the live oak tree. The only other sound was a car horn, somewhere off in the distance.

"Look at this," motioned Cathy.

There was a fresh set of initials just above where the tree limb had been.

RT+RR. The letters were surrounded by a heart.

Cathy reached up and traced the outline of the heart with her finger. She looked at Lisa.

Lisa just shook her head, slowly.

After a few minutes, as if following an unseen signal, they both turned and walked back to Lisa's car. Neither said a word after they got in. In fact, they were halfway home before either spoke.

12

Fading Fast

JOSE GARCIA WORRIED about his little sister. Her normally healthy complexion was replaced by a pallor the color of oatmeal, and her usual bright smile was missing. Maria had always been vibrant and alive, brightening up any room she entered, like a bouquet of beautiful flowers delivered on a dreary day. She was vivacious and outgoing. Her radiant smile, rich-brown skin, and long coal-black hair often made her the center of attention. And not only was she the center of attention of others, she was the center of Jose's universe.

Except for their maternal grandmother, Maria was his only blood relative. Orphaned when they were fourteen and eleven, Jose and Maria had been moved about between foster homes for months after their parents' deaths. The confusion had come because, even though their mother was from Puerto Rico, their father was undocumented. Jose had tried to explain to the Florida authorities that they were American citizens, but no one listened. They were finally located by their grandmother. Now, seven years later, everything was better. Having finished high school, Jose had enlisted in the Army. He had finished training and then spent one year overseas, and was now home on leave.

Maria was in her senior year, and was easily one of the most likely to succeed in her class. She was in the top ten academically, and the class vice-president. She was working toward a scholarship to the University of Florida. After earning her degree in political science, her goal was to study law, and then become attorney general of the state of Florida, if not of the whole United States.

Her favorite thing to do, however, was dance. She was a member of a high school dance team, the Eagle Feathers. They had recently won a national competition, and Maria was one of the featured dancers. She liked all types of dance, but Latin dance most. The competition in New York City had been strenuous, but Maria had come home happy and exhilarated.

In the past few days, however, Maria had not felt well. She was never one to complain and rarely sick, but this time it was different. The first day she felt bad, she had gone to school, but was sent home early by the school nurse. Ms. Donna had done a strep test on her, but it was negative. She told Maria a virus was going around the school and to go home and go to bed. Three days later Maria was almost unable to leave the bed and started to feel like she couldn't breathe. It was as if a great weakness had come over her. As she looked up at Jose and tried to smile, he could see the pain in her face.

No one would ever call Jose a procrastinator. Helping Maria get dressed, he then helped her to his car.

It was only a few blocks to Dr. Strickland's office.

Dr. John Strickland had been practicing family medicine for fifty years, forty-eight of them in this very spot. His office was on a corner in old downtown Tampa. He had been seeing patients in this same building Monday through Friday and most Saturday mornings for longer than many of the neighborhood's residents had been alive. He was on his fourth and fifth generations in some families.

At seventy-five, Dr. Strickland was still as sharp as ever. He was beloved by his patients, not just because he was a good doctor, but because he really cared. Dr. Strickland would not be considered a part of modern medicine, having stopped taking insurance, Medicare or other government-sponsored reimbursement years previously. He treated his patients for what they could pay him, ten or twenty dollars for an office visit, plus the cost of the medicine he gave. A penicillin shot, if indicated, cost eight dollars and not being able to sit down for a while.

He was known for his gentleness when shots were required, and many came to him for their flu shots, among others, for just this reason. He practiced alone and his wife was receptionist, office manager, and part-time nurse. Though he still had staff privileges at every major hospital in Tampa, and licensure in three states, he confined most of his practice to these local families, now treating minor illnesses, minor fractures, and stitching up the occasional gash from small accidents.

It was already after five, and Dr. Strickland was finishing writing in the last patient's chart when Jose carried Maria into the waiting room. Glancing up as the bell on the door tinkled, Mrs. Strickland jumped to help as Jose pushed the door closed with his foot. Maria was sagging in his arms, her face pasty-white, looking up at Mrs. Strickland with a small smile on her slightly blue lips.

As Mrs. Strickland showed him into one of the two exam rooms, she asked Jose, "How long has she been like this?"

"She came home early from school on Monday," he said worriedly. "The nurse said a virus was going around. She started getting worse last night."

Doc, after washing his hands with warm water at the sink, sat down next to Maria and began to talk to her about how she felt.

"I'm just so weak, and my chest is heavy," began Maria.

Dr. Strickland warmed his stethoscope with his hands and then started listening to her heart and breath sounds.

"Hmm," he breathed, the beginnings of a slight frown on his face, as he listened to the beat of her heart for several long seconds. The only other sound in the room was the slow ticking of the old wall clock just outside the door. Then, "Take a deep breath... again... now... again."

Mrs. Strickland didn't have to look at him to know he was worried. He glanced up at her.

"We need to do an EKG."

As she got the electrocardiograph from the closet, Mrs. Strickland tried to remember when they had last done an EKG on someone this young.

• • •

Dr. Strickland stood outside the door of the hospital room in Tampa General. He glanced through the chart, first checking the labs and chest x-ray, then flipping over to read the echo report. He finished by flipping back to the doctor's progress notes, squinting to read the cryptic handwriting of the cardiologist.

It was just as he had thought. Maria's heart was enlarged and failing, some sort of idiopathic cardiomyopathy.

Probably from a virus, he thought to himself.

He walked back down the corridor to the nurse's station.

"Would you page Dr. Watts, please," he asked the nurse.

"Yes sir."

Dr. Strickland waited, looking at the notes tacked to the wall of the nurse's station. There were several detailing new federal regulations on the nurses and doctors. He smiled as he noticed one about abbreviations. Many of the standard abbreviations that doctors had used for years were no longer condoned, and the note gave suggestions for the correct abbreviations. Dr. Strickland smiled again and shook his head slowly. He was glad he would soon be out of this business. He and Mrs. Strickland had lately been seriously discussing retirement.

He thought of the house they still had back in Alabama. It was in the small town where Mrs. Strickland had grown up and where some of her family still lived. They had built the house there several years before, thinking it would be a good place to retire. Though Dr. Strickland still saw patients, he was beginning to have a few health problems himself, particularly his hearing. The main issue, though, was Mrs. Strickland, who was not remembering things as well as in the past and was beginning to show signs of other problems.

She would be better off close to family, he thought.

At that moment, the unit phone rang. After a minute, the nurse held it up to him.

"It's Dr. Watts," she said.

Strickland took the phone, nodding a thank you to her.

"Alex, this is John Strickland. How are you?" He paused a moment. "No, we're all doing fine, thanks." Then his voice took on a more serious tone.

"I'm calling about Maria Garcia, the seventeen-year-old

female you did an echo on today. What do you think?"

Doc listened as the cardiologist detailed the problems with Maria's heart. The nurse watched as he listened, seeing him shake his head at one point.

"I was afraid of that," Doc said into the phone.

"When will you be by here?"

"Okay. I will be back at seven and we can talk about what to do next."

He hung up the phone, looking down at the nurse and shaking his head.

"She may end up having to have a transplant," he said, more to himself than to her.

"I was hoping we could get her better," the nurse said.

"We are going to try."

He thought a minute. "I may need to call Brighton," he said, again almost to himself.

"Brighton?"

"Probably the best heart transplant surgeon in the country. He was a resident under me, several years ago." Doc smiled at the "several."

"Is he here in Florida?"

"No, he's at the Medical College of Alabama in Birmingham."

"What about Shands in Gainesville?"

"The list for heart patients is quite a bit longer there, so the wait is longer. The doctors are okay, but Brighton is the best, and I'm afraid she can't wait very long."

He sighed, shaking his head.

"I'll be back around at seven; we'll see what Dr. Watts says."

Dr. Strickland turned to walk down the hall. The nurse watched him stride purposefully toward the skilled nursing wing, where he had several geriatric patients. She smiled and shook her head as she watched him go. She had worked at Tampa General Hospital more than twenty years and knew Dr. Strickland very well. He was probably older than many of the geriatric patients he was about to see. But he was as sharp as ever, and wise. She knew he treated his patients like family, and would send them to the best treatment programs, just like he would his own loved ones. She just hoped Maria would make it long enough to get there.

13

Mind of its Own

DAVID WALKED DOWN the hall of St. Vincent's hospital, looking for Sally Debardeleben's office. St. Vincent's, like so many other hospitals, was a maze of corridors and confusing numerology. Finally, with help from a custodian, David found the correct door.

David knocked, then opened the door. He saw Sally Debardeleben sitting behind a chic maple desk. Sally glanced up, then jumped to her feet, looking toward the clock on the wall.

"Oh, David, I didn't realize it had gotten so late. I'm sorry. I meant to meet you at the door downstairs and show you in."

"It's okay," said David, with a smile and a wry look. "I enjoy touring hospitals. You never know what you might run into."

"I'm sorry," Sally was chuckling at his remark. "This is an old building, and no one can ever make rhyme or reason of the room numbering. I want to be closer to patient care, so I'm stuck down here in never-never land. But I like it."

Then she gave a glance down the hall and whispered, "I like to be as far away from admin as possible."

She smiled again, giving him a wink.

"I understand perfectly," said David, looking around.

"This is a very nice office."

Sally's office was on a corner, and had a wall of windows on one side and several smaller ones on the adjoining wall. The hospital was on a ridge and her windows faced the valley, so she had a wonderful view of the city. The furnishings were all light maple, and the floor was maple as well. On the wall were several large photographs of what looked like small churches, all of which overlooked seas or lakes. The photography was breathtaking, beautifully done. One picture was exceptional, a white church against the background of a thunderstorm over the water, but with a vivid rainbow showing between the church and the sea.

"Wow," said David, "These photographs are beautiful. Where did you get them?"

"Somebody I know took them when she was on mission." Sally said, smiling at David.

"Somebody you know? Would that be you?"

"Yeah, it was me. When I was younger I used to dabble a little in photography."

David walked over for a closer look at the rainbow photo. The lighting was awesome, with the rainbow backed by the dark clouds, but bright sunshine framing it all.

"I'd say you more than 'dabbled.' This is a wonderful piece."

"It's a church on the coast of Sicily. I did a mission trip there when I was in college.

David walked over to another photograph. This one was not as large, and was not of scenery. It was of a group of children, all of them dressed in rags and all thin and gaunt. They were seemingly lined up for food, as each of them had a plate, and they were holding the plates out towards whoever held the camera. David's attention was drawn to the first little girl in the picture, whose eyes were a piercing gray, and whose face could have been in a modeling magazine. But she was in rags and obviously begging for something to eat. The other faces were also clear, a group of beautiful children, but the pathos was palpable. The picture perfectly captured the emotion of the moment.

"And the heart of the photographer is evident in this one. It's also amazing," said David.

"Did you take it?"

"I did. That was on a mission to Angola." Sally said softly.

"And those children still have a special place in my heart."

"I can see that."

Sally turned and walked over to the big window, silent for a moment as she looked out over the city below. Then she asked softly, "David, what do you think I mean when I say the children have a special place in my heart?"

She turned back toward him, her dark eyes smiling.

"What do you mean when you say the heart of the photographer is evident in that picture?"

David knew immediately where Sally was going, but was struck by her question. He looked at her, waiting for her to continue.

"That's why I asked you over for a meeting."

Sally smiled again. "I want to talk to you about hearts. Come sit down."

She led him over to the corner of her office, where two comfortable chairs and a small couch were situated across from each other. She had him sit down in one of the chairs. "You want some coffee or a Coke? I've even got green tea." There was a side bar with a sink and a small refrigerator.

"Sure," said David, "I'll have some tea. I've been reading about all the health benefits, and I'm encouraging my patients to drink it."

Sally placed teabags in two mugs and poured some hot water from a thermal pitcher. She handed David his.

"Do you have any sugar, just a teaspoon?" asked David.

Sally smiled and opened a cabinet above the bar. "You want some lemon, too? It's in a packet."

David nodded. "Thanks"

As she leaned close to spoon sugar into the mug, David could not help but notice her perfume, or maybe it was the smell of her long black hair. It was exotic, like some unusual flower. He inhaled, taking in the odor and the beauty of her hair. Sally was wearing a sky blue dress, and though it was business attire, the contrast with her hair was striking. David could not help but admire her.

She sat down in the chair next to him, angling it to face him better. She took a sip of her tea and then sat the mug down on a little table between the chairs. She slid back a little in her chair and looked up at him.

"David. Did you know that Aristotle and the ancient Greeks believed that consciousness resides in the heart?"

"No, I didn't know that."

"And did you know that when Chopin, the famous composer, died, they buried his body in France, where he had lived, but they sent his heart back to Poland, where he had been born?"

"No," David chuckled. "I wonder what his heart thought about that."

Sally looked at him, pleased at the remark. She was silent for a moment, then asked, "You wonder what his heart thought?"

"I was just kidding," said David.

"No, you weren't." Sally shook her head slightly.

She leaned over and picked up her mug, looking out the window as she took a sip of tea.

Then she turned and looked in his eyes. "Have you ever wondered what a heart thinks when you transplant it into another person?"

"I've wondered how so many of my patients know things about their donor," David said.

Sally leaned toward him, not letting him get away from the question. "Have you ever wondered why some patients do well and others don't, even when the transplant is fine and the patient is healthy?"

"I know that when the patient accepts the heart as theirs, it makes a difference. I've had patients who could not deal with the fact that they have another person's heart, or who can't deal with the fact that someone else had died for them to get a transplant. If they can't accept the heart, they will not do well."

Sally looked into his eyes again, seeking his full attention. "Have you ever wondered if it makes a difference if *the heart* accepts the patient?

David shook his head and said emphatically, "I've never thought about what the heart thinks. I've never thought that the heart *could* think."

Sally leaned back and took another sip of her tea. She then sat silently, watching and waiting.

David sat still a minute, looking out the window himself, thinking about what she had said, letting what Sally said sink in.

She watched him, smiling as she saw the idea begin to germinate in his mind.

He shook his head slightly. "No, I've never thought about it that way. It's always what the patient thinks about the heart. A heart can't think. It's a pump."

"Oh, I believe it can." Sally's dark eyes were glowing. "Where do the memories that the patient has of the donor originate?"

She stopped and took another sip of her tea. Then she sat up straight, sliding to the front of her chair.

"Let me tell you my hypothesis, Dr. McAllister, and this is based on years of research."

She tossed her dark hair and sat up even higher, again gazing out the window and then directly at David.

"I believe... that the heart has some kind of cellular memory. There is something there besides just a pump... You know that in every cell of our body we have the information to make any other part of the body. It's stored in the DNA. And we know that DNA has the ability to carry far more information than just the genetic information. I read recently that even with the mapping of the genome there is still an estimated sixty percent of the possible capacity that has an unknown function. Scientists used to call it junk DNA because no one knows its real purpose."

She leaned towards him. "Did you know that if the DNA strands in every cell in an average human were stretched out end to end, the strand would reach to the sun and back forty times? Isn't that amazing?"

Sally's eyes were flashing and David could see the fervor in her face as she attempted to verbalize her ideas.

She continued. "You told me the other day that the electrical potential from the heart is many times more powerful than the electrical potential of the brain. It was thirty years after the invention of the EKG that Berger thought to make a machine to record the electrical activity of the brain, an EEG. The signal is so weak that it took him that long to come up with it. The amplitude of the brain's activity was almost too small to measure with the instruments of the time."

David nodded.

She continued. "Information is transmitted in the body through electrical pathways, and the heart is the most powerful transmitter. Its current is far stronger than the brain's, both in voltage and in amplitude.

"I didn't know you knew so much about electricity," quipped David.

Sally shook her head and took a breath. Again, she looked into David's eyes.

"David, tell me about the S/A node in the heart."

David didn't even have to think. "That's where the electrical signal that causes the heartbeat originates. It works in conjunction with the A/V node. The electrical potential flows through the heart in a wave, causing the contraction of the atrium and the ventricle."

"Do you think that current can be felt in any other part of the body?"

"No." David shook his head.

Then he thought a minute, reconsidering what she had said.

He nodded, smiling at her.

"Sure it can. That's what we measure with an EKG. The electrodes can be placed on different parts of the body and will still pick up the heart's signal."

Sally nodded back. "So the heart can communicate with the whole body. And information is transmitted through electricity."

She paused for effect.

"Information is the key. Don't you see?"

David was shaking his head slightly again.

Sally smiled and continued. "Somehow, the heart continues to *think* after you transplant it." She shrugged her shoulders.

"It remembers. And it's communicating with the new body, the transplant patient."

She paused and took another sip of her tea, smiling. She could see that David was finally listening to her. David, on the other hand, had not touched his tea. He was too intrigued by what she was saying.

"Think about it." She sat quietly a minute, looking down at her cup of tea. Then she smiled at him and threw another curve.

"Would you say some of the hearts you transplant are dominant, and some are passive?"

David looked at her, shaking his head, nearly overwhelmed by her ideas.

"What do you mean by 'dominant' and 'passive?'"

Sally leaned forward again, her voice quieter.

"David, there is a give and take between the heart and the brain. Some people are dominated by their brain, it drives what they do, almost completely. Others are dominated by their heart, and are in tune with its signals. You know that."

Sally's dark eyes glowed as she spoke slowly.

"So some hearts are going to be dominant, and others are going to be passive. When you do a transplant, I don't think the passive ones make a fuss, they stay passive. But the dominant hearts—they may try to dominate again."

David was still shaking his head, thinking about what she said.

Suddenly Roy Huff came to mind. Mr. Huff was a patient who had had a heart transplant about two years before. Before his transplant, Huff had been an irascible sort, rough and tough. He was never happy. He was a guard at the state prison and a baseball umpire in the city where David grew up. Huff had a reputation for being difficult to deal with, and the players and coaches hated him. David didn't know, but figured that the inmates in the prison didn't like him either.

But, after his heart transplant, Huff had changed completely. He now worked as a volunteer at the Boys and Girls Club, and was a frequent speaker in area churches, talking about the miracle of his transplant, and his thankfulness for being alive. David knew that Huff's heart came from a young pastor, a charismatic man who had founded a ministry that had helped many needy people in the area. The young pastor had been known for his heart of love.

He looked up at Sally. "I guess a heart could be dominant."

He paused, thinking. "And the communication: maybe that's why the kidney and liver transplant patients aren't seeing as much of this."

"Exactly, David," she gave him a little nod of favor.

Sally smiled at him again, then continued.

"Okay, I've told you in the past that only about ten percent of heart transplant patients admit memories or feelings about their donor. But I think two things are in play here. Some of the patients are more open or in tune to the signals from the heart.

They are the ones that I call *sensitives*."

She paused a moment.

"The others are not necessarily sensitive themselves, but have a *dominant* heart, maybe a heart that came from a strong personality. They may not have dreams or memories, but their own personality changes. And that's probably another five or ten percent."

Sally stopped a minute, as if to organize what she was about to say. She took a deep breath.

"David, you say some patients do better than others. Some reject the heart transplant."

David nodded.

She paused again, gazing sideways out the window. Then she looked directly into his eyes again, leaning towards him, speaking softly.

"Do you ever have someone that the heart rejects?"

David looked at Sally, again having never thought of it this way. He looked away, toward the picture of the church by the sea.

A rush of memories came to him: images of patients, memories of midnight calls from the transplant unit. Walking down the hall in the hospital and hearing, "Code blue, code blue, room 442, CCU. Dr. McAllister, call 8822, stat!" Heart-rending memories.

David looked down, and both were quiet for a minute.

"Yes, maybe," he said softly, shaking his head, trying to clear the images. This time he was the one who took the deep breath.

"I've had patients who had perfect labs after a transplant, and no reason at all not to do well, no reason at all, but they declined and died. Good donor hearts, good transplants, otherwise healthy patients."

He let out a sigh. "And it happens to other doctors, too."

He shook his head slowly. "We've discussed it at meetings, but no one knows why those patients die."

He shrugged his shoulders. "Everyone thinks it's some kind of sub-clinical rejection process, but no one knows the mechanism."

"David. It's the heart."

The fire was glowing in her dark eyes. "You need to start thinking about how to keep *the heart* from rejecting *the person*."

14

Faithful

DAVID COULDN'T GET what Sally said out of his mind as he drove home. *How do I keep the heart from rejecting the person?*

Though it did not fit conventional science, and he knew that if he discussed this with some of his transplant colleagues they would laugh at him. *In your heart, you know it is true*, he thought.

Then he said it out loud.

"In your heart, you know it is true!"

He thought about that.

How do you know things in your heart?

He thought for a moment, first with his brain, then something deeper, trying to communicate with his heart.

And it came to him, a still, small voice.

Why, David, that's where love is.

He smiled.

Then his rational brain rebutted the heart's argument.

No! Love is in the amygdala, the part of the brain where emotions have been pinpointed by neuroscientists...

He paused a moment, shaking his head, collecting his thoughts.

Sally was right. The brain and the heart fight for dominance.

He smiled, almost laughing, and tried to get back in touch with his heart.

Elsa came to mind, and his love for her. He pictured her, her blue eyes smiling at him.

"Hmm," he said to himself, shaking his head slightly.

David missed the alone times with Elsa. Since Nicholas had been born, and his transplant schedule had gotten so busy, and she was in school, they just didn't have time together.

For the first few years after Nicholas, they had made a point to have a date night each week, but that had gone away as Nicholas started school and had homework, and Elsa started school again and had homework, and he was on call all the time.

He thought about Elsa, his beautiful wife, the love of his life.

They still had a good relationship, good sex, they were even good friends. She was beautiful and smart and talented, the mother of his child.

He shook his head.

Not just good sex... good lovemaking.

He nodded, smiling again.

He cared for her and she cared for him.

But there is something else, David thought.

Something else.

And then he knew.

It's her heart.

That's what I love the most.

He smiled at himself, bathed in a good feeling.

He spoke it out loud.

"It's her heart."

He could feel the good feeling in his own heart.

As he drove, he thought about that.

How could that be?

Then he thought, *Is there anyone else like that?*

He thought of Sally Debardeleben.

Yes, there was chemistry there, but it was different. She was fun to be around, but he respected Sally's choice in life. And, though she was beautiful, very beautiful, and desirable, and he enjoyed being around her, she was not Elsa.

It was like being in a garden of beautiful roses.

Someone else's garden.

Even if you couldn't pick them, you could still enjoy them.
David smiled at that.
And I like Sally's heart, too.

He thought of a couple of other possibilities, nurses who came on to him, other women who did as well.

He remembered a time, several years in the past. One of his best friends was a general surgeon, married, and Elsa was friends with the surgeon's wife. One day, he stopped by his friend's house to bring back a tool he had borrowed, and the man wasn't there, just the wife. She had been off exercising and was still dressed in her short workout outfit, and still flushed from the exercise. There had always been a little chemistry between them, too. She asked David if he wanted to come in.

That was a close one, David thought.

He remembered a roaring in his ears, and something, *his heart?* Speaking to him. He didn't do it, and they were still friends to this day.

What would things be like if he had given in?
He thought about another time.

He was on a trip, an organ transplant national meeting. During the meeting, there were different sessions on different topics, and participants got to choose the ones that best fit their needs. Most of David's sessions were clinical, particulars about transplant technique, or new medicines to combat rejection. But one morning he decided to attend some of the sessions dealing with donation issues, and there was one about communication and how to deal with families in grief. That's the one he chose.

He went down to the small meeting room, and there were only about twelve participants.

The leader, a Ph.D. in psychology, had them pair up with someone else to do some communication skills training. She called it "How to communicate on an emotional level." Somehow, David was paired with a cute nurse, a transplant coordinator from a program in the Northeast.

One of the exercises was to sit close, look at each other's eyes, and communicate nonverbally, no talking allowed. The cute nurse had sparkling eyes and perfect teeth, and a dimpled smile. They hit it off.

He enjoyed the other communication skills training sessions

with her immensely. Especially the nonverbal parts.

That night, the group went out to dinner, and David went along. They all sat together, and he sat next to the girl, talking to her about her life in New York City. There was another transplant coordinator, a guy, who sat on the other side of her. That guy was a jock, all muscled up, really good looking. He could have been a model. He joined the conversation about New York.

David went back to his hotel room alone.

The next morning, the girl came over to him at breakfast.

"Good morning, David," she said.

"Good morning. You have a good night?" he asked.

"No, terrible," she said, rolling her eyes. "Great body, but he must be taking steroids or something. You know. I had a boyfriend like that. He was a bodybuilder, too. Did you know steroids make them shrivel up?"

She shook her head in disgust.

David just looked down and chuckled, shaking his head slightly.

Then she smiled her dimpled smile at him and asked, "What are you up to tonight? Want to go to dinner?"

"I have a flight back this afternoon," said David. "I've got to get back to work."

"Well, here's my card," said the girl. "If you ever get to New York... "

She smiled, and her eyes twinkled.

David smiled back at her, shaking his head.

But he took the card.

David smiled again as he drove, remembering, and thinking, *I'm glad that one didn't work out, too.*

No, Sally, he thought, *Men can be dominated by more than their brain and their heart. There's another organ that's a factor, an important one.*

He chuckled.

He could imagine himself in Sally's office.

He said aloud, in a deep voice, "Sally, I have a theory on your heart thing, but it's a different thing. And sometimes it trumps the heart *and* the brain."

David laughed again.

He would never say that to Sally, but it was true.

He remembered the old poem by John Donne:
Down, wanton, down
Have you no shame
But to lift your ugly head
At the mention of love's name
David chuckled again, shaking his head. Human nature was what it was, and had been, forever.

He thought of the other doctors he worked with, some of whom had been married several times. Others were married, but had regular flings with nurses and other women, or men. One of them had recently been caught having sex with a nurse in a hospital lounge. Of course, it was after visiting hours.

He even knew of one doctor who had a pretty young wife, a son and a daughter, but also had a cute nurse on the side. He was renting a nice apartment near the hospital for the nurse, and regularly went by there in the evenings. You know he told his wife he was seeing patients at the hospital.

But maybe those guys had problems at home. Or they were married to a shrew.

Well, duh, of course they have problems at home.

If they didn't, they do now!

David was glad that he had Elsa. If you didn't count those two close calls, he had always been faithful.

Sure, he flirted with the nurses, and he loved working with Sally, but he knew Elsa was his only love.

She possessed his heart, completely. He smiled as he thought about that, the good feeling coming again.

She possessed his heart completely.

He started thinking about Elsa. About how they used to have more time together, just the two of them.

What can we do to have some alone time? Alone with her, that is. I know I need it, and she probably does, too.

At that moment, David saw the sign on the little storefront. In big, hand-printed letters it said:

LEARN TO DANCE HERE
BALLROOM, LATIN, HIP-HOP
ALL STYLES

15

Visions

THIS WAS SALLY Debardeleben's second meeting with Martha Lake. The first one had been at Dr. McAllister's office, and had really been just a short sort of "get to know each other" to establish whether or not Martha wanted to work with Sally and vice-versa. Sally had told Martha a little about her research, but purposefully had not gotten very much into Martha's story. They had set up a time to meet for what Debardeleben called a new client meeting. Since Martha was still an outpatient at the university hospital, they decided to meet there in one of the small consultation rooms at the clinic next door. The clinic had a lot of different specialists, and Debardeleben had had meetings there before. Sally had reserved her favorite room, the only one with a nice view. It was on the fourth floor and overlooked a fountain that was in front of the building.

Sally had arrived early and set up the room for her visit with Martha. The room had several padded armchairs. She had angled two of them towards each other with both facing the window. She felt that the view out the window would lend more of a comfortable aspect to the setting, putting her client at ease. She wanted to be as non-clinical as possible. There was a little side table back between the chairs. She already had a box of Kleenex handy, and had brought a small bag with a couple of bottles of water. She left the door open and sat down to go through some notes she had jotted down about Martha. She had purposely not done any research yet on Martha's donor. She did not want to be predisposed to coach Martha about anything. Some of the doctors actually thought that this is what happened in such situations and that the person counseling the patient might be leading them into answers. Sally always recorded her interactions with patients, as well as taking meticulous notes. She could document her methods, usually sticking to open-ended questions that could not be construed as leading the patients. She was glancing through a copy of Martha's history and physical from before her transplant when she heard a soft knock at the door. She had to turn in her chair to see the door. It was Martha. Sally smiled and stood up. Martha smiled back.

"Hey, Dr. Debardeleben, sorry I'm late."

"You're not late, Martha, you're right on time, and please call me Sally." Sally walked around the chairs and took Martha's hand, also reaching out to touch her shoulder.

"Thanks so much for coming. I'm glad to see you."

"I walked all the way from the parking deck." Martha was slightly breathless. Her cheeks were pink from the exertion.

"Are you feeling okay?" asked Sally.

"I'm feeling great," said Martha, with another smile. "I've been walking every day. I'm up to about a mile and a half. Alan has lost ten pounds in the last two months walking with me. And I really like this spring weather."

"It has been nice," noted Sally. "Please, come sit down. Do you want a bottle of water?"

"Yes, I would, thank you." Martha took the water and sat down in the chair opposite Sally. "Dr. Mac said I need to stay hydrated."

Sally smiled at her. "He's a good guy, isn't he?"

"Best doctor in the world, I think."

"I think you may be right, Martha. He certainly cares for his patients."

"You know, Dr. Debardeleben, he really does. He is concerned about me as a person, not just as a patient." Martha shook her head. "Most doctors wouldn't be concerned about my dreams. But look, I'm here to talk to you because he was concerned about that."

"Martha, I thought you had some sort of vision. Are you having dreams, too?"

Martha nodded, smiling at Sally. "Yes, I am. I had the visions of the girl several times right after the transplant. Those have gone away and now I have dreams."

"Are the dreams like the visions that you had earlier?"

"No, Dr. Debardeleben, the dreams are different."

"Okay, Martha, lets start at the beginning, and please call me Sally."

Martha looked at Sally. "Are you sure?"

Sally laughed and nodded. "Yes, I'm sure. It just makes things easier. I wasn't planning to call you Ms. Lake unless you want me to. I just want us to be able to talk about things together. But I would like to record our conversation, if you don't mind."

"Okay. Dr... Sally."

Sally smiled and nodded. She placed a small recorder on the table between them and turned it on.

"Just tell me what happened first."

Martha glanced out the window, then turned back towards Sally.

"I don't remember if it was right after I got my heart. You know that just before that I was sorta out of it. But I remember some things from then, like Dr. Mac standing over me and talking to Ms. Kim about how sick I was. It was sometime during then, I think, but I remembered it when I woke up after I got my heart. And, it happened two more times. All in the first week."

"What did you see?"

"I saw a young girl, maybe a teenager. She had sort of light brown hair and a pretty smile. She was in a helicopter—I told that to Dr. Mac. Well, not really in the helicopter. It was like I saw her face in the glass—in the windshield—but bigger." Martha shook her head. "She was smiling and happy, and I could feel her happiness. She looked right at me."

Martha's eyes began to tear up. Sally nodded at her. "She had on an orange T-shirt with blue on it. And something like a little lizard or something. I can still see her in my mind. And, and, I felt, like a shiver or something that was a good feeling. It was a good feeling all over... that I felt for a long time. I don't know how to describe it, but I told Dr. Mac I thought she let me feel it. I don't know. Maybe that is why she was happy."

"And this happened more than once?" asked Sally.

"No—just once, that night. The others were different."

"Okay, let's stay here a minute. Do you remember anything else about the girl in the helicopter?"

"Not really."

Martha thought a moment. "Well, one thing—she would look at me and smile and then turn her head and look up and smile, like she was looking at someone else. She had a pretty smile, a happy one. And I'll never forget the good feeling she gave me. "

Martha looked up at Sally and smiled herself.

"That's all I remember from the first one."

Sally smiled and nodded. "That's okay, Martha. There is something about dreams. Sometimes we remember them well and sometimes we don't. I've started placing a pen and paper on the side table by my bed. Sometimes I wake up after a dream and write down what it was about. I have to do that or I won't remember in the morning."

Martha was still smiling at Sally, a twinkle in her eyes. She reached down and opened her purse, a large bag, and pulled out a notebook.

"That's what I had to do with the dreams after that. I was still in the hospital and it was a few days after I got my heart. I was feeling good by then. I had a dream about the girl but then I couldn't remember much about it the next morning. The next night I had another dream. I think it was the same one, now. That night I woke up, and there was a paper and a pen on the table next to the bed. It had been there when I couldn't talk. I wrote down what the dream was about, but I didn't remember everything. The next night I dreamed it again. This time I wrote down some more about it. I didn't have that dream again after that, but I've been writing down what happens in my other dreams since then."

She opened the notebook and took out some loose papers, handing them over to Sally.

"These are the ones from the hospital. I've copied them in the notebook since then."

Sally took the papers. There were several short phrases in a scraggly handwriting written sideways across one of the sheets.

"That was the first one. Alan was asleep on the cot in the room and I didn't want to wake him so I didn't turn on the light."

The other papers were also covered in the handwriting, but a little neater. These had fuller sentences and were more detailed. Sally looked at them and then at Martha.

"It's amazing that you thought to do this."

"I worked for several years as a court reporter," explained Martha. "The dreams were so real I wanted to make sure I remembered them."

Sally looked up at Martha again. "Okay, let's talk about these dreams. You said they were different than the first ones."

"Yes, Dr. Debardeleben, um, I mean Sally... they were different. The girl came to see me, to talk to me."

Sally felt a little chill go up her spine. She had only heard this kind of story a few times before. She nodded, leaning a little closer to Martha.

"It was like she woke me up." Martha eyes filled with tears again. "I see her standing there in front of me: she is in a blue dress and her long hair is braided. She still has a smile, but is more serious this time. And she talks to me."

"What does she say?"

"Several things. I wrote them down so that I wouldn't forget."

Sally reached out and took Martha's hand. Martha looked down.

"Alan is the only one who knows about this, I haven't told anyone else. We were afraid to say anything."

"It's okay, Martha. This has happened before. And I am always discreet with this kind of thing."

"It's just so real, Dr. Sally. I don't know what to think. I want to do it, but I'm afraid. Is it just a dream that seems real? Or is it something I need to see about?"

"Tell me about it."

Martha took a deep breath. She looked up into Sally's eyes

"She says, 'Tell dad and mom I'm okay, I love you.'" Martha smiled again. "Then she says, 'Tell Susan not to worry, everything is all right.' I know she says Susan. The first night I thought she said Jane, but the other two times she said, 'Tell Susan.'"

"I wonder who Susan is," said Sally.

Martha shook her head. "I don't know. But there is also somebody named Tonto, she wants me to give him a hug. And one time, in the last dream, she said, 'Tell Ricky hi.'"

Sally looked at her and smiled.

"That seems okay."

Martha looked down, and pulled her hand back. She put her elbows on the arms of the chair and sank her face into her open hands. The tears came again, this time accompanied by soft sobs. Sally leaned forward and placed her hand on Martha's shoulder. Martha looked up, her eyes awash in tears.

"Why did she have to die? Did I cause this?"

"No, Martha. You didn't cause this. I don't understand either, but I know you didn't cause it. This is something that happens that we just don't understand, we don't know why."

"I don't know. I sure don't understand. And I keep asking myself why. Alan said everyone was praying that I would get a heart." Martha sighed and put her head back down in her hands.

They sat in silence for a minute. Then, Sally, still with her hand on Martha's shoulder said, "Martha, there are so many things we don't understand. Why young people die is one of them. Or why there are tragedies. But I believe that God is in control. He is in control, and one day, when we get to Heaven, we will understand. Right now, I don't know. But I am sure you are not the cause of the accident."

Sally paused a moment, thinking. Then she reached down and took Martha's hand again.

"This is what a mom told me one time, a mom who had lost a young daughter to an accident. She said, 'You know, God makes roses and God makes oak trees. We only have the roses for a while, but we would never want to be without their beauty.'"

Sally slowly stroked Martha's shoulder. Then she sat back. "One of my favorite quotes of all time is from a writer named Richard Bach." She smiled at Martha.

"He said something like this, 'The measure of our ignorance is our belief in injustice and tragedy... What the caterpillar calls the end of the world, the Master calls a butterfly.'"

Martha looked up at her, smiling at the thought. They both sat in silence for a minute or two. Then, suddenly, Martha sat back up straight. She reached over and took a Kleenex and wiped her eyes and nose. She looked back up at Sally.

"I want to go tell her parents about the dreams. I've made up my mind."

Sally thought a minute, then nodded. "I think it might be a good thing to do, if they want to do it, too," she said. "We can try to set that up if you want."

Martha reached out to take the notebook off of the table, then stopped.

"Oh, I forgot to tell you about the other dreams."

"Okay," said Sally, "if you think you can. Or we can wait till next time."

"No, this is not the girl, and it is a dream, a very real dream, sometimes a couple of times a week. I don't always wake up, but I usually remember it. In it, I'm riding a pony, fast, through the fields and woods." Martha closed her eyes and smiled.

"I can feel my hair blowing in the wind, and I can smell the fresh smell of pine trees. We're galloping along in the sunshine. It's a good dream."

Sally smiled back at her and nodded. "It sounds good."

Martha looked in her eyes.

"But I have never ridden a horse before, Dr. Sally. I'm afraid of them."

She looked to the side, then back at Sally.

"What do you think that is about?"

"I really don't know, Martha." Sally was smiling. "Maybe it's just a regular dream."

Martha shook her head. "No, it's about the girl again. I know it is."

She glanced to the side a minute, her eyes faraway. Then she looked back at Sally and shook her head, smiling. They sat in silence again.

Martha looked at her watch. "I have an appointment with Dr. Mac in a few minutes."

She bent to pick up her purse, then looked back up at Sally. "I would like to meet my heart donor's family if I can."

"I will start working on that." Sally stood up.

Martha stood up, too.

"Thank you for sharing your dreams with me, Martha. I look forward to talking to you again next week."

"Thank you, Dr. Sally. I'll see you next Thursday."

Martha gave Sally a hug, and picked up her notebook.

"Can I get a copy of your notes?" Sally asked.

Martha looked down at her notebook, then up at Sally. "Okay."

Sally nodded her thanks. "There's a copy machine right out at the nurse's desk. It'll just take a moment."

She reached down and stopped the recorder, then picked up her bag and notes. They walked out together.

16

Heart and Soul

IT WAS THURSDAY, and David was in the hospital checking on patients, both pre- and post-transplant. He enjoyed the visits with the post-transplant patients, all of whom were doing well after their transplant. Some were only a day or so out from the procedure, but others were nearing being released to the Townhouse. The visits with the pre-transplant patients were often much more difficult. Some of them were clinging to life by a thread, waiting for a donor heart. For some of those, this would not come about, and they would not leave the hospital alive. Most, though, due to the expertise of the medical team, would make it to get a transplant. If they could hold on and actually were transplanted, their chances were exceedingly good. At this institution, a patient's chances of surviving the transplant surgery were close to ninety-nine percent. The chances of living at least a year after the transplant were almost as good, and the great majority of patients could expect to live many more years after the procedure.

These patients had been given a death sentence by their extreme heart disease, and came to Dr. David McAllister with a survival chance of just about zero if they did not get a heart. David glanced up as he walked down the hospital corridor, smiling as he noticed a tall man coming down the hall towards him.

"Good morning, Bucky," he said.

"Mornin', Doc," shot back Bucky with a smile.

Actually, Bucky's smiles were more of a grin, his very white teeth contrasting sharply with his very dark skin. The smiles started in his eyes and spread down his face. You couldn't help but smile in response.

Bucky was a retired policeman, and a heart recipient about a year out. He was the picture of good health: tall, muscular, and fit. He had not stopped his regular workouts until his old heart was unable to keep up. Bucky had then spent a month in the apartments and a month in the hospital before he became one of the fortunate ones with a donor heart. His new heart had worked superbly, and he had been out of the hospital in just a few days, and home within a couple of weeks. He had resumed his physical fitness regimen as soon as possible, though slowly at first. Now he was back to close to where he had been before his heart failure.

Bucky would also be considered a poster child for a good attitude. He had made it his new life's task to help people in the transplant wards. He volunteered with the hospital chaplains and helped out with the transplant patient support groups. Most of all, though, he was at the hospital almost every day, going from patient to patient, telling jokes and stories, bringing them requests from the snack shop, and generally making himself a nuisance to the nurses.

Some of the Nurse Ratchet types thought that he conspired with the patients to get them what they wanted. Actually, Bucky was better at patient care than many of them. There were several cases that Dr. Mac knew about where Bucky had made the difference in people holding on long enough to get their needed heart.

"How are you today, Sergeant Parker?" David asked.

Bucky grinned at the formal greeting.

"I'm great, Dr. Mac, how are you and Ms. Elsa doing?"

"Good, thank you."

"And how's the young Einstein?" asked Bucky, eliciting a smile from David.

"Nicholas is doing fine, precocious as ever."

"Well," said Bucky, "I'm supposed to see you this afternoon. It's my one-year checkup."

"Okay." David nodded. "I look forward to seeing you."

"Doc, I've got a few questions," said Bucky, suddenly serious.

"Is everything okay?" asked David, immediately concerned.

"Oh, my heart's fine, it's just a few questions."

Bucky nodded back and turned to continue down the hall.

"That's fine, Bucky, I'll see you this afternoon," David said over his shoulder.

What was that about? David thought, as he walked into the next patient's room.

"Good morning, Mr. Riley," he said to the silver-haired gentleman sitting in the chair by the bed.

"How are you doing today?"

The day had gone fairly well for David. He'd spent the morning in the hospital, and then had gone quickly to the clinic to see follow-ups. He had a fast, stand-up lunch in the break room, making a note to himself to ask the nurses to think about some more heart-healthy lunches. Today it was pizza, bread sticks, and salad and was furnished by some drug company rep. She wanted a minute of David's time to discuss a new cholesterol-lowering drug. How ironic. The price for the doctor's time was to provide lunch for the clinic.

At least there is a salad, thought David, but he couldn't help but snatch a slice of with-the-works pizza before he left. He stopped by the medicine room, where samples were kept for patients starting new medications, grabbing a small packet of antacid. He went to the bathroom and brushed his teeth and rinsed with mouthwash, hoping it would take care of his pizza breath. The patient exam rooms were small and he had to be very close with his stethoscope.

After seeing several patients, he stopped at room three and pulled the chart out of the rack on the door.

"Parker, Samuel Roebuck," was typed on the label.

David glanced at the face page: *56 y/o male, African American, divorced, DOB 01/15/1955.*

On the medical history:

CAD

Three vessel CABG 11/2003

Idiopathic dilated cardiomyopathy
Heart transplant 6/02/2010
Mild GERD
On the social history:
Non-smoker
ETOH socially, rarely

Then, there was a list of recent lab test results. David glanced at his summary of the surgery and his notes on previous visits.

All of this took less than thirty seconds. David used the notes to jog his memory about each patient. For the first couple of years, he could keep up with everyone almost completely by memory. Now, however, as he approached 300 transplant patients, he found that impossible. He had asked the nurses to type a synopsis about each patient on the face sheet. He was still able to remember specifics about the patients with the synopsis as a start. He knocked softly on Bucky's door.

"Well, hello again, Bucky," David said with a smile, as he rolled a stainless stool from the corner. He pulled it close to Bucky and plopped down, spreading the chart out in his lap.

"Afternoon, Doc," Bucky said, from his uncomfortable perch on the exam table.

He sat up straight on the backless contraption and looked at David.

"Tell me how you are doing, are you having any problems?" asked David.

"Well, Doc, my college-age son is giving me a fit right now, can't seem to keep within his budget, and his grades are the pits."

"Really?" asked McAllister, smiling, used to Bucky's banter.

"And how about you and your heart?"

"I think I'm doing good, still working out every day. What did the damn biopsy show?"

McAllister smiled and nodded. "It was normal."

"That new cardiologist, what's his name... *Assanana?* He needs to learn how to put in that needle. He stuck me about ten times before he got it right."

"You mean Dr. Ahsunsana? Did he do the biopsy?" asked David.

"You know he did." Bucky shook his head emphatically. "And he is not nearly as good as the lady, Dr. Fey. And his bedside manner is really the pits. But the test was fine?"

"Yes, the biopsy was fine. Your EKG is normal and the echo was normal. All of your labs are good." David was looking down at the chart.

"Are you having any issues when you work out?"

"No, sir, the ticker seems to be just fine," smiled Bucky.

"Good, everything seems to be fine, then." David wrote a note in the chart, and then looked back up at Bucky.

"Are you having any other problems, besides the one with your son?" asked McAllister, smiling again.

"Well, there is something I need to talk to you about."

Bucky leaned forward.

"It's not something I want to go in my chart, though."

David also leaned forward, looking at Bucky with concern.

Bucky paused, like he was trying to decide whether to talk or not. He looked deliberately toward the door, as if to make sure it was closed and that no one was listening.

Then he leaned closer to McAllister.

"Doc, I think my heart came from a white person!" Bucky's voice was almost a whisper.

David chuckled, and rolled his stool back a little from Bucky, accustomed to his pranks.

"Doc, I'm serious."

McAllister laughed again, sliding his chair back some more and standing up.

"Dr. McAllister, I'm being serious here," said Bucky, louder, in his stern policeman's voice.

McAllister stopped laughing as he heard the tone and saw the expression on Bucky's face.

Bucky looked straight into David's eyes.

"Things are different. I mean really different. It's like I'm not the same person anymore."

He continued, "I know I'm always making jokes with the nurses and patients, but I am having some issues that I want to talk to you about. It's like something weird. It's like the heart has a mind of its own. Doc, I'm craving things that I never would have wanted before... I'm listening to different music... Hell, I watched the whole damn Indy 500 last weekend!"

Bucky paused a second, then lowered his voice again.

"I haven't been told anything about my donor yet, but I know he was white and he was a race fan."

The hair on the back of David's neck began to stand up.

He *did* know about Bucky's donor, and he *was* white and not just a race fan, but had been a race car driver. He had been in a bad crash at Talladega speedway and had been airlifted to MCA trauma center, where he had later died.

"Bucky."

David sat back down and rolled his chair closer. "It's okay. It's something I've seen before, but it's not something to worry about. I know someone who can talk to you if you would like."

Bucky let his eyes get wide, a look of horror on his face.

"You mean I could become like my donor?"

David shook his head. "No, not really, it's just a few unusual things. Not unusual, I've seen it before."

"Doc!" said Bucky, his voice quivering. "I crave hot wings and blue ribbon beer. I used to like soul music and now I'm listening to country! And I mean like... *Willie Nelson!*"

David didn't know what to say, and looked down a minute, trying to think. But then he saw the edge of Bucky's mouth begin to twitch upward and a sparkle start in his eyes.

He lifted his head and looked quizzically into Bucky's eyes.

Suddenly, unable to hold it any longer, Bucky roared with laughter.

He reached over and punched David on the arm. Then he was laughing so hard that tears started to roll down his face. He kept laughing, shaking his head in delight. It took him a minute to catch his breath, and he reached over to punch David on his arm again.

"I had you going there for a minute, didn't I, Doc? I got you. Reeled you right in. Hook, line, and sinker!"

He kept laughing to himself, proud at having fooled his favorite doctor.

"Hook, line and sinker!" he repeated.

David was laughing now, too, and shaking his head. He swatted Bucky softly with the chart.

"Yeah, you had me going there a minute."

"I know, Doc," said Bucky, enjoying the moment, still chuckling, and grinning from ear to ear.

Bucky wiped his eyes with his shirtsleeve, then looked at David.

"I've been around this unit long enough to hear *all* of the stories. And it was not hard to put two and two together when I read the papers after my transplant. The articles about that driver were everywhere... "

Bucky wiped his eyes again.

"I just can't believe you let me go that long." He chuckled again.

McAllister was still shaking his head and chuckling. He stood up to go.

"Well, you let me know when you want some hot wings."

David smiled at Bucky, then shook his head and walked out.

Kim Chou was standing right outside the door and looked quizzically at David as he left.

"What was it this time?" she asked.

"Bucky thinks his heart came from a white person." David was still chuckling.

"He what?" she said, with an incredulous look.

"It's a joke... just a joke."

McAllister walked away, shaking his head in disbelief.

17

Blood Type

THE TRANSPLANT COMMITTEE meeting was unusually contentious that morning. Dr. McAllister, as acting chair of the heart transplant program, was on the committee, as was Carver York. Dr. Brighton, though technically retired, attended, and was considered an ex-officio member. The chief of the liver program, Dr. Jackson, was the other transplant doctor on the committee. The committee was chaired by the university hospital's risk manager, a physician/attorney, Dr. Wanda Pruitt. There was also a psychiatrist, Dr. Federico Lopez, and a psychologist, Dr. Susan Kite. Elsa McAllister was on the committee, representing the organ donation agency, and so was Sarah Johnson, representing the transplant nursing staff. The last person on the committee was the hospital's assistant administrator, Mr. John Black.

The committee met on the second Tuesday of every month at six in the morning. It also met in special called sessions if there was an emergency patient listing. It was the committee's job to decide, after reviewing a patient's medical, social, and psychological profile, if they could be placed on the transplant list. It was also the committee's job to take a person off the list if he or she became too ill or otherwise ineligible for a transplant.

The big problem with transplantation in America is there are not enough organs donated, and many people die because an organ never becomes available for them. The committee was to decide, first of all, if the patient was medically suitable for a transplant. Then, was the patient mentally and psychologically able to deal with a transplant? Also, did they have some kind of social support, such as family and friends? Over the years the doctors had learned that people who had no support structure were less likely to do well.

Each prospective patient would have already met with one of the transplant doctors specific to the organ needed and would have been evaluated by a psychiatrist or psychologist. They would even have seen a dentist to make sure that they had no abscessed teeth or other major dental issues.

Transplant committees are not supposed to look at whether a patient is a good citizen, contributing to society, or a dastardly criminal. Even when it would seem reasonable to exclude someone it may not be possible. The U.S. Supreme Court has even ruled that prisoners serving life sentences for murder cannot be ruled out for transplants.

This morning, however, it was exactly that type of situation that caused contention among the normally amicable group.

The group had voted unanimously to list every patient brought up so far today, and then Dr. Pruitt introduced the case of Dominic DeMarco.

DeMarco was a nineteen-year-old male who had congestive heart failure. He had been evaluated by Dr. McAllister, Dr. Lopez, and Dr. Kite.

"As far as I'm concerned, he shouldn't be a candidate," said David.

"I've evaluated his heart condition, and I believe his heart failure is related to cocaine use."

"But he says that he has stopped using cocaine, and has been in rehabilitation for drug use," argued Dr. Lopez. He paused after a few skeptical looks from the group and added, "I really believe he has stopped."

"He has committed to stopping," confirmed Dr. Kite.

"Have you done a drug screen?" asked David.

"He will not agree to one," said Lopez.

"I thought our policy was that each patient had to be drug free before they could be listed." pointed out Elsa.

Dr. Jackson interjected, "That's true, whether it's alcohol use or drug use, and they have to demonstrate at least six months of no drug use before I will consider liver transplantation."

John Black spoke for the first time, "I think this is a case that we need to consider. After all, he is only nineteen years old, and Dr. Kite says he is committed to stopping."

Dr. Pruitt nodded. "Isn't he in good health otherwise?"

"Doesn't matter," David was shaking his head.

"If he gets a transplant and continues to use the drugs, we are wasting an organ. And we don't have enough hearts for my patients as it is."

"DeMarco. Where do I know that name from?" asked Sarah.

John Black looked down, a small grimace on his face.

"His father is Leo DeMarco."

"Isn't that the guy who just donated five hundred thousand for the new children's wing?" David asked, fixing Black with a piercing stare. "The guy who owns all the title pawn stores?"

David had seen the billboards emblazoned all over the city, *Pawn your car, keep your title!*

He had heard that they charged exorbitant interest, and targeted the neediest people.

"Yes," nodded Black slowly, not breaking eye contact with David.

David shook his head vehemently.

"No way that I'll vote to list him. His father is trying to buy a transplant!"

"Wait a minute, David," said Lopez, shaking his head. "We can't not list him because of his father. He has a legitimate medical problem and I think he is a good candidate. I've started him on an antidepressant and other meds and Dr. Kite thinks he will do well in counseling. We need to work together on this."

"Why is he refusing the drug screen?" asked Sarah, looking directly at Lopez.

"He is on probation and is afraid we will report him if it comes back positive," said Kite.

"Probation for what?" asked David.

"He was arrested for assault with a weapon two years ago and spent a month in a juvenile diversion program. He says he won't do the test because he had a friend who went to jail after a positive screen and the guy had been eating poppy seed muffins," said Kite.

"Give me a break!" cried David.

He started shaking his head. "No way, I will not agree, this is wrong!"

Carver, who had been quiet up to this point, spoke up. "How bad is his disease?"

David looked down and sighed. "Bad enough that he will need a transplant before long. I'd say within a year, even with medical intervention. Cocaine destroys the myocardium, and any continued use is going to accelerate the deterioration. That's why he has to be drug free."

Carver shook his head. "He's just a kid, David, and we don't know his family background. There are a lot of patients, as you know, that have contributed to their disease. Many lung transplant patients have emphysema from smoking, many liver patients were alcoholics, and most of my diabetic patients are overweight. And I bet some of your heart patients still eat bacon."

David did not smile at the jib. "*They* weren't criminals," he shot back coldly.

Dr. Brighton, usually silent during these sessions, asked, "May I speak?"

"Of course," said Dr. Pruitt.

Dr. Brighton stood up and walked around the table toward the front of the room. He took his time, as if gathering his thoughts. He looked out the open window for a second. Then he turned to face the group and in an uncharacteristically soft voice began to speak.

"Years ago, I was in a similar situation with a patient, a young girl who had been nothing but trouble her whole life. I knew her history because her mother was one of my nurses. The girl had done a little bit of everything and finally went too far one night and came into the hospital with cocaine overdose, in heart failure. They actually found her down, and someone started CPR. When she got to the hospital, she was barely alive, and her heart function was terrible. I saw the girl and knew that she would die, and soon, unless she got a transplant. That was when transplants were just beginning and there was no organ-sharing program. Plus she was blood type AB, the rarest kind, and her history ruled her out, anyway."

"Her mother had not given up on her, even after years of trying to help and only having heartache in return, and pleaded with me to do something. But there was really nothing we could do and the girl was basically left to die in the unit. When I saw her mother the next morning, she pleaded again for her child. I told her there wasn't anything that would help."

"That evening, though, there was a fifty-five-year-old man who died in the same unit from a brain aneurysm. He was a donor, according to his wife, and so was being assessed for kidney and liver donation. During the consent, his wife told the coordinator he had always said he wanted his heart to help someone. Of course fifty-five was quite beyond our age limit but the nurse called me and asked if I was interested in the heart. At first I said no way... but then stopped her and asked if she knew his blood type."

Dr. Brighton paused a moment.

"He was AB."

He paused again, shaking his head slightly.

"I went up and reviewed the chart and he had no other medical problems, very healthy in fact. His wife said he was a runner and worked out regularly. His EKG was normal."

He smiled. "When I did an echo, it was perfect."

He paused, and then spoke slowly, looking up at David.

Brighton continued to look at David. "We went to surgery, and I transplanted a fifty-five-year-old heart into a twenty-year-old girl."

He looked around the room and shook his head.

"That heart was almost three times as old as the girl!"

He looked out the window, still shaking his head slightly.

"That girl is alive today... turned her life around... got married and has a child of her own... and is a nurse herself. She works in the critical care unit. I saw her recently for her annual checkup, and the heart is still working fine, twenty years later!"

He looked around the room for a moment.

"I remember a quote from Mahatma Gandhi. Something like, 'Whatever you do will be insignificant, but it is very important that you do it.'"

Brighton was silent a minute, then shook his head emphatically.

"Gandhi was wrong! What we do, what she does now, basically whatever we do as humans is significant in some way... And you never know how significant."

He smiled, almost to himself.

"How old is that heart now?"

He looked directly at David, and answered, "Seventy-five?"

He nodded his head.

"And she is forty."

He thought a second. "The heart is less than twice her age now, so she's catching up." He chuckled at that.

Brighton then continued, serious again. "Since then, I rule in, if possible, particularly with young people. You never know what will happen."

Brighton moved back to his chair and sat down.

The room was quiet for a minute.

Dr. Pruitt spoke up, "Thank you, Dr. Brighton."

Black, with what David thought was a small smirk, said, "I think it's time for us to vote on DeMarco."

Pruitt immediately said, "All in favor of placing him on the list raise your hand."

David gave Carver a wry look, but finally raised his hand like everyone else.

18
Potential

THAT EVENING, DAVID and Carver were sitting across from each other at the table in the McAllisters' kitchen. Nicholas was busy putting together a puzzle at the other end of the table. They had just finished a dinner of salad and homemade spaghetti. This had become a tradition over the past five weeks. Elsa was taking courses at the university, trying to complete her Masters and Nurse Practitioner degrees. She had classes on Tuesday and Thursday evenings, and David was in charge of dinner and of Nicholas on these nights.

After the meal, Carver, with a twinkle in his eyes, asked David what he thought about the transplant committee meeting.

"Don't get me started... I was not happy with the decision today."

David shook his head. "I don't think the kid deserves a transplant. He's destroyed his heart through his own behavior and no matter what he says now, he isn't going to stop using drugs. *And* his father is trying to buy a heart, and that's just not right! In fact, it's illegal. I can't understand Pruitt in this situation. She knows it's wrong. And I wouldn't put it past Black even offering a heart if he knew that DeMarco would donate some more money."

"But you don't know the kid hasn't stopped using cocaine.

Lopez thinks he has."

"No, he said he says he has," corrected David. "Remember, I evaluated the kid. He's cocky and smug. He looks like a hoodlum. I think he expects his father and his money will fix this problem, just like he did the arrest for assault."

"I didn't know that you were clairvoyant, David." Carver's gaze was piercing.

"I'm not, but I am a doctor of medicine and a student of human nature, and I know what I see here," retorted David.

"What is a clair-voy-ant, Uncle Carver?" asked Nicholas, not realizing that he was breaking into a very serious conversation.

"Nicholad," said Carver, with a sigh, "it's like when somebody knows something is going to happen before it happens."

"Like Mom does?" Nicholas asked.

David and Carver both laughed, the tension between them breaking.

"Yeah," David grinned, "like Mom."

"She was sure right about Hannah," said Nicholas, shaking his head.

"Hannah who?"

"You know, Dad, Hannah Crumpler. She was my girlfriend."

David looked at Carver and shook his head, a puzzled look on his face.

"But I don't think she's right about broccoli. She says I'll learn to like it," Nicholas said wryly, looking back down at his puzzle.

David smiled and looked back at Carver, resuming the original conversation.

"Out of respect for Dr. Brighton, I didn't say anything else. But I don't think this kid will be anything but a thug. Just like his father."

Seemingly letting the conversation end on that note, Carver slid over to the chair next to Nicholas. "Nicholad, let me tell you a story about clairvoyance."

"Okay, Uncle Carver." Nicolas was always interested in Carver's tales.

Carver reached over and grabbed his mug. He sat back more comfortably in his chair. He took a slow sip of hot chocolate, and a far-away look came into his eyes.

Nicolas, forgetting about the puzzle, grabbed his own mug of chocolate and watched in anticipation, knowing this would be a good tale.

Carver began the story, his deep baritone voice resonating, like a Baptist preacher preaching, preaching to his little congregation.

Just after the Civil War, there was a poor farmer who lived in southern Missouri. He lived in a small house on the farm with his family, and he had a few pigs and cows, and three or four horses. He and his family tilled the land that they had, and eked out a sparse living.

His farm was near the border with Arkansas, and it was known in the area that he would allow freed slaves to stop there on their way north, for he was a kind and gentle man. He believed that the Constitution really meant "all" when it said "all men are created equal, and endowed by their Creator with certain unalienable rights, among which are life, liberty, and the pursuit of happiness."

There was a woman staying at his farm, a former slave. This young woman had a little baby boy, and he was just a few months old. They had stayed with the farmer for a while, probably because the baby was so small, and it was winter. The winters in Missouri can be especially harsh, with all of the plains to the west for the cold winds to gain speed. And this one particular night there was a terrible blizzard, with snow blowing fiercely, and everyone staying inside to keep warm.

Though the slaves had been freed by President Lincoln's Emancipation Proclamation, and the Civil War was over, there were still vigilantes who tried to take the former slaves back and force them to work.

This night, a band of these bad men, vigilantes, came to the Missouri farm on horseback, and abducted the lady and her baby boy. They took them away into the cold, cold night, unseen and unheard by the farmer because of the terrible blizzard. No one saw them, and the snow covered the tracks of their horses.

The next morning, when the farmer realized that the lady and her baby were missing, he sent out searchers to try and find them. It was still very cold, and the farmer knew that if he didn't find them soon, they would perish.

The farmer had only one thing of value, and that was a racehorse, the fastest horse in the county, if not the whole state. This beautiful, jet-black pony, with a white blaze on his forehead, was only two years old, but had already won several races. It was the farmer's prized possession, and very valuable at the time. Several rich men around the area had tried to buy it, but it was not for sale, for the farmer had raised the horse from a colt, and loved it.

The leader of the vigilantes knew of the horse that the farmer owned. He sent a message to the farmer that he would trade the baby boy for the horse. If the farmer would trade, he was to meet them at midnight that night, down at the old arch bridge, where the road crossed the river.

Carver paused and took a sip of his hot chocolate. Nicholas was leaning forward in anticipation, now totally entranced by the story. Taking another sip of his chocolate, and clearing his throat, Carver continued, a twinkle in his eye.

Bundled up against the cold, and with a heavy heart, the farmer led the beautiful horse down the road. Down to meet the vigilantes. As he journeyed down towards the river, the woods got thicker and the shadows heavier. They had only the light of the moon to show the way, and the snow got deeper as the drifts piled up in the woods. It took them a while in the deep snow, but the old arch bridge finally came into view in the stark light of the moon. When he arrived there, there was no other person to be seen, and the farmer stood shivering in the cold wind, and the little horse stamped its feet and snorted by his side, as if to say "what are we doing here?" They waited.

Suddenly, out of the darkness, the band of vigilantes rode up, crossing the wooden bridge with a clatter of hoof beats. They circled around the farmer and the little horse, as if to close off any escape. They all wore long, leather cowboy style coats, the kind that are split in the back to fit over the saddle. And they had masks made from rags, covering their lower faces. Their spurs and saddles jingled and creaked. Some carried rifles and some carried shotguns, and pistols and knives festooned their belts. Their horses were wild-eyed and breathing hard, winded from the journey, their breath coming in snorted clouds of steam. They bucked and stomped, frightened by the shadows of the rushing clouds and the darkness of the midnight. The men pulled hard on the reins, and the horses cried out in pain.

The leader of the vigilantes, who did not wear a mask, was an ugly man with only a few crooked, yellow teeth. He stopped his big horse just short of the farmer. He turned and spat, right at the poor farmer's feet. He then glared at him with a baleful eye, and chuckled.

"I knew you would come, you slave-lover."

He looked down at the farmer, and spat again, the yellow tobacco-juice staining the snow. Then he looked around at his henchmen.

"We should just kill him and take the horse," he snarled.

"Yeah, just kill him," said one of his men, and they all laughed, horrible cackles, like witches in the wind.

The leader pointed his rifle right at the shivering farmer's face. He pulled the hammer back, and it clicked into its place.

One of the vigilantes grabbed the reins from the poor man's hands, jerking as the little horse balked.

The farmer stood still, his hands at his side, his heart in his throat.

All was silent for a moment; even the wind seemed to hold its breath.

Then the leader spat again, and grumbled, "Bah—we made a deal."

He dropped the barrel of his gun and nodded his head to the riders.

The mob turned to ride away, their laughter cackling in the night.

The farmer stood still, heart racing, finally able to breathe again.

Suddenly, a small bundle was flung at him out of the darkness by the last of the riders, something wrapped up tight, like an Indian papoose. The farmer caught it in his arms, barely.

It was the little baby boy, wrapped in a flour sack.

Nicholas' eyes were wide. He waited in anticipation.

"What happened then, Uncle Carver?" he asked.

Carver smiled. He took another sip of his chocolate, and continued, his voice changing, now soft and quiet.

The kind farmer took the little baby boy back home to the farm and took care of him. He raised him as if he were his own son.

Carver looked up, staring into space, and his dark eyes started to grow moist. Then he spoke slowly.

The boy grew up. He went to school with the other children. Then he went off to college. He spent years learning about plants and farming.

Carver paused, looking down at Nicholas.

Then he became a great teacher. A great teacher... He was such a good teacher, and knew so much about plants and agriculture, that he became famous for his ideas. He developed many new methods of farming. His methods are credited with saving the lives of thousands of people during the great depression. His farming techniques have been used all over the world. They say that in Africa millions of people are alive that might have starved if it had not been for the teacher's special hybrids and methods of crop rotation.

Carver paused again, a far-away look in his eyes.

"Is this a true story?" asked Nicholas.

"Yes it is, Nicholad."

"You see, the little boy's name was George Washington. The farmer's name was Moses Carver. When the farmer adopted the baby, the boy's name was changed to George Washington Carver."

"I've heard of him," nodded Nicholas. "We studied George Washington Carver in history class. I remember because the teacher gave us peanuts that day."

Carver smiled and nodded, too.

"He made a lot of difference in a lot of people's lives," said Carver. "He was a great man."

The room was silent for a minute.

Carver finally broke the silence. He looked back down at Nicholas.

"Nicholas. Who do you think made a lot of difference in George Washington Carver's life?" Carver glanced sideways over at David as he asked the question.

"Why, the farmer did. He saved his life."

"So did Mr. Carver, the farmer, save other people's lives?"

"Sure he did." Nicholas nodded again. "When he saved the baby, the baby grew up and helped others. If the farmer had not saved the baby, many people could have died."

Carver looked over at David again. He spoke slowly, as if he were a teacher asking a student a question.

"Nicholas, do you think the farmer knew that the little slave baby would grow up to be a great man and save thousands of lives?"

"No sir. He wouldn't know that in advance."

Carver continued to look at David, not breaking eye contact.

David sat still, looking back at Carver.

Everything was quiet a minute.

Finally it was Nicholas who broke the silence.

"Uncle Carver," asked Nicholas. "Was that farmer your grandfather?"

"No, Nicholas," said Carver, a tear in his eye. "But the little slave boy was my great uncle."

19

Billboards

IT WAS ABOUT a week later that David noticed a new billboard on the way to the hospital. It was in the same location as the old Title Pawn sign. This one had a large picture of Dominic DeMarco. DeMarco was sitting in a wheelchair, and looked pale and sick. His family stood behind him: his mother, father, and two young sisters.

In huge letters across the top, the sign read:

I NEED A HEART

Under the picture it said:

Our Son Dominic DeMarco Is On the Heart Transplant List. Please Pray For Him.

Then in large letters at the bottom:

BE AN ORGAN DONOR.

David nearly crashed into the car in front of him. He pulled onto the shoulder of the road, took a deep breath, and called into the office.

"Please get all of the committee members together, ASAP," he instructed his assistant.

• • •

David walked over to the administrative conference room with Elsa and Carver. David was furious, going on about the sign.

Carver just nodded. He didn't tell David he had seen the billboard in two other places that morning.

Though it was a hastily called meeting, almost everyone had made it. Mr. Black had also brought along Deborah Chapman, the hospital public relations director. Everyone was seated and Dr. Brighton, with his characteristic curt manner, cut right to the chase.

"So, Dr. McAllister, I think we all know why we're here."

"Yes, the billboards about Dominic DeMarco... it's reprehensible," David said. "And just so you know, we have called a meeting of the hospital ethics committee as well. It will start at one o'clock."

Dr. Pruitt weighed in first: "Mr. Black and I have reviewed some similar cases that have happened around the country. The most recent one was a liver patient in Texas. That patient did the same thing, billboards all over town. He did receive a liver, a direct donation to him by a family that had seen the sign. So, even though he had just been listed, he went to the top of the transplant list, a de facto number one. Of course there was an outcry by the transplant community, but there are no regulations or laws to cover this. The direct donation rules say that a family can designate the recipient, within reason, and that is what happened. Mr. Black and I have discussed it, and there doesn't seem to be anything we can do."

"Wait a minute," David blurted. "What do you mean *billboards all over town?*' Is there more than the one on the expressway?"

He looked around the room.

"I saw two on I-20," confirmed York.

"And there is one as you come in on I-65 South," Sarah said.

"It's on the new electronic billboard at malfunction junction," said Black. "That's the only one I saw. But that sign alone costs about two thousand a month for a four-second slot that rolls around every minute or so."

"Great!" David sputtered. "So they're all over town!"

He turned and angrily glared at Black and Pruitt. "And

there's *nothing* you can do?" he demanded.

At that moment, Faye Eastmark, Black's secretary and personal assistant, charged into the room.

"WBHM-TV is here," she said. "They want to interview you, Mr. Black, and they want to interview Dr. McAllister. It's about a patient named DeMarco. I told them I didn't know anything about it, and that you were in a meeting, and it was hospital policy not to release information about particular patients. But they are insisting on seeing you."

She was looking at John Black.

Black turned to Deborah Chapman.

"Go with Faye and tell them we do not have any comments at this time," he directed. "Reiterate what Faye said, you know the drill."

Chapman nodded and left with Faye, a tense look on her face.

After the two ladies left, Black turned back to the group. David thought he heard him mutter "Well, it's hit the fan," to Pruitt as he sat back down.

David glanced over at Carver, and Carver just shook his head side to side, a slight smile on his face.

"Okay," said Dr. Pruitt. "Because of HIPPA regulations, we cannot say anything to the news. Even if we had Dominic DeMarco's permission, I don't think it's wise to comment. It's sure to be on the six o'clock news tonight, though."

"That's just what DeMarco wants," muttered David. "And I won't allow an interview, anyway."

David looked around the room. "Reprehensible. I think he needs to be delisted."

"He can't be delisted," said Pruitt, glaring at McAllister. "The transplant bylaws say a patient can be taken from the list only for health-related reasons."

"I thought it said 'or at the committee's discretion'," David retorted.

"Well, that means 'for health-related reasons,'" said Pruitt.

"Dr. Pruitt, that's not what it means," this was from Dr. Brighton.

Everyone looked at Brighton.

"While I agree with you that we do not need to take Mr.

DeMarco off of the list, the phrase 'or at the committee's discretion' means exactly that. I put it in there. If someone, for any reason, becomes ineligible for a transplant, we can take them off the list. I have done it once or twice when a patient started smoking again. Dr. Jackson regularly takes people off the liver list if they start drinking again."

"Thank you, Dr. Brighton, but I still think those are health-related," said Pruitt.

"No matter what is in the bylaws, we would be setting ourselves up for a massive lawsuit if we took DeMarco off the list," said John Black.

"You don't think that DeMarco, whose father just gave the hospital five hundred thousand dollars, would sue us, do you?" David couldn't resist.

"In a heartbeat, for something like this," said Pruitt, not picking up on David's dig. She looked around the room. "We need to all be on the same page."

"Well, in my opinion we wouldn't be in this predicament if we had not listed him in the first place," said David.

"You are right, Dr. McAllister," said Pruitt, "but we did, and we are." She continued, heatedly. "While I still think he should have been listed, I do not like being put into this position. In my opinion, the signs are despicable. However, we still have to agree on what to do about this."

"I don't think there is anything we can do about it," said Carver.

Pruitt nodded. "At this point, we cannot say anything, except 'no comment.' We cannot even admit that DeMarco is a patient here, and certainly can't admit that he is on the list for a heart transplant. We will see what the ethics committee says, but I think it's going to be the same thing that we have decided." She stood up, as did John Black.

"Thank you for your time, ladies and gentlemen. I will let you know if and when there needs to be another meeting." She and Black walked out.

"What's this 'we' stuff?" David quipped to Carver as they started out together.

20

Bomp... Bomp

ELSA, DAVID, KIM and Carver walked down the jet way in Bozeman, Montana. As they passed through the terminal on their way to pick up their luggage, they were astounded at the piles of snow outside. Montana had just been through a snowstorm, and the snowplows had pushed up huge piles to clear the runway.

David and Carver grabbed the bags as they came around on the baggage carousel, and then they all headed for the door. As they neared the exit, they were spotted by a young man holding a sign with *York* printed on it.

"Dr. York?" he said.

"Yes," said Carver.

"I'm Roger Lightfoot, and I'm here for Dr. Hawkins. He sent me to pick you up."

Lightfoot had his black hair back in a ponytail, and a deeply tan face and wrinkles around his eyes from years in the sun.

Carver introduced Kim, David, and Elsa.

Roger greeted them warmly. "Welcome to Montana."

Lightfoot took one of the bags. "Follow me," he said, and led them outside.

"Wow," Carver gasped, as the frigid air took his breath away, "it's really cold!"

"Just ten below today," smiled Lightfoot as they hurried

toward the U.S. Park Service Chevy Suburban waiting at the curb. "It was twenty-four below zero last night." Lightfoot opened the back hatch for them. "It may get that cold again tonight."

"Yeah, but it's a dry cold," quipped David.

They threw their luggage in the back.

"That's why I stay in Alabama," laughed Carver, as he slid into the passenger seat.

"And I thought it was cold in Pittsburgh," he quipped, glancing at David.

Kim, Elsa, and David jumped in the back seat, and Elsa snuggled close to David after they buckled up. They had all brought heavy parkas in anticipation of the cold, but the wind seemed to cut right through.

"It's normal out here this time of year," Roger Lightfoot said. "You get used to it."

"Are you a native Montanan?" Elsa asked, and then shook her head at her blonde moment. "I didn't mean it that way," she said.

Roger laughed.

"Yes, I am a native, but I grew up in New Mexico," he smiled. "I'm a grad student at U. of Montana, studying wildlife management. I'm working on a project with Dr. Hawkins, his hibernation study. He said you guys were interested in that, too."

"We are," nodded David eagerly, "We're hoping to learn about how the bear's metabolism slows and how it affects the bear's heart. Do you know anything about that?"

"Sure. I'm the senior assistant after Dr. Hawkins. But I can't tell you much. He wants to meet you first. I had to take a vow of secrecy."

"Okay," David laughed, glancing at Carver.

They were driving south from Bozeman. The surrounding countryside was absolutely beautiful. Everything was covered in a thick blanket of pure white snow. They passed a huge ranch to the west of the road. They could see bison, clustered in groups of eight or ten. Small signs recurred on the fence about every half mile. David thought he saw *Turner* on the sign.

Roger looked back over his shoulder. "It's the Turner Ranch, you know... Ted Turner. He owns several hundred thousand acres out here."

They passed the turn for Big Sky.

Carver pointed out the sign for the others. "We plan to spend a couple of days there."

Lightfoot nodded his approval.

"The skiing is great, and it shouldn't be crowded. You'll probably have fresh powder the way it's been snowing lately. We come up a lot for the day from West Yellowstone."

He looked over towards Carver.

"What kind of skiers are you?"

Elsa chimed in, "I like the blue slopes. But David and Carver may do some black diamonds. They're better skiers than I am."

David shook his head. "I don't know about that, I think you're pretty good."

Carver looked back and nodded.

"I've only skied in Europe," said Kim, "And they don't mark the slopes the same way. But I started when I was four, so I think I'll be okay."

"Well," Roger stated, "I may have to come up with you guys and show you the best runs. You have to be a good skier to go to the top of the mountain, all the runs down from there are black, but it's a beautiful, breathtaking view. I could show you the easiest way down. Maybe after you've skied the first day we can do that."

They were driving alongside a swift river.

Roger gestured towards the stream. "That's the Gallatin. Do you remember the movie *A River Runs Through It*? That is the river that's in the movie. In the summer we raft it. It's a lot of fun."

"It sounds like a terrible place to live," laughed Carver.

"Well, it can get really cold, like now, but it is so beautiful that you don't mind. I mean, people pay to come here on vacation. Dr. Hawkins keeps us real busy in the winter, anyway, so you don't have time to think about much else. The grant runs out next year, so we are really hustling to finish."

They continued south, once having to slow down as a bull elk crossed the road in a couple of bounds.

"We have some cabins close to West Yellowstone, and that's where Dr. Hawkins has you staying. He has a meeting until two o'clock. I will take you there first, and you will have about an hour and a half before we leave again. You can unpack and change, and then we'll go over to meet him at the west lodge. You need to dress warmly, several layers, because we will be outside some. We may take a short snowmobile trip, but they will give you coveralls to put over your parkas, and heavy mittens. Be sure to take your gloves and headgear. You will need sunglasses or ski goggles as well. You actually picked the best time to come. The bears are as close to hibernation as they get."

They passed through the little town of West Yellowstone, and then entered the park. It was just a short way to the cabins, and the road was not plowed beyond the entrance. Lightfoot had to put the suburban in four-wheel drive to make it up the narrow road.

They had not thought to put on their pacs, and so had to slog through the snow in their street shoes. It wasn't far to the steps, though, and the cabin was warm and cozy.

It was simple but nice, constructed of logs, and of course with Southwestern décor. There was an open living area with a big stone fireplace. There were three bedrooms and a small loft.

Carver let Elsa and Kim choose which they wanted, and then took the last room for himself. Then they all started to unpack and change. Roger waited in the kitchen, heating up some hot chocolate for everyone.

Carver came in first, wearing thick khaki pants and a dark blue flannel shirt. He carried a ski bib, pullover, and thick wool toboggan. Roger gave him a steaming mug. They talked about the weather again for a moment, and the appropriateness of the clothes Carver was wearing.

"Most of time we wear regular clothes for work in the lab, but if we expect to spend any time outside we wear something like ski garb. Long underwear, sweats, and bibs, and I may do a fleece coat under my parka. It's not so bad when you are moving around, but sometimes we have to be still for a long time while we are doing the tests on the bears. It's better to have too much so you can take something off than to have too little and freeze. Especially remember to protect you head, your hands, and your feet," said Roger.

"You'll be fine to go to the lab with just your parka, but be ready to dress in the over-clothes when we go to the study site."

Elsa came down next, in a sleek blue body suit, her blond hair back in a braided bun. The suit matched her eyes perfectly.

"Wow," said Carver, "That's a nice outfit."

Then Kim came in the kitchen. Her ski suit was red trimmed in black, and also fit her like a glove. Her dark hair was in a ponytail and her black eyes sparkled.

As he looked at her, Carver took in a deep breath and said "Wow" again.

"Sorry," he said, blushing.

"That's okay, York, you don't look so bad yourself," smiled Kim.

Carver pulled out chairs for the ladies, and then sat down next to Kim.

David came down and they all enjoyed a cup of cocoa and talked to Lightfoot about his background. Roger had grown up in New Mexico and gone to college in Colorado, majoring in wildlife management. He had joined Air Force ROTC to help with his college expenses and had then been stationed on Kodiak Island, Alaska.

Uncharacteristically, the Air Force actually assigned him within his area of training, making him wildlife officer for the base in Alaska. This is where he first became interested in bears. He had to develop plans for dealing with the bears and other wildlife on and around the base.

"It was funny, there was a group of specialists there who were also experts on bears. The Russian *Bear* bombers, that is," he said with a smile.

He was an avid hiker and camper, and had had numerous encounters with the bears on Kodiak Island, some of the biggest in the world.

Lightfoot had joined the park service after leaving the Air Force, and was working on a PhD at the University of Montana. He had gotten a fellowship to study with Dr. Hawkins.

Hawkins was renowned, considered to be the world's expert on bears and wolves.

David became more and more impressed with this young man and was eager to meet his mentor. He was also pleasantly surprised, again, at the amazing contacts his friend and colleague, Carver York, had.

After Elsa and Kim went back to their rooms for their fleece and parkas, they all got ready to go to the lab. This time each of them had on clothing appropriate for the task at hand, including fur-lined boots over thick wool socks. As they tromped through the snow to the Suburban, Roger began to tell them about Hawkins's research.

The lab was part of a group of buildings that comprised the veterinary clinic for Yellowstone National Park. Yellowstone has one of the largest varieties of wild animals of any of the national parks. Of course there were several veterinarians on staff, as well as experts in wildlife management.

After they had driven a few miles on the main road, Roger turned off on a side road that lead into an area with several buildings, some big and some small.

Roger pointed out the building housing the large animal clinic, with a fenced-in area alongside containing several bison. He showed them the small animal facility, and when Elsa asked, he said, "It's for wolves, foxes, weasels and such. Sometimes those doctors have a harder task than the large animal guys."

They drove up to a newer looking building, though it was still designed to match the cabin style of the others.

"This is the large animal lab," said Roger.

"It was designed by Dr. Hawkins, and is about as state-of-the-art as a park service facility can be. We can monitor animals remotely from here."

He parked the suburban in front of the lab, and everyone bailed out, crunching in the snow as they walked to the door.

When they walked into the building, they were impressed by the soaring timber-frame ceiling. The beams were thick and solid, and looked like they were hand-hewn.

In the center of the wall across from the entrance, towering to fourteen feet, stood a huge bear, arms lifted high. Everyone walked over to get a closer look. None of their group had ever seen a bear this big.

"Wow, that's a big bear," said Elsa, looking at David with a questioning look on her face.

Roger smiled, "It's a Kodiak, *Ursa Horribilis*."

"Is a grizzly as big as this?" Elsa asked

"Almost," nodded Lightfoot, "But the bears can get really big in Alaska, and some of the Kodiaks are huge. They're not quite that big down here."

Carver pointed up at of one of the bear's claws and exclaimed, "Look at those claws!"

They were several inches long, and as sharp as steak knives.

"Where did you get this one?" he asked

"It came from a hotel lobby in Anchorage, Alaska," said Lightfoot. "The hotel had closed, and the owner owed some back taxes."

He smiled. "We were able to negotiate a deal: the bear for the tax bill."

"It was shot when it attacked some fishermen on the island, sometime in the sixties. One of the fishermen was the owner of the hotel, and had the bear mounted. I've actually seen bigger ones on the island, but this may be the largest mounted like this."

"I was back in Alaska for a holiday last year while the building was being built here. I knew the hotel owner and knew about the bear. I happened to see the owner at a party and we began to talk about the research I was involved in. I asked him what had happened to the bear, and he said it was still in the lobby of the closed hotel. He wanted to know if we wanted to buy it, but I told him we had no funding for that."

"He called the next day and asked about a trade with the bear. I called Dr. Hawkins and told him the situation and he called someone he knew high up in the IRS and got it all got worked out. I couldn't believe it. The bear was in good condition and perfect for this room."

"The hardest thing was getting it down here in one piece, and without damage. That was done on a C-130. It was already coming south, flown by a friend of mine in the air force, so the bear made the trip."

Roger grinned.

"I'm glad I am still in the reserves, because of course a wildlife officer had to come along with the bear."

"And that was you?" York asked, with a smile.

Roger nodded. "It was really amazing how everything fell into place."

As they finished talking, a large man with a handlebar

mustache, full beard, and a crop of bushy brown hair came into the lobby. He was way over six feet tall and dressed in heavy boots and dark brown coveralls. As he strode towards them Elsa couldn't help but compare him to the grizzly.

"Carver!" he boomed. "It's great to see you!"

He grabbed Carver in a bear hug. Then he turned and grinned at David, thrusting out his hand.

"And this must be the Dr. McAllister that you told me about. I can't believe I'm meeting such a renowned heart surgeon."

"Please, it's David," said David, as he shook the huge paw of a hand. "Thank you for letting us come talk to you about your research on hibernating bears."

Hawkins looked over his glasses and down at David, a small smile on his face. Then he looked around.

"And who are these beautiful creatures?" he asked, looking down at Elsa and Kim.

"That's Elsa, David's wife," said Carver with a grin.

As she stepped forward to shake his hand, Hawkins swooped Elsa up in a hug.

She said "Nice to meet you" as she caught her breath. Then she smiled in spite of herself.

"And this is Kim Chou," said Carver. "Kim is David's echocardiogram specialist—she's the best!"

Hawkins glanced at Carver with a raised eyebrow, and then hugged Kim as well, almost lifting her off her feet.

"Hello," she gasped, her voice coming out a squeak.

Hawkins smiled down at them.

"It's so nice to meet you all. I've been looking forward to this ever since Carver called me. It's not every day that I get to talk to a heart transplant surgeon, and world-renowned at that. I've got some questions for you."

David smiled and winked at Carver.

"It's just a damn pump," said Carver, under his breath.

"What?" asked Hawkins.

"Nothing, just a joke," said Carver, looking back at David.

Hawkins gave David a sly glance, then said, "Everybody, come on back and I'll show you our little operation."

He led them past the secretary/receptionist's desk and scanned his badge to open the door. They followed him down a hallway and then into a large room that spanned nearly the whole building. It was full of laboratory equipment, rivaling some that David had seen in hospitals.

There were several technicians working on various tasks, from microscope slides to blood work.

As the group looked around the room, Hawkins turned to David.

"David, the first thing I need to tell you is that bears don't actually hibernate, not in the truest sense of the word."

David stared at him, the blood nearly draining out of his face.

"What do you mean?" he asked.

Hawkins laughed at David's obvious reaction. "Don't worry, I've read your proposal and I've talked to Carver, and the research we do is pertinent to your study. In fact, I think we can contribute a lot of useful information."

He continued, "Bears do go into a state in the winter that is *similar* to hibernation. Their body temp goes down some and their heart rate slows dramatically. And their metabolism slows by more than sixty percent. It's just not the true hibernation of some smaller animals."

"We see about a six-degree-centigrade decrease in temp, and a dramatic decrease in heart rate. Down to about ten beats per minute. Some of their other body functions shut down completely: the kidneys, for instance."

He glanced over his glasses toward Carver and smiled.

Then Hawkins looked at David. "And a colleague of mine at Washington State is documenting some changes in heart function. You're going to need to talk to her, too. I have copies of two echoes that she did. You won't believe what you're going to be seeing."

"The other thing is that normal bear heart function is close to that of humans, about the same rate and so on, unlike that of the smaller mammals, so you're doing the right thing looking at bears."

Hawkins looked down at them, a toothy grin showing through his whiskers.

"Don't worry, I still call it hibernation."

The he turned back toward the lab.

"Let me show you what we can do."

One wall of the lab was taken up by computer screens with multiple readouts. David could see scans, similar to what would be in a hospital ICU, with heart rate, ECG, respiratory rate, even oxygen saturation and body temp displaying on the screens. The info was broken down into windows of four to a screen.

"This is the monitor station for the hibernation study," said Hawkins.

"We currently have fifteen bears outfitted with a device to monitor their vital signs as they hibernate."

He held up a small rectangular box, about the size of a pack of cigarettes.

"These are the senders. Each bear is outfitted with one, and it receives the signals from the sensors that are implanted just beneath the bear's skin."

He then picked up a small disk that looked like a silver dollar. "This is one of the sensors. The sender relays the information to the receivers here in the lab and then it is displayed on the monitors. We record it all and can correlate the info, looking at trends. Of course we can also keep up with where the bears are, which is not a problem in the winter, but helpful the rest of the year.

"We also have infrared video and audio monitoring in five of the dens. We can look at the bears at any time, and record them. I'll let you look at one. They snore just like humans, but the rate is so slow that you almost hold your breath waiting for them to inhale."

Dr. Hawkins continued around the lab, showing the group some of the other equipment. He had a portable echocardiogram machine and even portable X-ray equipment.

"We had already scheduled an echo on a female tomorrow morning, and that will give you a chance to have some hands-on experience."

He grinned at David.

"We'll get out bright and early."

He smiled at all of them as they stopped at the back door of the building.

"Now I'm going to let all of you go back to the cabin. I know you're tired from your long flight and the drive down, and I've got a conference call with some bozo from D.C. We'll plan to get together for an early dinner, and be back here early tomorrow to go visit a wild grizzly."

"I'll see you all in a little while." He waved a little salute as he turned and went back into the lab.

Lightfoot led them back out to the vehicle, and they piled in. Carver looked at David as they headed to the cabin, then spoke to Lightfoot.

"How often do you guys do echoes on bears?"

"That's only the third one like that, I think," grinned Lightfoot. "The wild grizzlies would eat you!"

Everyone laughed, except David.

That evening they went out to eat together at a restaurant that Hawkins had chosen. When they all walked in, Hawkins was already seated at the head of a long table, with his wife, Patsy. They both stood up and Hawkins introduced her to Elsa and Kim. Patsy was a pretty lady, her shoulder-length dark hair streaked with gray. She was wearing a long dress and had silver and turquoise jewelry. Carver gave her a hug.

"You look nice, Patsy. You haven't aged at all, unlike your husband here."

Hawkins smiled, looking over his glasses at Carver.

"And this is Dr. McAllister, the famous heart transplant surgeon," Hawkins stated with emphasis, motioning toward David.

"David, please," said McAllister, and shook her hand.

"He's saved hundreds of lives with heart transplants," said Hawkins. "And he is doing research on a new heart perfusion machine, to keep hearts viable outside the body."

"I just can't imagine the skill required to sew in a heart. I could never do it, not with these paws." He held up his huge hands.

Patsy looked at Carver.

"And are you still doing kidney transplants?"

"He is," said Hawkins, butting in, "But I think any reasonably good surgeon could do that. I mean, if a kidney doesn't work, you can still do dialysis. But a heart, you know, if it doesn't work, you're up the proverbial creek!"

Carver was turning red.

"It's just a damn pump. A plumber could do it."

Hawkins let out a roar of laughter and slapped his leg, winking at David.

"He's kind of sensitive about that, isn't he, David?"

Kim was standing over to the side.

"He does pancreas and liver transplants, too," she blurted.

Hawkins smiled down at Kim.

"I know, Kim," he said, looking down over his glasses again. "And I know Carver York, probably the best hands I ever saw in surgery. I'm just pulling his chain.

"Sometime I'll have to tell you the story of when I first met Carver. I was a senior fellow at the vet school in Auburn and Carver was a new vet student, just graduated from Tuskegee. He was a great student. He only changed to medicine after working with some doctors who were doing experiments with kidney transplants. They started out transplanting kidneys in dogs at the vet school. Remember those days, Carver?"

Carver smiled and nodded. "And how many times have you sewed back the vessels on an injured bear?"

"A few." Hawkins gave them a sly look. "But only if they will be still."

Everyone laughed and started to sit down. The waiter brought the menus, and Hawkins ordered a bottle of wine, a Pinot Noir from a local vineyard.

"The elk is excellent, local, grain fed, but lean," said Hawkins.

"And get it with the béarnaise sauce." He smiled.

David chuckled at the double entendre.

"Elk? I've never had that. What's it like?" asked Elsa.

"Tastes a little like chicken," laughed Carver.

Hawkins looked up.

"It's tender and lean, sorta like beef. But better for you, they say."

He continued. "Actually almost everything on the menu is good."

"I like the trout," said Patsy. "And they have a great Greek salad."

The guys and Kim had the elk, and it was very good. Elsa and Patsy had fish, and were not disappointed.

The conversation was about many things, the park, medicine,

bears, and of course the government. Hawkins was not at all happy with the current state of affairs, and was against how the park service was making certain areas that had been public off limits to people.

"The parks were set up for people to see nature close up. People need that. And we need the people to see and be a part of nature, that's how we get our funding. It's as if the government wants to save the wilderness for only an elite few."

He shook his head in disgust.

"And now we have bureaucrats in charge instead of real rangers. They only know how to have meetings and pass new regs."

"Just like the hospitals," quipped David, and Carver nodded his head.

The next morning they were up early, had a quick breakfast of sweet rolls and coffee, and Roger picked them up again in the Suburban. Hawkins met them at the back door of the lab. They were dressed for the cold, but Roger had them don coveralls and mittens at the lab.

They trooped back out in their heavy clothes, walking like astronauts in the deep snow. There were several snowmobiles in a small building beside the lab. Helmets were passed around as Roger showed them how to operate the machines.

There were four, so Elsa rode with David and Kim with Carver, but only after both the girls received promises that they would get to drive, too.

The park was absolutely gorgeous in the winter. David and Elsa had been to Yellowstone in the summer, but this was like a completely different place. As they rode along, it seemed like everything was covered in a blanket of snow. Even the bison they passed were blanketed in white. Carver felt sorrow for the big animals as he watched them paw in the deep snow for the grass underneath. Once Hawkins stopped for a minute and pointed out a wolf up on the ridge above them. He stated that his next project would include trying to monitor the wolves' vital signs as well.

After traveling about fifteen miles along one of the perimeter roads in Yellowstone, they turned off on a side road that was marked "No Trespassing: Park Service Personnel Only." This road had not been plowed, but the snow was packed from recent use.

The going slowed quite a bit. It took another few minutes to go up over a ridge and then down into a small valley. There were two snowmobiles already parked in an open area.

At this point they dismounted from the snowmobiles and followed a lightly packed path. Lightfoot and Hawkins were both carrying backpacks, and they led the way. There were boot prints from others passing this way, but the snow was still deep enough that it required some effort to slog through it. They trooped along again, in single file, like ducklings following their mother. David almost wished for snowshoes. It was very cold, and their breath came out in clouds.

The path led them down a small draw and then up a low ridge. It was convoluted, moving around large rocks and through undergrowth. The trees formed a snow-covered canopy above them. The air was so cold that it felt like ice crystals were biting against their skin.

"It's beautiful, so beautiful, like a winter wonderland," said Kim.

"Yes, it's beautiful, but cold," breathed Carver.

"I don't think I've ever been anywhere this cold."

Lightfoot turned and said, "It's still about eighteen below, but the temp is headed up. The weatherman said it may get up to ten below, today. It just stays cold when the sun is low like this."

They topped the ridge, and the view was magnificent, with the snow-capped mountains to the west standing out in stark relief in the bright morning sun. It was crystal clear, with only a few flurries of snow when the wind would dip through the trees.

Just after they started down from the ridge, they came to a bow-shaped cliff that faced south. It was about eight feet high, and sloped down towards the valley below. There were two other park rangers standing by it, stomping their feet in the cold. Lightfoot and Hawkins stopped, greeting the two.

The trees and undergrowth above grew right down to the edge of the cliff, which was topped by an overhang, where dead leaves had accumulated on long grass and fallen limbs. There was a deep recess under the edge of one area of the overhang, and what looked like an opening, but everything was covered by the fresh powder.

"The bear is in there." Hawkins' voice was low. "And this is Sam Cloud and Jane Allgood. They are part of my field team, the ones who keep up with where the bears are."

Everyone nodded hello.

"This is a three-year-old-female, a twin, her first year away from the mother. She weighs about one hundred eighty pounds. Her mother was raised in captivity, and the cub and her sister are used to people. They were just released last year. We want to do some blood work, were actually supposed to do it last week, but I knew you were coming and thought you might want to participate."

He grinned at the doctors.

"Jane has worked with this bear since it was born. Her name is Elsa."

Hawkins smiled and winked at Elsa McAllister.

"Elsa and Emma, both females."

"Emma's den is somewhere over that ridge," he pointed toward the west.

"Usually they are not too upset when we check them in their dens, and we hope she will cooperate. She will be asleep, but if she wakes up, she will be very groggy. Everything should be okay."

Hawkins looked down at the group.

"Let's let Jane check her out first."

He looked back past them.

"You all need to stand back over there." Hawkins pointed toward the trail coming in.

Carver, Kim, David, and Elsa stepped back up the trail, Carver climbing almost back up to the ridge. They all turned to watch. Kim slid back towards Carver, shivering, and glanced up at him. He put his arm around her to help her stay warm.

As they watched, Allgood began to lightly move away the fresh snow at the opening of the den. She was talking in a low, soothing voice, like someone trying to wake a small child. She kept digging, and as she got further in, David and Elsa thought they heard a muffled *woof*.

"The den goes back about ten feet," said Hawkins.

Jane continued to slide in, but was obviously ready to jump

back out if she had to. She signaled to Sam Cloud and he handed her a small pistol-type syringe. She continued to talk to the bear, and then reached in with the syringe. They heard a small pop as she activated the mechanism. She backed back out of the den, brushing the snow off of her parka.

"It'll just take a minute or two to work," whispered Hawkins.

"She was only half asleep. We hope we can keep her in the hibernation state, like she's asleep."

He continued. "Animals that go into true hibernation are difficult to arouse, it takes them a long time to wake up. Bears wake up faster, but they are still groggy. We've given her something to keep her sleeping, but it will not slow her heart any more, and should not affect the echo."

He looked at David. "I have the portable echo machine in my pack. It's really basic, just a transducer and module that we attach to a laptop. But you can see the image. When we get it back to the lab, you will be able to plug in to the real echo machine, and it will enhance the image. I could do it for you: we need one on her anyway. But if you want to and she cooperates, you may do it yourself, and Carver, if he wants."

At that moment they heard another muffled "woof" come from the den.

"Okay," said David, nodding, looking at Elsa and Carver.

Carver shook his head. "I don't think so. I don't do many echoes."

Hawkins was looking at them with a smile.

Jane Allgood went back into the opening of the den. She started to dig some more of the snow away. Then she turned and nodded toward Hawkins.

"We can go in now," whispered Hawkins.

The group, with Hawkins in the lead, tromped back down the slope toward the den. As David got close, he could see the brown fur of the bear. He showed Elsa, and they stood and watched while Allgood and Cloud cleared out more of the snow. Carver and Kim came up beside them.

They could all smell the strong odor of the bear, and could now see clearly into the den. The bear had made a bed of grass and leaves at the back of the den. It was lying on its stomach, its feet splayed. It was nodding its head slowly up and down and back and forth, sniffing the air. It squinted its rheumy eyes at the light coming through the opening.

Jane continued to talk in low tones to the bear, and it sniffed at her parka. After figuring out who she was, it rolled over on its side, as if to go back to sleep. She knelt down beside the bear and gently placed a muzzle on its snout, tying the leather strap in back into a bow. Jane called its name, but the bear stayed quiet.

Allgood took off her backpack and took out a blood draw kit. She laid it out on a cloth in the snow beside her. She swabbed an area on the bear's arm, felt for a vessel and then deftly inserted a needle into the vein, all the time talking softly to the bear, as if it were a child. The needle was attached to a short piece of tubing with a blood draw port, and she started filling blood tubes.

Just like a nurse would do in the hospital, thought David, looking at Elsa and shaking his head.

Hawkins was climbing down into the den with a stethoscope in one hand and his backpack in the other. Lightfoot followed. While Hawkins began to listen to the bear's heart, Lightfoot put down a small plastic sheet and set out the computer and echo device. He opened the laptop and turned it on, then waited for it to start up. He typed in a code to start the system. Then he plugged in the module for the echo and started the echo program. Next, he pulled a small USB stick drive out of his jacket pocket and plugged it into the computer.

Hawkins sat down on the grass and leaves behind the bear, and Lightfoot handed him the transducer for the echo. Reaching around the bear, and watching its head, Hawkins placed the sensor on the bear's left chest. David could see the computer screen, and lo and behold, the image of the bear's heart started to appear.

"Can you believe that?" he whispered to Elsa.

She shook her head, as much in awe as he was.

Hawkins looked up. "Come on down here, David,"

"Are you sure it's safe?" asked Elsa hesitantly.

Hawkins smiled at her.

"The bear's asleep, he'll be fine."

David slid slowly down into the den, now crowded with bear and people. The odor was much stronger, and reminded him of a wet horse after a long day's ride. Jane was holding onto the bear's front legs and Lightfoot had the rear legs. David could see the bear's sharp claws. He glanced at the bear's head, and noticed a collar with the monitoring system.

The bear didn't move.

Hawkins grinned at him and gave him the stethoscope.

"Take a listen."

David took the stethoscope and moved down beside the sleeping bear. He stayed away from the head. The bear's smell was strong in his nostrils.

Squatting beside Hawkins, and reaching over the animal, he began a routine exam of the bear's heart and breath sounds, just like he would do on a human patient.

Everything sounded normal at first, except for the heart rate and the respiratory rate. He could not believe how slow the heart was beating, hearing one beat and waiting nearly six seconds for the next. It was a loud *bomp*, then a long pause, then *bomp*. But the beat was strong when it did happen. Very strong. The rate would increase as the bear took a breath. He listened to hear the valves close, but something was different. He bent down, moving the stethoscope to hear better. It was like there was only one thump, not the normal lub-dub of a mammal heart. He glanced at Hawkins, whose face was only about a foot away.

Hawkins grinned at him, and whispered, "I told you there was something unusual. Listen again."

David listened again, moving the stethoscope around, looking up and nodding at Hawkins. It was amazing. Just one loud *bomp*, each time. He bent over to hear better. Now he could hear a little of a first beat, but it was very soft. The pulmonic and aortic valve sound was good, no murmur, but it was odd to just hear the "dub." It was as if only the ventricles were working. As he moved the stethoscope, he could feel the small sender that kept up with the bear's heart rate. It was implanted just under the bear's skin.

After a minute, Dr. Hawkins tapped him on the arm, and motioned to him to move around and take the echo sensor.

David slid around behind the bear, into the place where Hawkins had been, sitting in the leaves and snow. He placed the transducer on the bear's left chest, the same place he would on a human patient. He was thankful that this bear wasn't much bigger than some of his regular patients. But she sure smelled bad. He looked at the monitor, and could see the shape of the heart in black and white, just like normal, but beating slowly. Taking his time because of the slow rate, he moved the echo sensor around, trying to see the heart from every angle. He would move the sensor, take a minute, and then move it again. It looked like a fairly normal echo, but again, the atria did not move much. The wall motion of the ventricle was strong, and if he had to guess an ejection fraction it would be at least fifty percent.

David was in his echo mode, concentrating on the monitor, pressing in on the transducer, trying to get the best picture.

Suddenly the bear snorted and tried to roll over.

David jumped, realizing where he was. The bear shifted again, and David dropped the echo transducer and scrambled to his feet. The bear huffed, but did not struggle against Allgood and Lightfoot. It opened its eyes and looked over at them.

"Let's get our stuff and get back out," hissed Hawkins, picking up the computer with the echo module still attached.

David grabbed the small tarp and scrambled out, Hawkins close behind him.

Allgood was talking to the bear. Soothing it, in a small quiet voice, she was almost singing a little song. After a minute, she let go of the bear's paws with her right hand and reached up and pulled the loop on of the strap holding the muzzle. It had been tied with a bow and the binding fell down, loose. She and Lightfoot then counted to three and let go of the bear together.

Roger moved away quickly and climbed out of the hole, carrying the backpack and blood tubes with him. The bear rolled over on its stomach and watched him.

Allgood continued to soothe bear with her voice, and then reached over and pulled off the muzzle. The bear rolled its head around again and then yawned, like a cat waking up from a nap. Jane Allgood slowly backed away, talking softly.

David could hear her now.

"It's okay, Elsa, we're all done. It's all done, you're fine. Good girl. Good girl. You can go back to sleep now," she said, climbing backwards out of the den.

The bear watched her closely, but allowed her to move some

of the snow back into its place. It shook its head and yawned again, then rolled back onto its side. They all watched it gradually disappear from view as Jane closed the opening with leaves and limbs and fresh snow.

It seemed that everyone let out their breath at the same time, as if they had been holding it.

Hawkins looked at Elsa and grinned, and then nodded at David.

Then Hawkins and the rangers started packing up the gear.

David was standing beside Carver, speechless, his heart racing.

"Damn, if that's not the weirdest thing I've ever seen," said Carver.

"But I'm glad I'm not a heart surgeon. You won't see us kidney guys doing anything like that!"

Elsa hugged David and held up her camera.

"I got it all." She grinned. "Nobody's going to believe this."

Then she backed away and looked at him, sniffing.

"Man, you stink!" she said with a laugh.

David laughed back, finally finding his voice.

"I had her in my lap! Damn, a full-grown grizzly bear in my lap! Can you believe it?"

"She's just a cub, David," laughed Carver.

"I didn't see you down in that hole." David's eyes were sparkling.

He shook his head.

"I just did an echocardiogram on a grizzly bear!"

Everyone laughed at his enthusiasm.

The rangers finished gathering up their stuff, and came back up the trail.

They all started back over the ridge, the rangers in the lead.

David looked back, then stopped and turned around.

"Goodbye, Elsa," he called. "I had a nice time."

Elsa McAllister punched him.

"I get to drive back!"

When they got back to the lab, they went in the back door, tromping in in their snow packs, then shedding their mittens and heavy coveralls, then their parkas, scarves, and toboggans. The coveralls were hung up for another time, or another team, and David hung his up last, to air out. He was glad his street clothes didn't smell like bear sweat.

So was Elsa.

After cleaning up, they all sat down in the staff break room. Patsy Hawkins was there, and passed around mugs of steaming coffee, laced with a tad of brandy. She had made a huge crockpot full of chili, with cheese and peppers on the side. She had also brought baked potatoes, and a thick loaf of garlic bread. They toasted the bread in the oven, covered it with butter, and cracked open the potatoes and covered them with chili and cheese. They were all hungry, and it was a feast fit for a king and his knights.

After they had all eaten, and taken a little time to rest, Hawkins came back in.

"David," he said, looking down over his glasses, "I want you to look at these echoes. Carver, you can come too, if you want. Roger can take the girls back to the cabin."

David shook his head.

"Elsa is in charge of the research project, Joseph. And Kim does all the echoes in my office. She's the best sonographer in the state. They need to participate, too."

"Now Carver, like he said, doesn't do many echoes. He may want to go shopping or something."

Everyone laughed, except Carver.

"I've seen a few echoes," said Carver, "and we do sonograms all the time. You know that! Why, I could have done a sonogram on that stupid baby bear cub."

They all laughed again, and then Hawkins boomed, "Fine! Let's all go. Then you can take the rest of the afternoon off, together."

They spent about another hour and a half in the lab, and afterwards Hawkins gave them copies of all of the echoes they had, including the one David had just done, and the two from Washington State. Then he had to go to another meeting.

"What do you want to do?" asked Lightfoot, as they started out to the suburban.

"How about the snowmobiles?" asked Carver, and the ladies nodded.

Roger thought a minute.

"You promise to be careful, and stay on the roads?"

"Absolutely," Carver said, and they all nodded, again.

They went back in to get the coveralls, mittens, and helmets. David got there first, and handed them out. He made sure Carver got the first set of coveralls.

They spent several hours riding in the park, going all the way to the Old Faithful geyser. It was a beautiful day, but cold. The lodge was open at Old Faithful, so they took a break and warmed up with hot chocolate, and watched the geyser erupt. While they were sitting down with the chocolate, Carver suddenly sat up and sniffed, looking around.

"Do you smell that?" he asked. "Smells like there's a bear in here."

David nearly fell out of his chair, he was laughing so hard.

On the way back, they rode the snowmobiles a different route around. It was amazing to see the steam from the hot springs, sizzling in the ice cold air. The girls got their fill of driving, and everybody's thumbs were sore from holding the throttle open.

They got back to the lab just before sundown, and Roger brought them home. They made plans to go skiing the next day, and he said he would pick them up early. Roger told them the cafeteria would be open, and since it was Wednesday they would have homemade minestrone soup. He said it was the best thing they made. He also said there would be music.

After showering, they rested for about an hour and then tromped over to the cafeteria.

The place was almost full of park employees, finishing their day or starting their evening shift. Some were visiting after their day at work, but others were just sitting around, waiting.

The four of them were in a corner booth finishing up their dinner. Just then, two guys and a girl walked in, carrying guitars. They uncovered a set of drums in the other corner and started setting up to play. Both guys had hair down their backs, and the girl was nice-looking and animated. She went around and talked to some of the other park people as the guys got ready to play. Some of the workers started to clear out the area in front of the band, moving the chairs and tables back out of the way.

"This looks interesting," said David. "Do we want to stay awhile?"

"Let's see what they're like," nodded Elsa.

After a few minutes, the group tuned up and started the first song.

It was just as they expected: a folksy mix of rock and country. And they were pretty good, the girl especially.

The group sat and listened to the first two songs, and then Elsa said, "Let's get a glass of wine and listen awhile."

The lodge had a small bar, so David and Carver went over to check out what they had. They only had two kinds of wine, a merlot and a chardonnay. It wasn't expensive. They bought a bottle of each and grabbed four glasses from the bartender. They knew they could take what was left back to the cabin.

As they sipped their wine and talked, the music continued. The girl had a nice voice, and one of the guys was really good on the guitar. They played a couple more folksy tunes and then the tempo of the songs sped up. The band was getting warmed up. Some of the people in the audience got up to dance, couples and singles.

Then band started a familiar song, an old rock-and-roll tune.

David looked at Elsa and smiled.

"Want to dance?"

"Yes, I do." Elsa had a smile on her face, and a sparkle in her eyes.

Carver and Kim watched as David took Elsa by the hand and led her to the dance floor. David then grabbed both of Elsa's hands in his, and took a moment to get the beat. Then they started into a swing dance, rocking back and forth and stepping back from each other in rhythm to the beat. David would let go with one hand and lift his arm and Elsa would turn, or they would do a turn holding both hands where Elsa would come out beside David, cradled in his arms, and then go back out away from him.

Carver and Kim watched, and Kim smiled and laughed. "They're pretty good!"

Some of the other couples were doing the swing dance, too, and the other dancers gave the group of swing dancers room.

When the song was over, David and Elsa came back to sit down, smiles on their faces, both of them a little out of breath.

"That was good." Kim quipped as they sat down. "I didn't

know you could dance."

Elsa smiled again, obviously pleased at the compliment. "David signed us up for dance lessons. We've been getting somebody to come over and stay with Nicholas on Friday nights. We go out to the lesson, and then go out to dinner together."

She snuggled over close to David, looking up at him and smiling.

"We've learned the swing, and the rumba, and a little of the waltz. So far the swing is the one we do best."

"Wow," said Kim. "That's romantic."

She glanced over at Carver. "We used to do the swing dance when I was in college."

Carver was looking at David, and shaking his head. He knew what was coming next.

The band started another song, and Kim looked at Carver. "Wanna dance?"

"Sure."

Carver stood and took Kim's hand.

David and Elsa watched with interest as they walked to the dance floor.

Carver stopped Kim on the dance floor, took both her hands just as David had done with Elsa, counted a minute, and away they went.

Elsa's mouth nearly fell open, and she looked at David and clapped her hands. Carver had obviously done the swing before.

They walked out to the floor and joined in.

As Carver brought Kim around in turn, he winked at David, a big grin on his face.

21

Frat Boy

JUST ABOUT EVERYONE at the Alpha Kappa house had a buzz on from the beer and the shooters. By around midnight, the party was winding down. Dominic DeMarco, however, was just getting into full stride. He had actually been partying pretty much continually since Thursday night.

The Alphas were the big dogs on campus. Most were sons of prominent or wealthy parents, elites, and were the up and coming, destined by fate and wealth to inherit the status of their elders. Many majored in political science, aiming for law school and then politics, or maybe plaintiff law. Some were already leaders on campus. The last two SGA presidents had been Alphas, and there was hope in the group that they could make it three in a row. Dominic was a contender for that spot, having already been elected pledge chairman in just his sophomore year. It had helped that his father was well placed in local politics, was on the college board, and had donated a hundred thousand towards renovations at the fraternity house.

This was a special party, celebrating the engagement of the current fraternity president with one of the most eligible women on campus, who happened to be head cheerleader and homecoming queen. She was vice-president of the Phi Mu sorority herself.

Someone had made a poster with two hearts intertwined. One of the hearts had the Greek letters for the Alphas and the other had the logo for the Phi Mus. The wedding date had not been set, but it was still a reason to have a party. The brothers had dates and had invited friends, and several of the other fraternities on campus had sent envoys to honor the occasion.

Dominic had been partaking freely of the cold beer from the huge keg that had been set up in the house's spacious kitchen. He had also had several of the strawberry Jell-O shooters that were being passed around on a tray by Sam, the butler.

Dominic and Misty, his current girlfriend, were sitting on a couch in the large living room that adjoined the kitchen. She was also a sophomore, majoring in nursing. They had been together about six months. The widescreen TV was tuned to a rock station and blared the music through the surround-sound system, the thump of the bass resonating through the building. The partiers were gathered around the room in small groups, laughing and talking, trying to hear over the din of the TV and the noise of the others.

Misty drank red wine, which was also plentiful, and strawberry shooters. She was sitting close beside Dominic, her bare legs stretched out on the couch. His right arm was draped over her shoulder, and he was twisting her hair around his finger. Her pupils were dilated from the wine and vodka. She still held the wineglass, now tilted, and some of the cabernet splashed onto her shoes below.

"Do you have any?"

Dominic looked down at her and smiled. He reached into his coat pocket and took out a small container. "I do, baby, but remember our agreement."

"Agreement?" Misty looked at him, her head lolling sideways a little.

"You know. You can't have any until after the tests."

"Aw, baby, please. It won't hurt anything. They're not going to call you yet."

"We're just not going to until after the appointment," he said, smiling down at her.

He moved his fingers down to the smear of the red liquid in her cleavage.

She looked at him and smiled, and reached down to pull his hand closer and deeper.

"Wanta go upstairs?" he asked.

She nodded slyly.

She sat up, then slowly stood and walked toward the bathroom, focusing on her balance. She nearly ran into the door, and turned and giggled at him, winking and reaching up to unbutton another button on her blouse.

She did not see him open the can and reach in for a pinch of the white powder. He frowned when he noticed it was almost empty. Where had it all gone? He spread the powder in a line on the small glass table next to the couch. He waited until the door closed before he took out a straw and bent over the table, inhaling with practiced ease.

When Dominic awoke, he felt like there was a heavy weight on his chest. He could hardly breathe. His skin was clammy and damp, and his head ached terribly.

He slid out of the bed, noticing Misty for the first time. Then he remembered last night. Something had been wrong then, too. He remembered not being able to do anything with her, the first time that had ever happened.

He went into the bathroom and got a glass of water, gulping down three aspirin for the headache. He was breathing hard just from the exertion of walking across the room. His chest felt tight. He could feel his heart pumping fast. He washed his face and, glancing up, gasped when he saw himself in the mirror. His skin was pale as an eggshell, and almost blue. He noticed the veins in his forehead, and didn't remember them sticking out so prominently. He washed his face again, splashing the cold water over the counter and the floor. He couldn't find a towel on the hook, and turned to get one from the shelf.

He moved slowly back into the bedroom, looking for the clock on the bedside table. Misty's lacey bra was draped over it, hiding the numbers. He removed the bra. The clock said 9:15.

"Oh, shit," he hissed. "Misty, wake up. Wake up."

He shook her, but it only elicited a soft moan.

"Misty. Get up. We've got to get ready to go."

He shook her again, harder this time. She sat up slowly, shaking her head back and forth. She could not open her eyes at first, rubbing them with both hands. When she did they were red and rheumy, and she squinted against the light.

"What? What's wrong?"

"We have to get ready for the doctor. It's 9:15 and my appointment is at ten."

She lay back down, her face in the covers.

"Just go on without me," she mumbled, her voice muffled by the pillow.

"No, you have to go, too. They're doing the test."

"Aw, shit," she moaned. "Just give me a minute to wake up."

She sat back up, eyes still shut, tousling her hair with her hands. Her naked breasts were thrust out prominently, but he didn't care.

"Damn, my head hurts," she moaned. "It feels like it's about to explode."

"I don't feel good, either," he said.

Misty rolled over to the edge of the bed and let her feet slide over the side. She stood up slowly, still rubbing the sleep from her eyes.

DeMarco watched her stumble to the bathroom and close the door. He heard the water running and then heard the toilet flush. He found his jeans on the floor and sat on the bed to put them on. Every movement seemed to make him breathe harder. He found his sandals, but had trouble telling which was left and which was right. It was like his thinking was fuzzy. He sat on the bed again, catching his breath.

Misty came out to get her bag. She had brought some clothes over the night before, knowing that he had a doctor's appointment.

"I need to clean up a little, too," he said, not looking up.

Misty looked at him, seeing him for the first time that morning.

"Damn, Dominic, you look awful," she gasped.

"I don't feel good," he said, again.

They walked in the clinic at ten past ten. Misty had had trouble finding a place to park, ending up in a handicapped space.

"Dad can fix the ticket," Dominic had said.

He was winded from the short walk into the clinic.

After they had signed in and sat down he looked at her.

"Don't forget what we practiced."

She nodded and held his hand, noticing again how pale he was.

They had only been waiting a few minutes when they heard his name called and a tech opened the side door and motioned them in.

"I need to go to the bathroom," said Misty to the girl. "Which room will he be in?"

"In room six, and the bathroom is down the hall."

Misty went into the small bathroom and closed the door. She looked around and found what she was looking for on a shelf above the toilet. It only took a minute to fill the small plastic container to the line, and then finish in the toilet. After placing a lid on the container she tucked it in the elastic of her pants under her baggy sweatshirt, then washed her hands and fluffed her hair.

She walked to room six just as the transplant nurse arrived at the door.

"I'm Misty. I go with Dominic," she said.

The nurse nodded at Misty and followed her into the room, looking at the chart as she walked in.

"So you're here for that drug screen?" Then she looked up.

Donna Tankersley had been a heart transplant nurse for fifteen years. Before that, she worked in critical care at the University Hospital, taking care of patients in the cardiac intensive care unit.

It only took her a second to see that things were not right with Dominic.

"Are you okay, Dominic?" she asked.

"No, Ms. Tankersley, I don't feel very good."

Donna sat down beside Dominic and took his wrist. His skin was cold and clammy. His pulse was racing.

"What's wrong, Dominic?" she asked.

"I just have this weight on my chest. I can barely breathe, and it feels like my head is bursting."

"Let's get your blood pressure."

Donna reached over for the cuff in the wall holder. She wrapped it around Dominic's arm and started pumping it up.

She moved the earpieces of her stethoscope into her ears and placed the diaphragm on his arm. She watched the liquid in the tube as it moved up the scale and then down as she let off the pressure. She frowned.

"What?" he said.

"Your pressure's really high." She moved the stethoscope to his chest. "Let me listen to your heart."

She moved the stethoscope around his chest, listening to his heart and lung sounds.

She stood up and stepped to the door.

"Jenny, ask Dr. McAllister to come down here for me," she said.

After a minute they heard a knock. It was Jenny. "He'll be here in ten minutes, he was over at the hospital."

Tankersley sat back down, writing in the chart.

"Let's go ahead and get that urine sample while we wait."

She looked at Dominic. "The bathroom is down the hall."

Dominic got up and left. Donna continued writing in the chart for a minute.

Then she looked up at Misty. "So you are Dominic's girlfriend?"

Misty nodded. "Yes, and his driver today."

"He may need to stay in the hospital."

"I was afraid of that."

They heard Dominic back at the door.

Misty got up to open it, saying, "I need to go to the bathroom, too."

It was a classic bump pass as they went by each other in the doorway, and would have been perfectly executed if Dominic hadn't stumbled slightly.

Tankersley wasn't sure what she had seen, but something had happened between the two. And she had seen Misty come out of the bathroom not ten minutes ago.

His back to her, Dominic closed the door. Then he turned and held out the little container of warm yellow fluid.

"Here you go, Ms. Tankersley," he said.

Donna sat the container on the table beside them, then waited for him to sit. She looked at him, thinking about what she had just seen. It wasn't the first time someone had tried that trick. She thought a minute, then smiled and checked several additional boxes on the form in her hand.

"This is the release for the test." She held out the clipboard with the form and a pen.

"Okay." Dominic signed the form with a flourish and handed it back, a sly smile on his face.

Donna took the form and pen. She then labeled the container with one of the stickers from Dominic's chart.

"Let me get this to the lab." She stood.

"I'll be right back. Dr. McAllister should be here by then."

They admitted Dominic DeMarco to the hospital.

McAllister had ordered a chest x-ray and echo in the office as soon as he had arrived and talked to Donna Tankersley. Of course he was worried about the blood pressure and the shortness of breath, as well as Dominic's heart rate. He also saw significant fluid around Dominic's heart and lungs on the x-ray. The echo had been more difficult, with the fluid buildup and hypertension, but showed that the cardiomyopathy was worse.

The clinic was connected to the hospital, in fact, almost all of the clinics around MCAMC were connected in some way to the hospital. Dominic had been taken by wheelchair to the cardiac floor, and was admitted to McAllister's service. They had drawn blood for labs and started an IV. McAllister had already ordered medicine for the fluid buildup and hypertension.

By the end of the day, Dominic felt better. His heart rate had come down, his chest pain was gone, and he could breathe normally again.

He was sitting up in bed eating frozen yogurt with Misty when Dr. McAllister and nurse Tankersley walked into the room.

"How are you feeling, now?" asked David, taking out his stethoscope.

"Better, Dr. McAllister," said Dominic.

McAllister took a minute to listen to Dominic's heart and lung sounds.

"You still need to stay overnight, Dominic, but if things stabilize you may get to go home tomorrow."

"Thank you, Dr. McAllister."

McAllister nodded and smiled, placing his stethoscope back in his pocket.

"Oh, Ms. Tankersley has some information for you," he said.

Donna stepped forward with the chart in her hand.

"I've got good news," she smiled, "your drug screen came back negative."

"I told you it would, Doc," said DeMarco, smiling back.

He looked over at Misty, nodding. She smiled back at him.

"But one other thing," said Donna.

"What?" asked Dominic.

Donna looked down at him.

"Your pregnancy test came back positive."

This time it was Misty who turned white as a sheet.

22

Heartthrob

DAVID AND CARVER were sitting in the corner of the medical library at MCA hospital. They had both just been to a lecture at the university forum. The lecturer had been Dr. Sollinger from the University of Wisconsin, one of the pioneers in kidney transplant. He had been discussing tolerance, the idea that a transplant patient could somehow be made to accept the transplanted organ without the regimen of antirejection drugs. They were both very interested in the topic, and had sat together for the lecture.

David had been thinking, a lot, about what Debardeleben had said about the heart rejecting the recipient. He needed someone to bounce the idea off of, and Carver seemed to be the one. They often discussed common problems with transplantation, and it was not unusual for Carver to have some eccentric ideas, so David had no trepidation in bringing up the ideas with him. They each had a cup of coffee, and there was no one else in the library since it was now after four on a Friday.

They had been discussing the lecture when David suddenly stopped.

"Carver," he said. "I have something else I want to talk to you about."

"You know how over the years some of my patients have

had strange dreams or memories about their donors that were uncannily close to reality."

"Yes," Carver nodded. "I've had a few of those patients myself, we've talked about it."

"Well, I've been working with someone who is interested in the subject and is studying the phenomena, and I think she may be onto something."

"Sally Debardeleben?"

David looked at Carver, surprise on his face. "Yes. How did you know?"

Carver smiled. "David, old man, the great Doctor Carver knows all."

David shook his head. "No, now really, Carver, how do you know Dr. Debardeleben?"

Carver looked him straight in the eye. "I have served on two ethics committees with Sally, and we attend the same church. I have also consulted her about a couple of patients. You heart guys think everything revolves around you, but we, the other guys, have some similar issues, believe it or not."

David shook his head again, ever amazed at Carver's connections.

"I think she has some interesting ideas about rejection."

"Like what."

"She believes that the heart... " David smiled. "Umm, the organ... can reject the recipient."

"Cellular memory?"

"Exactly."

"I haven't talked to her about that, but it sounds interesting," said Carver, his eyes looking slightly right as he thought about it.

"You're left-braining it, aren't you?"

"What?"

"I've been reading. When you shift your eyes right like that it is your left brain that is computing. If you shifted to the left it would be the right brain."

"What difference does that make?"

"Right hemisphere is more rational, left is creative. Cellular memory is a left-brain concept. I'm trying to tap into that side."

"David, you continually surprise me."

Then he smiled and shook his head. "Have you mentioned

this to any of the other docs?"

"No," laughed David. "I bet Brighton would have me committed."

Carver thought a minute.

"No, he wouldn't. He's smarter than that. He has to have run into this before."

"I've just talked to Sally and a little to Elsa."

Carver looked at his watch. "I've got a date tonight or I would stay and talk. I am very interested in this, David. Let's schedule a time for a discussion, and I'll tell you about some of the cases I've seen and what I think is going on."

"I've got an appointment with Sally this Thursday," David said. "Do you want to come along?"

"Absolutely. I'll call you Monday about it."

"Good," said David as they both got up to go. "Maybe we can talk about it some more Tuesday night. Nicholas wants tacos."

"Sounds good to me."

• • •

They met in the small conference room next to David's office during lunch again, and everyone had brought something, either from home or a takeout. David had asked Sally if it was okay for Carver to attend, and of course she had said yes. Elsa was at the office that day and joined in. She had just opened a salad with baked chicken for her and David when Carver walked in, a large brown paper bag in his hand. It had "Dreamland" written on the outside.

"I was coming through Five Points and decided to stop by Dreamland," said Carver, with a grin.

"I got two slabs of ribs."

The aroma of barbecued ribs filled the room as Carver opened the bag. Elsa was shaking her head, but David was smiling.

"These are the best ribs in the country," said Carver. "Better even than Chicken Comer's in Columbus."

"Everybody dig in."

David reached over and grabbed a couple of ribs, turning them over in the sauce first. He sat down and started eating.

Sally and Elsa took a rib each, and sat. Elsa passed Sally a plastic fork and knife.

"Uh, uh," said Carver, shaking his head.

"You can't eat these ribs with a fork. You have to pick them up."

He got a plate and took three ribs, some stew, and a piece of bread.

"I'll be right back."

"Where are you going?" asked Elsa.

"I'm taking some to Kim."

Elsa looked at him, a sly smile on her face. "Why don't you just ask her to come in here?"

"Okay," said Carver.

"Kim?" Sally looked at Elsa.

"Just David's nurse." Elsa said, glancing over at David.

Carver came back in, holding the door for Kim.

"Kim, this is Dr. Sally Debardeleben. She's the psychologist I've been telling you about who studies some of our heart recipients."

Sally stood and shook Kim's hand.

David continued, "Sally, this is Kim Chou, the best cardiac nurse in the state." Kim smiled at Sally, shaking her head at David's remark.

"Nice to meet you, Dr. Debardeleben, I've heard a lot about you."

"It's Sally, Kim, and it's nice to meet you, too."

Carver grabbed a plate and covered it with ribs, then covered them with more sauce.

He took a bite.

"These are the best ribs. Tender and lean. And you can't beat the sauce."

"Too bad they started in Tuscaloosa."

David laughed.

"Speaking of ribs," Sally interjected.

"In his homily last Sunday, Father Gallagher was speaking of how God created Eve from Adam's rib. He said God could have used anything to create Eve, but He chose a rib from Adam.

"Father told the old story of how it came from Adam's side, so that Eve would stand by him as an equal, and it came from under his arm, so that Eve would be protected by him. And it came from close to his heart, so that Eve would be loved by him.

"Father Gallagher said that love is from the heart. In fact, there is a scripture that says that when we accept God in faith, he gives us a new heart. He replaces our heart of stone with one of flesh."

"Sounds like some of my patients," quipped David.

Sally smiled at that, and nodded at David. Then she continued.

"The heart is mentioned quite a bit in scripture. In fact, when the teachers asked Jesus which is the greatest commandment, He says to love the Lord your God with all your heart, all your soul, and all your mind. He differentiates between the mind, the soul and the heart. Why does he do that?"

"Because the heart is the most important organ in the body," David interjected, smiling and winking at Carver.

Sally continued, not allowing David to derail her thesis. "You hear people say things like 'her heart was not in it' and we all know what that means. I teach my counseling students to listen with their hearts."

She paused, thinking, then continued, "When I work with patients or families in grief in the hospital, I try to communicate on the level of the heart, not the mind. It just doesn't work if you are clinical or analytical. You have to be compassionate, to empathize. It has to come from your heart."

Elsa and Kim were nodding.

"David, your love for Elsa is not just mental or physical, it is spiritual, on the level of the heart. Then why are we surprised when a heart is transplanted and the recipient can feel things about the donor?"

Sally paused again, then went on. "There is something there beyond just an organ. The heart is not just an organ, not just a pump, it is the lighthouse for the body. Its signal is not visible, but it is felt throughout the body, by every cell, with every beat... And the signal is strong, much stronger than the signals from the brain."

"It's going to be the same for a heart transplanted into a recipient. The signal is going to be felt throughout the new body. Every beat of the heart is going to resonate. And the heart itself can sense what is going on in the body. It changes its rate to accommodate the body's needs. The heart is like a concert pianist, who does not need to look at the keys on the keyboard, but knows their exact location."

Kim spoke up for the first time. "What about the cases that I hear about where they dream about the donor before the transplant? We have one patient whose daughter had a vision of the donor the night before her father got the heart, and the vision is too real, too true to life to be just a dream. She describes the donor perfectly, and he speaks to her in the dream, telling her everything will be okay. The donor was not even in the same state, but I had the history in the donor record, including a picture from the donor's driver's license. And the dream occurred after the donor died but was before the heart was transplanted."

David looked at her quizzically.

Kim looked at him, then looked down, as if revealing a secret. "It was Mr. Nelson, he got a heart last year. His daughter is a nurse and had a dream the night before about his donor. She told me about it, that the donor was a young man and what he looked like. It was too close to be made-up."

"I see those, too," nodded Sally, "But I think that those are different. That is more of a spiritual thing. I know of several cases where transplant recipients, or even family members, have had dreams about the transplant before it occurs. I've been studying those, too, and it happens more than we think."

She looked at David.

"Martha Lake has been having dreams about her donor."

David looked at her. "Really? I knew about the helicopter thing."

"Yes, that happened. But this is different. We've met a couple of times now and she has told me about a dream about the girl. The girl is always wearing a blue dress and actually speaks to her. She says something like, 'Tell Mom and Dad and Susan I'm okay.' She says 'Tell Ricky hello for me.' And she asks about someone named Tonto."

David was shaking his head.

"So there could be more than one phenomenon going on here?"

Sally smiled at David's word choice. "Yes, Dr. McAllister,"

she stated, in her most clinical voice, "There could be more than one 'phenomenon!'"

Everybody laughed, including David.

Sally looked around the room. "There is an unseen aspect to life that many people do not even realize." She smiled, almost impishly, then looked up at them. "I have a special study that we are doing on Wednesday nights. Maybe you all would like to participate. We are investigating some of the common spiritual aspects of everyday life: prayer, meditation, dreams, that kind of thing. Exploring how they fit into our lives, their meaning and significance."

"I think that would be very interesting," said Carver, who had been sitting in the corner, quietly listening to the whole discussion.

Kim nodded.

"I would like to go, too.

"Perhaps we could go together," said Carver, to everyone's amusement.

"Are you asking me on a date?" Kim chided Carver.

"Well, I guess so... yes," he said embarrassed.

"Carver, is your heart beating a little faster?" Sally quipped.

23

He Knows

MARTHA LAKE FACED the day with some trepidation. There was excitement over finally meeting the family of her donor and learning something about the young girl who had donated her heart. And there was uncertainty about communication with a mom and a dad who had lost their daughter, the emotions involved, and if there might be some kind of blame towards her.

She still felt guilt.

Even though it had been several months since her transplant, the thoughts of the girl still came to her regularly.

In her heart, she often asked why. *Why did the girl have to die? Was it really just chance, like Dr. Mac said?*

Or did the girl die for me?

Martha had always believed in God, and had always thought that He had a plan for her life.

Was this in the plan?

Dr. Debardeleben had told her that she didn't cause the girl's death, and she knew that this was true. But still, there would always be the why. She wondered if she would ever get over it.

Martha glanced over at her husband, Alan, who was humming along with a song on the radio as he drove. They were heading south towards Florida. Lisa Kelly had set up the meeting for them with the Raines. Actually the Raines had asked if they could meet, and Lisa had called the family counselor in Birmingham and asked her to call Martha and see if she wanted to meet them. Amazingly, the call had come only a few days after Martha's meeting with Dr. Debardeleben. Martha had written a letter thanking the Raines, and telling them something about herself and her situation. The Raines had responded almost immediately. The counselor had told her that a meeting was totally her decision, that she might want to wait a little longer, or maybe not meet at all. The counselor knew that for some transplant recipients it was just too difficult.

But Martha did want to meet them. Most of all she wanted to thank them, to tell them about how sick she had been and how they had saved her life. To tell them about all the things she could do again, about Kristi... and about the dreams.

How do you do this? she thought as they drove along... *How do you meet the mom and the dad of the girl who died and gave you her heart?* Her eyes filled with tears again, and Alan looked over at her. He reached over to take her hand, giving it a squeeze.

Martha sighed.

At least Dr. Sally will be there, she thought. Just then she glanced up and saw the big sign.

"Welcome to Florida—the Sunshine State."

Martha smiled. That was Alan's nickname for her: *Sunshine*.

She sat up straight, wiped the tears from her eyes, and turned and smiled at Alan. Things were going to be fine.

Martha and Alan stopped at the rest area just inside Florida. They were to meet Lisa there and then follow her to the Raines' home. Then she and Alan were going on down to Panama City Beach for a vacation. They had honeymooned at the beach and tried to come back down every couple of years. This visit with the family had given them another reason to come, so they would spend a little time with the Raines and then continue down to Panama City.

After meeting Lisa, they followed her for the twenty minutes or so that it took to reach the Raines' home. Lisa had told them that Dr. Debardeleben was going to be there when they arrived. Sally had been down to meet with the Raines the day before, and then had spent the night with her own family in Dothan.

The first thing Martha noticed as they pulled up was the live oaks that ringed the little house. She had always liked live oaks. She glanced over at Alan and smiled as she unbuckled her seat belt. She took a deep breath and started to open the door. Then she stopped and reached over to Alan. She held his hand and bowed down for a second to say a prayer.

Then she opened the door and stepped out of the car.

Sally Debardeleben and a man and a woman had come out of the house, and were standing on the small porch watching as she and Alan and Lisa walked up. They stepped down from the porch and walked out to greet them. They were smiling.

Sally Debardeleben looked at the man and woman. "Tom and Leslie," she said, as they stopped in front of Martha. "This is Martha Lake, the lady who received Rachel's heart."

"I've been wanting to meet you," Martha reached out to take Mrs. Raines' hand.

"We've been wanting to meet you, too," said Leslie Raines, ignoring Martha's hand and hugging her. Mr. Raines joined in the hug, and Alan stepped up behind Martha. Sally and Lisa stood to the side, smiling.

"Thank you," said Martha, stepping back just a bit from the hug and looking at Leslie and Tom.

Leslie shook her head and started to cry, pulling Martha back into a hug. Martha started crying as well.

"Thank you," said Martha, again.

They all stood for a moment, a small circle, and Lisa and Sally joined in the hug. Everyone was sobbing.

Tom was the first to pull back a little.

"Please, let's go inside. We want to get to know you, Martha."

"Oh," said Sally. "This is Alan Lake, Martha's husband."

"Nice to meet you, Alan." Tom shook Alan's hand.

Leslie said hello as well. Tom motioned for them to go into the house, stepping up and holding the door open as they filed in. Leslie and Sally went in first, and Martha followed. She looked around at the small living room as Leslie motioned her towards a chair. When Martha turned around to sit down, she suddenly caught her breath.

"It's her!" she exclaimed softly, gazing at the portrait on the wall.

"Yes, that's Rachel," said Leslie. "That picture was taken the same night she had the accident."

Martha caught her breath again and sat down, her legs wobbly. She looked down a minute and then over towards Sally, who had sat down across from her. Tears came again to Martha.

"She's beautiful."

She looked at the other pictures around the room, pictures of the girl with her mom and dad and others of her by herself. But her eyes kept coming back to the portrait on the wall, the blue eyed girl in her sky-blue dress, smiling, her braided blond hair over to one side.

"I am so sorry," she said, looking over at Leslie and Tom.

"She was a beautiful girl, and full of life," said Tom.

Leslie looked at her, silent for a moment, then leaned toward Martha.

"We are so glad to get to meet you, thank you for allowing us to."

Martha smiled at her.

"I'm alive because of you."

Martha smiled again through the tears.

She looked back up at the portrait.

"Rachel?"

"Yes. Rachel," said Leslie.

"What a beautiful name."

"You didn't know her name?"

"No, I only knew that my heart came from a girl, and that she was in her teens."

Leslie looked over at Sally. Sally spoke up.

"The information is always anonymous and general at first. Later, if the family of the donor and the recipient both agree, they can communicate."

Tom looked at Martha. "Rachel was a junior in high school. She had just turned sixteen."

Leslie added, "She was a majorette and in the band. And she was an honor student. She had planned to go to Chipola College after high school and become a nurse. She always wanted to help people."

"She had put 'organ donor' on her driver's license," stated Tom. He glanced up at the picture on the wall. He shook his head, looking down.

Leslie looked at him and then at Martha.

"You said in your letter you have a daughter."

"Yes, her name is Kristi. She's seven."

"Do you have a picture?"

"Yes, but I didn't bring my purse in." Martha looked at Alan.

"I have one," he said, taking out his wallet.

"Here she is."

Leslie took the picture from him.

"She is pretty."

'She's smart—she's smart, too," smiled Martha.

Leslie handed the picture back to Alan.

Martha looked back the picture on the wall, then over toward Sally.

Sally nodded slightly.

"Leslie, Tom?" said Martha.

"Yes?"

"She loved you a lot."

"What?" asked Tom.

Martha spoke louder. "Rachel loved you a lot."

Leslie looked at her quizzically. Martha looked back at Sally, then at Leslie.

"Did Dr. Debardeleben tell you about the dreams?"

Leslie nodded her head. "She said you had a dream about Rachel."

Martha smiled through her tears, leaning towards Leslie. "Rachel told me to tell you she loved you, and that she was okay."

Both Leslie and Tom were staring at her.

"In my dream she is wearing a blue dress and her hair is braided, just like in the picture. She came to me and said to tell you she is okay, and that she loves you."

Tom was shaking his head. Then he looked up at her.

"When did this happen?"

"Right about the time of my transplant."

Everyone was silent for a moment.

Then Leslie spoke up.

"Did she say anything else?"

"Yes."

Martha looked at Sally again. Sally nodded at her.

Martha smiled at Leslie.

"She said, 'Tell Susan not to worry. Everything is okay.'"

Leslie drew in her breath quickly, and she and Richard looked at each other, a surprised look on their faces.

"Is there somebody named Susan?" Sally asked.

Leslie nodded, tears welling up in her eyes again.

"Susan James was her best friend," she spoke slowly. She shook her head again and smiled.

Tom was looking down and shaking his head as well.

Martha smiled back and then spoke slowly and clearly.

"She said to give Tonto a hug."

"Tonto?" Tom shook his head and looked at Leslie.

"I don't know who that is."

Leslie shook her head as well.

She and Tom looked at each other.

Martha glanced at Sally again, then continued.

"And one more thing. She said to 'Tell Ricky hi.'"

Leslie nodded at her and smiled. "Ricky is one of the guys from her school. I think he had a crush on her."

Tom and Leslie looked at each other again, then Tom looked at her.

"This was all in a dream?"

"Like a dream or a vision, I don't know which. And more than once. But I saw Rachel clearly and she talked to me. Dr. Sally thought I should tell you."

Sally nodded. "We wanted you to know. I have seen transplant recipients have visions like this before, and I wanted you to know."

Tom looked at Martha, leaning forward.

"Did she say anything else?"

Martha shook her head, slowly. She looked Tom in the eyes.

"No. But she was smiling when she told me, and she said everything is okay."

Martha then looked at Sally, who nodded to her.

The tears were coming again in Martha's eyes.

"I know that I would want to know if I were you."

They talked a little longer, the Raines asking Martha about why she had to have a transplant. Martha told them how sick she had been and how the doctors had not expected her to live.

Then she asked them some more questions about Rachel. Tom asked Sally if dreams like this were common among transplant recipients, so Sally explained some of her research. Finally, it was Sally, sensing that Martha was tiring, who stood first, thanking the Raines for letting them come.

Martha stood up, the tears coming again, and Leslie stood and hugged her.

"Thank you."

"Thank you," said Leslie.

Everyone else stood up.

They slowly walked out the door, Leslie and Martha still holding on to each other.

As they got to the front steps, Tom suddenly stopped them.

"Wait a minute," he said. "Wait a minute."

He looked at Martha and Alan with a strange smile on his face.

"Come around back, I want you to meet someone."

Leslie looked at him quizzically, but he had already started around the house. She glanced at the others, and they all followed, walking along the neat fence beside the house to a small gate. After everyone got to the gate, Tom whistled, and a horse that had been in the back of the lot started towards him.

"Come here, Quando!" said Tom.

The little horse came forward, then backed up a ways, snorted at the strangers, and looked sideways. He stuck his head up a little and sniffed the air.

"Come over here, Martha." Tom motioned her towards him.

Martha stepped towards the gate. She stood beside Tom.

The little horse eyed them, sniffing the air again.

"He's nice, he won't hurt you,"

Tom, seeing Martha's trepidation, put his arm around her.

"He's been sad, too. He misses Rachel."

"Didn't eat anything for several days after she died... he just kept looking for her."

The horse sniffed the air again and stepped forward. Tom opened the gate. He took Martha by the hand.

"It's okay."

The horse came toward them, slowly. He stopped a little ways in front of Martha, then stretched out his neck and sniffed her.

"It's okay, Martha," Tom's voice was quivering. "This is Quando."

He smiled at her, the lines around his eyes wrinkling—the first time he had smiled in weeks.

"It's *Quando*, not *Tonto*."

He looked at the horse.

"Quando, this is Martha."

Martha looked at him and at the little horse.

"Quando and Rachel were inseparable," said Tom. "She loved him."

The little horse sniffed Martha, nodding his head. He stepped a little closer. She reached out and stroked the side of his head. Quando came even closer, nuzzling Martha's chest. He whinnied, a soft sound in his throat. He looked sideways at Martha, then moved his head against her, not hard enough to make her fall but enough to make her wrap her arm around him. Martha laughed and wrapped both her arms around his head. The little horse whinnied softly and drew in his breath, turning back to sniff at Martha, nuzzling her chest again.

Leslie was standing close beside them.

"I wonder if he knows?"

She looked around at the others.

"He usually doesn't take to strangers."

Everyone looked at Sally.

Sally just smiled and shook her head.

"I don't know," she said. "Maybe."

She was smiling through the tears.

24

Chi

LISA KELLY WAS in the Surgical Intensive Care Unit of the regional hospital in Dothan. She had been paged that morning for a potential donor, a twenty-six-year-old male. The patient had cardiac-arrested after an overdose of narcotics. A friend had found him and called 911. When EMS arrived, they found him down without pulse or respirations, but they did CPR and established a heartbeat. He was intubated and brought to the emergency room. He had been admitted to the hospital, but had never awakened or responded in any way. His brain had been without oxygen for too long. Lisa was called after he had been declared brain-dead.

She sat at the nurse's station reviewing the patient's chart. The young man had a psych and drug abuse history. He had been diagnosed with schizophrenia as a teenager and the chart also mentioned he had previous issues with multiple personalities. He had had numerous stays in the hospital's behavioral medicine wing and his main doctor was one of the local psychiatrists. Otherwise, there were no major medical problems.

Lisa glanced at the lab page and saw that, while his liver numbers were elevated, most of his other labs were normal. He was now on one medication to keep his blood pressure up, and his vital signs were normal. Lisa's only worry was about the drug history. If there had been IV drug use, such as heroin, he would have to be considered a high-risk donor, and may come back positive for HIV or hepatitis.

She waited until the nurse taking care of the patient came out of his room.

"Good morning, Russell," she said.

"Morning," said Russell, with a smile.

"This is going to be a good one."

Lisa smiled back. "What do you mean?"

Russell shook his head slowly, his eyes sparkling.

"Just wait until you meet this family. This guy definitely inherited his psychological problems."

"Really?" asked Lisa.

"Well." Russell smiled at her. "You saw that he has... well... had a psychological disorder, including multiple personalities. His mother and sister are here, and they are his only next of kin. The mother has been hospitalized for psych problems herself, and the sister as well. Pam almost had to call security last night, they were carrying on so. They went home about midnight and got back here a little over an hour ago. Right now they seem to be functioning okay, but that could change at any moment."

"Has Dr. George told them he is brain-dead?" asked Lisa.

"Yes, he talked to them this morning and they seem to understand. We were waiting for you to come in, but I really don't think this one will work out. We know he used drugs, he was positive on toxicology for cannabis and opiates. His sister doesn't think he used IV drugs, but she can't say for sure. And, he recently got out of rehab for alcohol abuse."

"Great," mumbled Lisa, making a wry face. "But I will still talk to them and we can do serology. Even if he is high risk, we may still be able do something."

"Okay," shrugged Russell.

"Let me go get them in the quiet room. It may take me a minute. Last time I tried to find them they had gone down to smoke."

Lisa sat back down at the nurse's desk and continued to review the chart. Then she called the organ center main office and asked them to check if the man had "donor" on his license. It took a minute, but she was pleased when they told her that he was on the registry. At least that was one positive thing. She asked the coordinator to fax the donor verification form so that she could show the family.

A few minutes later Russell came back in and told her the family was waiting for her. He walked down to the little conference room with her. When he opened the door, Lisa saw a middle-aged woman and a twenty-something girl, both of whom were dressed in jeans and sweatshirts. They both looked somewhat disheveled, like they had slept in their clothes, and smelled strongly of cigarette smoke.

Russell introduced her.

"This is Lisa. We ask her to come in at times like this to help families with some of the decisions that they have to make."

Lisa shook hands with the mother and sister, and then sat down to face them.

"I am so sorry about your son," she said to the mother. "And I understand you are Jason's sister," she said, looking at the girl. "This is such a tragedy. Can you tell me a little bit about what happened?"

"We think he overdosed last night," said the sister. "He had a problem with his back... he was injured in a car accident... and had been taking pain meds... hydrocodone or something. He always took more than the prescription, and they said he had been drinking, too. His roommate found him passed out and not breathing, and they brought him here. They said they were still doing CPR when they got to the hospital. They say it was accidental."

The girl looked at the mother.

"But I think Rick did it."

"Rick?" asked Lisa.

"Yeah, Rick was the bad one," said the sister.

"Rick would make him do things to hurt himself. He almost died from an overdose one time before, and afterwards he always said it was Rick made him do it. Probably to get back at Chris. I don't think Jason did it himself."

"Is Rick his roommate?" asked Lisa.

"No."

"Rick was him... or he was Rick." The girl thought a minute. "Umm... Jason had... he was more than one person. Rick was one of them."

The mother sort of nodded, like this was understood.

Lisa looked over at Russell.

"Is the coroner going to investigate?"

Russell shook his head. "They think it was accidental. He probably took a whole bottle of pain meds, and he had been drinking a lot. His blood alcohol level was really high."

The sister looked at them. "They couldn't do anything, anyway."

Lisa nodded at her, then glanced back at Russell.

"Well, I'm sorry about this. I'm sorry that I have to meet you like this. But, like Russell said, they call me in to talk to families about some of the things that you have to think about when someone dies. Did the doctor tell you that Jason is brain-dead?"

"Yes," said the mother, "And he said we had some decisions to make."

"Do you understand what brain death means?" asked Lisa.

"He said he is legally dead... they did tests and he is gone."

The mother looked down and shook her head.

"I knew he was gone when we got here last night. When we went in that room and I saw him, I knew he was gone."

The mother put her head down in her hands.

"I am so sorry about this, Ms. Jones." Lisa said.

She took the mother's hand in hers.

"Thank you," said the mother.

Lisa looked toward the sister, then back at the mother.

"Ms. Jones, brain death is rare. It is not often that someone can be kept on the ventilator like this after they have died. I want to talk to you about how you can help other people, perhaps save another person's life."

Lisa continued to hold the mother's hands.

"Ms. Jones, did you know that Jason wanted to be an organ donor?"

"I didn't, he never said nothing to me about it."

"It's in times like this that we can do organ donation. Do you know anyone who has had a transplant or is waiting for one?"

"No."

The mother shook her head and looked toward the daughter.

"That doesn't sound like Jason," she stated, firmly.

The sister shook her head, too.

Lisa continued. "I have a printout of the registry. It says that Jason had 'donor' put on his license when he renewed it year before last."

The mother took the paper, still shaking her head. Then she was still for a moment.

"Do you have his driver's license?"

Russell spoke up. "We have his things in the safe. I was going to give them to you before you left. Let me go check and see if the license is there." He walked out of the room.

"Jason never did anything for anybody," said the sister.

"It could have been Brucey," said the mom, quietly, as if to herself.

"It sounds more like Brucey," the sister nodded.

"How does organ donation work?" asked the mother, looking back at Lisa.

"Jason will stay here in the unit until I can do the matching and do some tests to see if we can do donation. Then the surgical team would come here. The machine that is breathing for him, the ventilator, would be turned off in surgery. We would do the surgery, then the organs that can be used would be taken back for the patients who need the transplants. This will not affect Jason's funeral, but it could save several people's lives."

Russell came back in, a wallet in his hand. He gave it to the mother. They all watched as she opened it and flipped through. The driver's license was behind a little window. They could all see the little heart that denoted organ donation.

"It just doesn't sound like Jason."

"Let me see it!" said the sister, taking it from the mom. She looked at the license closely.

"It was Brucey," she said emphatically, nodding her head and holding the license out for the mom.

"See, it says his eyes are hazel."

The mother looked closer. "Yep, it was Brucey."

Lisa looked at her, a puzzled look in her eyes.

"Jason had green eyes, but Brucey always said his eyes were hazel," said the sister, as if everything was solved.

Lisa still looked puzzled.

The mother looked at her and smiled.

"Jason had personalities. One of them was Brucey. Brucey was gay. It must have been Brucey who renewed the license."

Lisa just nodded. What else could she do? She tried to ask delicately, "How many personalities were there?"

The sister spoke up. "The main ones were Jason, Rick, Brucey, and Chris. Jason had an addiction problem. Chris and Brucey were the nicer ones. Chris was the nicest and was getting to be the strongest. He was taking lessons from a guru or something. Rick was just mean, he would cuss you out in a minute."

She looked over at the mom.

"I think Rick was jealous."

The mother sat quiet for a minute, then she looked at Lisa.

"Will the transplant patients get the spirits... the other personalities?"

"I... I don't think so," Lisa glanced over at Russell.

The mother looked at the sister.

"It might be the first time he did anything positive for anybody else in his whole life."

The sister nodded.

Lisa started to explain in more detail how donation worked and then spent a long time asking questions about Jason's medical and social history.

Sometime later, all of the paperwork had been done and blood had been sent to Birmingham for testing. She had let the coordinators in Birmingham know Jason's height and weight. He was a small guy, just five foot-five inches and one hundred and forty pounds. They were already running the list to see who would match.

Jason's mother and sister had spent some time in the room with him and had then said their goodbyes. Lisa had told them she would call them when everything was finished. They had been gone about an hour when Russell walked up, just back from the front desk.

"There is someone at the door of the unit who wants to see our patient," said Russell.

"Who is it?" asked Lisa.

"You won't believe this," said Russell with a smile. "The fellow says he is Jason's tai chi instructor, sorta like his minister."

"Stacey mentioned that he was seeing a 'guru' of some kind," said Lisa.

"It's okay with me if it's okay with you. We would let his minister in."

"Okay," said Russell. "But this gets stranger by the minute."

The man who walked in the door did not look that different to Lisa than anyone else. He was Asian, dressed in slacks and a nice sport shirt. His head was shaved and he smiled and bowed slightly to her as he entered the room.

"I am Wu Chen," he said, his voice soft and melodious.

"I'm Lisa Kelly. I'm sorry about your friend."

"Chris was student of mine. Very good student."

Chen reached in his pocket and pulled out a card and handed it to Lisa. She looked down at it. The plain white card had only his name and address, followed by the words "Tai Chi."

He looked at her, with dark, piercing eyes.

"I too am sorry. May I stay a moment?"

"Yes, you may stay. I will be just outside at the nurses' desk."

Lisa watched closely through the window, but the tai chi instructor just stood by the bed. First he looked around at the machines and pumps in the room, then down at Jason. He stood there, completely still, for several minutes, then turned and sat down in the chair next to the bed. He sat straight for a minute, then folded his hands and seemed to bow slightly. Then he straightened again and opened his hands, resting them on the arms of the chair. He closed his eyes and just stayed there—for a long time.

Lisa just watched for a while, doing her charting. Finally, she went into the room to check the heart monitor. She had been having trouble regulating heart rate and blood pressure all morning. Mr. Chen looked up at her, and stood. He stepped over to the bedside.

"Chi has gone," he said, shaking his head slightly.

Lisa thought that he said "*He* has gone."

"He was declared brain-dead this morning," she said.

Chen nodded once, then looked at her. "What will now happen?"

"We hope to do organ donation," answered Lisa. "We may be able to save several people's lives."

A troubled look came onto Chen's face. He turned and sat back down. Lisa left to make a call.

When she came back in, Chen was standing over the bed, his head bowed. His hands were folded together at his chest. He heard her come into the room, and looked up.

"How long has he died?" he asked, looking toward Jason's— Chris's face.

"We think he was probably brain-dead last night, but it was confirmed with tests early this morning. He has probably been brain-dead nearly twenty-four hours now. I'm sorry."

Chen sighed and was quiet again for a minute. Lisa continued her duties in the room, checking the IV pumps. When she finished, she came over and stood by him, standing silently. He lifted his head and turned towards her.

"It is good that he will save others."

She just smiled and nodded.

She left the room again, sitting at the desk to work some more on charting. She watched as he continued to stand by the bed, in silence, for several more minutes.

Chen then came out and walked over to the desk. He smiled down at Lisa. She stood up.

"Thank you," he said, with a slight bow.

He then turned and walked out of the unit.

Lisa watched him leave, and felt a curious calmness, a feeling of well-being. She stood there a minute, wondering about the man who had just left.

Then she went back into the room.

As she did, she glanced up at the monitor. Surprised, she looked again, staring at the monitor for several seconds.

The heart rate had slowed, settling into normal sinus rhythm. The blood pressure was just about perfect.

Lisa walked back out and looked down the hall, but Mr. Chen was gone. She continued to gaze down the hall for a few seconds, still feeling an aura of calmness.

Then she shook her head, turned, and got back to the business of charting.

Lisa waited for a call from Birmingham, crossing her fingers that serology would come back negative. The coordinator in Birmingham had said that the prospective heart recipient was an eighteen-year-old girl. Lisa was used to hearts going to older patients, men or women in their forties or fifties who had bad heart disease. She had had a few that went to younger people, and was always pleased if a younger heart went to a younger patient. The coordinator had also told her that the liver was to go to a Birmingham patient as well. Of course, all of this was pending negative serology results.

When the unit phone rang about eleven thirty, and they said it was for her, Lisa thought it was Birmingham calling in the results. She picked up the phone, but said a little prayer before she punched the button.

"Dear Lord," she said. "Let everything be negative."

She punched the button by the little blinking light on the phone.

"This is Lisa," she said.

"Ms. Lisa?" said a female voice on the other end.

"Yes," said Lisa.

"This is Stacey, Stacey Jones, Jason's sister," the voice quavered.

"Hi, Stacey, is everything okay?"

Lisa wondered why she was calling so late.

Oh, no, she thought. *I hope they're not going to withdraw consent.* She knew this was a squirrelly family.

"Ms. Lisa," the voice continued. "Mama and I were talking a little ago, and we remembered last week when we were in Birmingham we saw a sign about a teenage boy who needed a heart transplant. It said he was really sick, and we've been thinking about him all night. Mom has tried to go to sleep and it just keeps coming back to her."

Stacey paused a minute, then continued, her voice still quavering.

"Mom says to tell you she wants to give Jason's heart to him."

Lisa thought a minute, then answered, "Stacey, I'll have to check on if we can do that. First of all, he has to match, *and* he has to be on the list, *and* the doctor has to approve it."

"We understand," said Stacey hurriedly. "But Mom says she knows it will work, she knows Jason's heart is for him."

"Just give me a little time to check," said Lisa hesitantly, shaking her head. "How much longer are you all going to be up?"

"Oh, we're up. Neither one of us can sleep. We're headed to Waffle House now to get some food. You can get me on my cell. We'll be up for a while."

"Okay, I'll see what I can find out. But it may not work out. Everything has to match," Lisa repeated helplessly.

She heard Stacey talking to someone in the background. Stacey finally said, "Mom says 'okay, if it won't work for him, that's okay.' But please check and see."

"I'll call you as soon as I know," said Lisa, and hung up the phone.

She immediately picked it back up and punched in the number for the Organ Center.

25

Damn Signs

MARIA HAD BEEN in the cardiac intensive care unit at MCAMC now for several days. Though she had been stable for several weeks after coming to Birmingham, her heart function had suddenly taken a turn for the worse. Dr. David McAllister was growing increasingly worried about her. She was almost to the point that he was going to have to either install an LVAD, the mechanical device that did the work of the left ventricle, or do a totally artificial heart. He really did not want to do either one, for several reasons. First, it was an additional open-heart surgery, and there would be scar tissue and other issues. Second, she would begin to develop additional antibodies, hindering her ability to keep a donor heart when one came available. Third, there were issues with the medicines that had to be given when an artificial device, either heart or LVAD, was placed, and these would also be an issue when a donor heart was transplanted. Even now, Maria was on strong medications to keep her heart function as good as possible, but he could not continue those forever. Maria's current status did, however, make her first on the list for any heart that matched her in the region. She was considered a Status-One since she was so ill. The problem was that, by its very nature, being listed as a Status-One meant that if she did not get a heart soon she would die.

This particular day, David had reviewed her labs in the morning, had made a few changes in her meds, and then was back by the unit later in the day to check on her. When he walked into the room, Jose was sitting in his usual place, the chair by the window. He had been pretty much a permanent fixture since Maria had come into the hospital, there every day or evening, usually several hours at a time. David and the nurses had given him a special dispensation for visiting, since Maria was so young and he was generally her only visitor. The hospital was more open anyway to patients' families staying in the rooms on the transplant unit. As long as they did not interfere with the patient's care it was thought that family members and other loved ones would increase the transplant patient's chances of lasting long enough to get the transplant.

"Hey, Dr. Mac," said Jose as David walked into the room.

"Hello, Jose, how are you today?" David asked.

"I'm okay, but Maria... " Jose shook his head. "She is not. She's worse today."

"I know," said David, walking over to the bed and taking out his stethoscope. They had Maria sedated to allow her heart to recover as much function as it could. David was trying not to stress her heart with any extra requirement other than just keeping her alive. At this point, he was hoping for a donor heart soon, as soon as possible. As he listened to her heart, he looked at the monitor. She had a line placed that allowed him to monitor her cardiac output and the pressure that her heart developed as it pumped. Though her heart rate was fairly normal, the output was not, a symptom of the cardiomyopathy. Her heart had enlarged so much that, though the muscle was moving, it was not pumping efficiently. Her oxygen saturation was low and David was beginning to worry. It would not be long, if she continued to decline, that the oxygen level would not be sufficient to support her brain and organ function. Somehow, though, something was telling him to wait just a little longer. Though he was tempted to go ahead and schedule her for the LVAD, he still had hope that a heart would become available for her. But she could not wait more than a few more days.

Maria had been in Birmingham less than a month. Dr. Strickland had talked with Dr. Brighton and she had been

accepted as a patient at MCAMC. The Tampa cardiologist had
been okay with a transfer, even though he would have preferred
her to go to Shands in Gainesville. Unfortunately, the Shands
heart transplant program had been temporarily shut down due
to a tragic accident involving their primary heart transplant
surgeon. He and a transplant coordinator had been killed in an
aircraft accident just days before. The charter jet had gone down
in the Gulf somewhere between Gainesville and Pensacola as
they flew up to procure a heart. Both Brighton and McAllister
had known the surgeon.

Maria had been transported to Birmingham, and had actually
been doing reasonably well on arrival. David and Brighton
had seen her. Brighton was now semi-retired. He was chair of
several committees and continued as chief of the heart program,
though he had not done a transplant for a while. David was the
de facto chief. Maria had been admitted to the hospital, her case
had been reviewed by the transplant committee, and she had
been approved to be listed. Her heart function had improved a
little on the meds that the transplant cardiologist had placed her
on, and she had been able to move out of the hospital and over
to the transplant townhouses, checking in for assessment every
day, but otherwise able to get out and about.

Maria's grandmother had been up and met with Brighton
and David. The grandmother was an imposing lady, her father
a former territorial governor of Puerto Rico. She had originally
questioned the move, but after meeting Dr. Brighton, she changed
her mind. She had done some research on heart transplants
herself, and learned that Birmingham was nationally recognized
for its excellent heart program. She had also been charmed by
Brighton during the meetings. They were close to the same age
and she had liked him from the start. Brighton, who had lost his
wife to cancer two years before, also enjoyed the meetings with
Maria's grandmother, who did not look her age at all. Plus, she
had the elegance and poise of a territorial governor's daughter.
David had come away from the second meeting smiling, having
picked up on the chemistry between her and Brighton. Ms.
Hernandez wanted Brighton to do Maria's heart transplant, but
he had declined, telling her that he was retiring and no longer
taking calls. He told her that Dr. McAllister was the best to do

the case, and she was satisfied with that.

David went home that evening worried about Maria. It was his and Elsa's date night, and they went out to eat at a nice Thai place in Five Points, an area of Birmingham close to the hospital.

Elsa could tell that David was preoccupied. He was usually able to leave most of his work at work. She knew about Maria: she had met her when she was listed. As they sat at dinner, David discussed with her the pros and cons of placing the mechanical LVAD. Though she would have preferred to talk about them and their issues, Elsa was understanding, knowing Maria had become special to David.

It was just a little later, as they were driving home, that David's pager went off. It was the organ center.

"We have a heart donor down in Dothan," the coordinator said. "It's a twenty-six-year-old man, blood type is A." He continued with some other pertinent information.

"How much does he weigh?" asked McAllister.

"He's small, Dr. Mac," said the coordinator. "About sixty-five kilos."

"And his height?"

"Five feet five."

David drew in his breath, and Elsa looked over at him.

"Maybe a heart for Maria," he said, glancing her way.

The coordinator barked, "Garcia is printing up first."

"Good," said David.

"Dr. Mac," said the coordinator.

"Yes?"

"The donor may be high risk."

"What?" asked David.

"He overdosed on pain meds, and there may be an MSM history."

"MSM?"

"Male who had sex with a male," said the coordinator.

"How about IV drugs?"

"No, according to his family."

"Okay," said David, letting his breath out with a sigh. "When will serology be back?"

"About midnight."

"If serology comes back negative, we'll look at it," said David.

He turned to Elsa after he hung up. "We may have a heart for Maria," he said, again.

Elsa smiled at him.

"I hope so," she said.

David and Elsa were in bed by ten, having paid the babysitter when they got home and spending a little time with Nicholas before getting him to bed. David anticipated only a few hours of sleep, knowing that they would probably be setting up to leave pretty soon after serology was back. The coordinator had told him that Vanderbilt was supposed to be coming for the lungs, so he knew he might get in one extra hour while they got set to come down. He had already called the transplant cardiologist and told him that he may have to come in and explain things to Jose and to Maria's grandmother, who was in town. They had already talked about this possibility, while Maria was still coherent, and had decided that if she was critical and if there were a high risk heart that she would take it. David lay in bed, on his back, thinking about the day's events. He was glad there was at least a chance for Maria. He knew that this was probably her last chance. It took him a little while to go to sleep.

He may have been asleep for an hour when his pager beeped once and then vibrated. He always set it that way in hopes that it would not wake up Elsa, but in this case she was not fully asleep either and sat up as he reached over to turn the pager off.

She watched as he grabbed his clothes from beside the bed and went into the other room to make the call.

"Let me know if you have to go," she mumbled sleepily.

Then she remembered who this case involved and dragged herself out of bed as well.

David was already on the phone with the coordinator when she got to the kitchen.

"Dr. Mac, this is Joe," said the voice on the other end. "Serology is negative. And the echo is good, ejection fraction sixty-five or better, normal wall motion, normal valves, normal in every way."

"Great!" exclaimed David, nodding to Elsa.

"Yes!" she said.

"There is one change, though, Dr. Mac," said Joe.

"What is it?" Mac anticipated that the change was a delay,

maybe Vanderbilt had something going on.

"The family wants to do a direct donation of the heart. They want it to go to DeMarco."

David couldn't believe his ears.

"What! No! This heart is for Garcia. She may not have another chance. She's a Status One!"

"Actually, Dr. Burch had DeMarco changed to a Status One today. But the family is adamant. They want the heart to go specifically to DeMarco."

David sat down in the kitchen chair. He looked at Elsa and shook his head, then spoke into the phone, "See if the family will change their mind."

"I'll call Lisa back and see," said Joe. "But everyone is to meet at the lab at two a.m. Surgery is set for four a.m. Is that okay with you?"

"That's fine, but call me back when you know what the family says." David hung up the phone.

"Shit!" he exclaimed, looking at Elsa.

She looked at him, shaking her head. It was unusual for David to curse, but she had heard the conversation and figured out what was happening.

"The donor's family wants to give the heart to DeMarco," he said. "It's those damn signs! It's just not fair. Maria needs this heart *now*." He stood up. "Dammit!"

"Are they going to talk to the family again?" asked Elsa.

"Yes, but I doubt they'll change their mind. Once they pick someone, it would be hard to change. A specific person versus someone anonymous on the list—you know they won't change."

"Would DeMarco have been the backup patient?"

"Probably."

"Then he may have gotten it anyway. You never know, this heart might be meant for him. It may be the wrong one for Maria."

David looked at Elsa.

"Have you been talking to Sally Debardeleben?"

Elsa smiled. "Some. But that's not why I said it. Do you remember Mr. Moore from Alexander City?"

He shook his head.

Elsa sat down across from David.

"It was back when I was working as a coordinator. Mr. Moore was at a transplant function I went to, the mayor was doing a proclamation about organ donation. Mr. Moore was waiting on a heart. He was in a wheelchair and on oxygen. After the program we talked, and as I started to leave he looked at me and said, 'Elsa, if you guys don't get me a heart soon, I'm... I'm not going to make it.'" Elsa looked down. "What he said really troubled me, though I knew that I couldn't just 'get him a heart.'"

"Well, about two weeks later I had a heart donor who matched Mr. Moore. It was a young man who had been in a car accident. Everything looked good, and I was excited that Mr. Moore would finally get his heart transplant. But when we went to surgery, Dr. Brighton had to rule out the heart. It had an injury from the accident that we couldn't see on the echo. I went home sick that night, feeling responsible."

"But you weren't responsible for that," reasoned David.

"I know, but I still felt that way. Well, about two weeks later there was another donor, and the heart went to Mr. Moore. They said it was a perfect match. He did great after that. I saw him sometime later and he had already been on a trip to Europe. He thanked me." She smiled.

"And it wasn't a donor of mine. I just know that he got the perfect heart. God works things out."

David's pager went off again. He called the number.

The heart was going to DeMarco.

26

Long Distance

THE NEXT MORNING, JUST before McAllister started
DeMarco's transplant, another heart came available in Puerto
Rico. The transplant coordinator who took the call expected
that David would turn it down for time. The distance was just
too great. They had had other heart offers from the Puerto
Rico donor program, but had never accepted one. It would be
impossible to get a heart back and transplanted within anywhere
near the accepted time limits. But the donation coordinator in
Puerto Rico told the transplant coordinator in Birmingham that
the donor's family wanted the heart to go to Maria Garcia.

This type of case was called an *import*, since the organ was
coming from out of the organ procurement agency's region.
The program had imported organs from Puerto Rico before, in
fact it was not uncommon for a liver or kidney to be imported
from there to Alabama. Alabama and Florida were among the
closest states to Puerto Rico, and the transplant program down
there was small, so it was not unusual for there to be organs
available for recipients in the southeastern states. It was a long
flight, however, over eighteen hundred miles. In most private
jets, which cruise at about four hundred and fifty knots, the trip
would take close to five hours. This was far too long for a heart,
even without adding the time in surgery. Most programs would

turn down hearts from Puerto Rico for this reason, though sometimes a recipient would be transplanted who was on the list in Miami.

Charles Perry, the transplant coordinator called McAllister and was surprised when David said that yes, he would consider the heart. Perry started thinking about the distance, and how to get the heart back as fast as possible. He was a private pilot himself, and knew the average speed of the jets that they commonly used. He knew that they would take too long. He really needed something very fast, supersonic. He knew that in the past the military had flown organs in emergencies, but knew that he would have to go to assist Dr. McAllister. Even if the military would help, which was doubtful these days, they would not have a supersonic jet large enough for two or three passengers and their equipment. He wasn't sure that a military jet could even fly that far at supersonic speed without having to land and refuel, which would negate the advantage in time.

Perry remembered an article he had recently read in a magazine about flying that discussed a new private jet, made by Cessna. It was supposed to be the fastest in the world. It wasn't supersonic, but was faster than most of the others by about one hundred and fifty knots. This would save about an hour on the trip back, and might be enough to make the difference in the heart functioning or not. He started checking around with the charter services to see if the Cessna jet was available.

David immediately knew that this was a case where he was going to have to use the pump. They had already completed the research transplanting pig hearts. He had transplanted several successfully after using the pump, one after eight hours and two after twelve hours on the pump. He had also had several human hearts that were not transplantable but had been donated for research that had worked well on the pump. One of those was a heart that had been procured by Carver. They had all worked well on the machine. David had applied for approval from the government to go to clinical trials with human patients, but had not been approved yet. He was expecting word any time now, but the government was not known for being quick in its approvals of new medical technology. David knew he would have to try anyway, and started the process for an expeditious approval.

First, he called Dr. Brighton and explained the situation, asking him to contact the members of the hospital transplant committee and the ethics committee and ask for approval. Then he called Elsa at the lab and explained where they stood, and told her to get in touch with UNOS, the United Network for Organ Sharing, the agency that oversaw the transplant programs. He thought that they might give him a provisional or temporary approval in this case. He told Elsa to stress the patient's critical status, the family's direct donation to Garcia, and the distance. The fact that the heart would not be used anywhere else would be a major factor. Then he went down to scrub in for Dominic's transplant.

27

Autopsy

THE FLIGHT TO Puerto Rico much longer than usual. The pilot had told Charles Perry and David that they would be fighting a headwind all the way, and they had. The pilot tried different altitudes, but to no avail. The best altitude was high, almost as high as the jet was certified. Perry had not been able to get the faster Cessna jet. There were none available. David just hoped that they could use the same winds going back. That would help them instead of hinder them, and may make the difference between the heart functioning or not.

The copilot turned around and told them the new ETA, and it was thirty minutes later than the last. They were trying to get on down to get in and hopefully out ahead of a storm. The pilot had assured them that even if the weather started to go down that they would still make it out.

David looked across at Carver and shook his head. Carver just looked over and shrugged, then closed his eyes. He was glad Carver was along on this trip, even though it might increase the time in the OR slightly. Carver was coming to procure the liver for one of their patients. David knew it was an advantage that Carver was there if there was an issue with the pump. Carver had a lot of experience with the kidney profusion machines, and would be of help if something happened to the heart pump.

David sat in his seat and tried to nap, but he was so wound up that it was almost impossible. Would the donor make it till they got there, would the pump work, would the heart work, would they get back in time, what about the weather? There were too many variables.

Then, when they were past halfway down, there was suddenly some commotion in the cockpit. It went on for several minutes. Finally, the copilot came back and sat down across from David and Carver.

"Docs," he said wearily. "We just got a message from our dispatcher. He said to tell you that the coroner in San Juan has called off the donation. He is going to do an autopsy instead."

"What?" David was groggy from being half asleep.

The copilot looked at them both, letting it sink in, then he sort of opened his hands as if asking what to do. "Do you want us to turn around?"

"Say again?"

"It seems that the coroner wants to do an autopsy instead of donation," the copilot said again.

David looked at Carver and Perry and shook his head.

"What else can happen in this case?"

Perry shook his head, too, and said, "He can still do an autopsy, donation won't change anything, it's a gunshot wound to the head."

"Just give us a few minutes," said David, looking at the copilot.

He sat up, gathering his thoughts.

If we turn around now we lose the heart for sure. But if we continue maybe we can work things out when we get there.

Carver said briskly, "How far out are we?"

"About another forty-five minutes."

David just sat there, still thinking.

Then it came to him.

Ah! Maria's grandmother. Maybe she can help.

He looked back up at the pilot. "Can I get a message out to Birmingham through the dispatcher?"

"Yes, sir, we can do that."

"Okay, ask them to get in touch with our Birmingham office. Have them call with this message."

The pilot took out a pen and paper. He wrote down the number.

David continued, "Tell Elsa that the coroner in San Juan wants to stop the case, that he wants an autopsy. Tell her to ask the organ center coordinator to call the coordinator in Puerto Rico and get them to hold the donor, not to stop management. Then she needs to call Dr. Brighton and have him get in touch with Ms. Hernandez, Maria's grandmother. Let her know the situation and see if she can appeal to the coroner or someone else in Puerto Rico. Tell Elsa that we are continuing on in the hope that it can be worked out."

David looked at the copilot. "Did you get all of that?"

"Yes, sir," he said.

"Is that okay with you, Carver?"

Carver nodded.

"Okay," said David, looking back at the copilot. "Continue to San Juan. And I want a verification that the message got to her."

Of course there was no sleeping the rest of the trip.

When they landed in San Juan the weather was already starting to deteriorate. The first bands from the storm were supposed to be several hours away, but the wind was picking up and the clouds were already starting to form. The pilot made a good landing, and as soon as the wheels touched Perry was calling the local coordinator and David dialed Elsa on his cell. She picked up on the first ring.

"Hey," he said. "We just landed in Puerto Rico. Could you get Dr. Brighton? Do you know if he was able to get Maria's grandmother?"

"Hey, babe," she said, "Glad you are there safe. Yes, Dr. Brighton got Ms. Hernandez. She's at the hospital with Maria and he went over to talk with her. He called me back and said that Ms. Hernandez has a call in to the governor of Puerto Rico. She's waiting for him to call her. Evidently she knows him well. She has also talked to the territory attorney general, and he's checking with the coroner on the autopsy. He may actually be the best bet, as he can make a legal determination."

"It shouldn't be a problem," said David. "He can still do an autopsy of the man's head, and will be able to determine cause of death. When Perry talked to the coordinator here there are no other injuries to the body."

"I know," said Elsa. "If anyone can work it out, its Maria's grandmother."

"Okay," said David. "We are going to head on to the hospital. We'll wait there to hear from you."

"How is the weather?" asked Elsa, worry in her voice.

"It's fine now, we just need to do this case and get the heck out of here as soon as possible."

"I'll call as soon as I know anything," she said. "Love you, be careful."

"Thanks, love you, too." David looked over at Perry, who was just ending his call as well. "What's going on here?"

Perry shook his head. "They're on hold at the hospital, waiting for word from the M.E. The coordinator is going up the chain of command. She says she is waiting for the chief medical examiner to call, but he is in a case. Shouldn't be much longer, though. We just need to head that way."

Rain was starting to fall as they moved the stuff over to the ambulance, big, heavy drops.

They got to the hospital and were met by the local coordinator. She was a young Hispanic nurse and was obviously stressed. She introduced herself as Rebecca.

"I still have not heard back from the medical examiner," she said. "The coroner is really being difficult. I've explained to him that this is a direct donation, but he says the criminal case is more important. He says the local district attorney agrees with him."

"Have you heard from anyone else?" asked David as they walked down the hall with the equipment.

"Who else? I have talked to everyone I can think of."

"We have someone back home working on the situation as well."

She took them into the surgery doctor's lounge.

Just as she turned to leave, two official-looking men walked down the hall toward her. "Rebecca!" the first one said loudly, then continued with something in Spanish.

"It's the coroner." Rebecca looked upset.

When the men stopped in front of them, they both started

talking to Rebecca in Spanish, as if they were chastising her.

Perry, who was fluent in Spanish, looked at David and Carver and shook his head.

"They want everything turned off right now."

The first man turned toward David, who was at the front of the group.

"Who are you?" he said, now in English.

Rebecca said, "This is Dr. David McAllister, heart transplant surgeon, and his colleague, Dr. Carver York, liver surgeon. Mr. Charles Perry is the coordinator who came with them."

She looked at David. "And this is Mr. Orlando Merced, coroner, and his assistant, Mr. Peck."

"I'm sorry you came all this way for nothing," said Merced. "But we are going to do an autopsy on Mr. Garcia. He is the victim of a homicide."

Carver spoke up first. "Mr. Merced, it is still possible to do an autopsy after organ donation. This is a victim of a gunshot wound to the head. Your medical examiner can still autopsy the head for cause of death even if we do donation. We do this routinely in Alabama."

"This is not Alabama, this is Puerto Rico, and it is my jurisdiction. The law says that I have authority, in fact am obligated to order an autopsy in cases such as this. And what if there was a problem with the heart and it is the cause of death? How would we ever know?"

"Mr. Merced," said David. "I respect your need for evidence in this case, but we have an eighteen-year-old female who will probably die if she does not get this heart."

"That is not my concern, doctor." Merced said. "I am now ordering the hospital to discontinue the life support on Mr. Garcia. We will do a complete autopsy."

At that moment both Merced's and McAllister's cell phones rang.

When David answered his, it was Elsa.

"Ms. Hernandez has talked to the governor of Puerto Rico and he has talked to the territory attorney general. The AG has been on the phone with the chief medical examiner. They have okayed donation, but the M.E. wants one of his examiners in the room for chain of custody and evidence issues. I told her to tell them that that is fine. You should be getting word at the hospital any time now."

"Thanks, Elsa," said David, with a sigh of relief. He glanced up at Merced, who was talking quickly and fervently in Spanish on his own cell.

"Thanks," David said again. "I'll call you before we leave."

"There's another thing," she said. "There's a storm. It's turned east. Puerto Rico is going to catch the edge. Be careful."

"Okay, we will. Love you."

David hung up. Merced had also hung up and looked as if steam was about to come from his ears. Then he turned, stood tall, and spoke to David and Carver.

"Doctors, it seems that the governor and the attorney general have ruled that you can go ahead with donation."

David nodded to him, then smiled and held out his hand. "Thank you, Mr. Merced," he said.

Taken aback, the coroner reached out to shake David's hand. "It was a pleasure to meet you," he said. He then turned to his assistant and barked a command in Spanish.

David and Carver just watched them leave. When they turned back around, Perry was nodding to him, having just finished his own phone call from Birmingham. "They say go ahead and get ready for surgery, the governor has okayed everything."

David stood still a moment, his own heart beating ninety miles an hour.

Rebecca asked to leave to go check on the donor. Perry went with her to review the donor situation while David and Carver changed into scrubs.

When Perry came back, he said, "He's still stable, but may not be for much longer. She has had to go up on the meds and his heart rate is starting to climb. We are just waiting for the medical examiner."

"Okay, but we've got to get going as soon as possible. If we lose this donor we will probably lose Maria," said David.

Rebecca knocked on the door. "We have a go-ahead from the medical examiner," she said. "He is on his way and will observe the case."

"Good," said McAllister.

They picked up the equipment, including the case that the heart perfusion machine was in. Rebecca told them they would be in OR number two, and that she would go get the donor.

Perry said, "I'll go with her to bring him down."

"Okay," said David.

He sank down in one of the chairs. Looking over at Carver, he said, "What a couple of days. I don't think I've slept more than an hour or so since night before last."

Carver was still shaking his head over the drama.

"I'll go as quickly as possible," he said. "We need to get done and out of here before they change their minds."

The case itself actually went smoothly. A local transplant surgeon was there to procure the kidneys. Carver knew her from a medical meeting.

Both Carver and David reviewed the chart, a little more thoroughly than usual, since so much had happened.

"So this is Maria's cousin?"

"Yes sir," said Rebecca. "Alberto Garcia. He was registered as a donor, and his family had been praying... In fact, most of the city has been praying for Maria since we found out about her. Senora Hernandez, Maria's grandmother, is loved by the people of San Juan."

"And what were the circumstances of the gunshot wound?" asked David.

"He was at a salsa party. When he started to leave with some friends, there was a gunfight in the parking lot. They say a stray bullet struck him in the head. It was an accident. They have arrested the shooter. He was just a teenager as well."

"Damn." muttered David.

McAllister had asked Rebecca to have the echocardiogram so that he could view it. The echo had been done earlier, at his request, and had been reviewed by the local cardiologist. The cardiologist had read it as normal, but McAllister always wanted to look if he could. The OR had a monitor that could access the echo, and Rebecca took it out to show it to him. As McAllister paged through the different views, he looked at Rebecca and shook his head.

"Look," he pointed at the view of the heart motion. "There are some changes in wall motion. I was afraid of that."

Rebecca looked at him, consternation in her face. "Can we not use the heart?"

"We have to," said McAllister. "It's her only hope."

"What would cause that? Is it something I did?"

"No, Rebecca, we see this sometimes with a gunshot wound to the head. No one understands it fully, but it could be related to the sudden increase in blood pressure when a wound like this occurs. It overtaxes the heart. But it is not a huge change. I think we will be all right. He is young and healthy."

The medical examiner walked in. David was thankful when he introduced himself cordially. The M.E. was a retired surgeon who was now working for the territory forensics department. David was glad he was a surgeon, as he had worried about a pathologist who may not be used to sterile technique. There was no mention of the drama with the coroner.

After everything was set up and everyone scrubbed in, David stepped up to his side of the table.

"Do you do a timeout, here?" he asked the circulator in charge.

"Yes, sir," she said.

"Carver, would you oversee the timeout?"

"Sure," said Carver, and began the process where the patient identity was verified, the type of surgery reviewed, and other information addressed.

David stood in his spot and bowed his head during the process.

"Please, Lord," he prayed to himself. "Be with us and let this work for Maria." He stopped a minute thinking, then continued, this time in a whisper, "And... thank you, Alberto, for your gift of life."

It was crowded with the four doctors and Perry plus the scrub nurse at the table, but that was not unusual.

David looked up, making sure there was a sterile cover on the light handle. He reached up to adjust the light, then he looked up at Carver, who nodded.

David nodded back.

He placed his gloved left hand on the landmark that he used to guide the cut.

"Scalpel," he said, and the case began.

At the end of the case, there were only a few things to be done differently for the heart to be placed on the pump. About fifteen minutes prior to cross-clamp, David began to give a medication that caused the heart rate to slow. They monitored the oxygen saturation, making sure it did not decrease too much as the heart slowed. He had already gone to 100% O_2 on the ventilator. By the time they cross-clamped, the rate was down to about thirty-five, which had still been sufficient to maintain good O_2 saturation. David knew from his previous trials that enough of the medication would remain in the heart cells after it stopped that when it was restarted it would still beat slowly. At cross-clamp, David began the heart perfusion as usual as he quickly finished removing the heart, but then immediately took the heart around and placed it on the pump. The pump had been set up at the beginning by David, but Perry had done some adjustments as the case went forward. As soon as David had the heart on the pump, the machine was started, perfusing the still heart with an oxygen and nutrient-rich solution. In only a few seconds the heart was warmed up to the pump temperature, about 32 degrees centigrade, close to 90 degrees Fahrenheit.

After a minute or two on the pump, David took a set of sterile defibrillator probes and gave the heart a small shock. It started to work immediately, though it was still very slow. David monitored the rate and oxygen saturation closely, watching as the heart continued to slow. By the time Carver was done procuring the liver, the heart had slowed to a rate of about twelve beats per minute, though it was not a stable rhythm. David knew that there would be a sinus arrhythmia from his previous trials. But the oxygen saturation was good.

As Carver and Perry packed the liver in its cooler for transport, David continued to work with the machine, making sure the heart was okay. Everyone in the room was amazed, particularly the medical examiner.

With the heart stable, David and Perry started to get everything ready to go. The machine was about the size of a large cooler with the heart in the cassette on top. The cassette was clear so that it was possible to visually monitor the heart as well as to monitor its vital signs through the computer.

David had a portable table with wheels on which to transport the machine. The machine had its own power supply, and the battery was supposed to be good for about eight hours.

When everything was situated and the liver was also ready to go, David took one last look at the heart and then covered the machine with a top that would restrict anyone from seeing it as they transported it through the hospital. After thanking Rebecca and the OR staff, they stopped by the surgeon's lounge to grab their clothes and then ran, pushing the heart pump and pulling the wheeled cooler to the E.R., where the ambulance was waiting to take them back to the airport.

It was raining heavily, with wind blowing the rain almost horizontally when they got on the road. David took the cover off the machine to keep a close watch on the heart. The ambulance trip to the airport was delayed by traffic and the weather, taking over forty-five minutes instead of the usual twenty, but Perry had called the pilot and the aircraft was ready to go when they got there.

They quickly loaded the heart machine and the cooler with the liver into the plane and got in themselves. The pilot had already started the right engine and began to taxi almost as soon as the doors were closed, telling them that the airport was about to close, that it had only stayed open long enough for them to depart.

As they taxied, David buckled the heart machine into the seat across from him, taking the cover back off so that he could see the heart. It was still beating its slow rate. He sat a cooler filled with ice and cold perfusion solution next to it. This was his last resort. If the heart machine failed for any reason he could still fill the cassette with cold sterile solution and place it in the cooler, thus preserving the heart the old way. He even had a surgical gown and a set of gloves ready to open in case he needed them. He buckled in himself just as the jet started its takeoff roll into the driving wind and rain.

The climb to altitude was as bumpy as any flight David had ever been on. He actually had to loosen his seatbelt a little and lean forward to hold onto the perfusion machine in front of him. The cooler beside it kept trying to walk away with the vibrations until he secured it between the seat and the bulkhead. He watched the heart closely, but the vibration and rocking did not seem to disturb it. It just kept up its steady rhythm, vacillating a little between nine and twelve beats per minute.

Carver was in the seat beside him, and also watched the heart closely. Though he had been consulted in the initial development of the pump, he had not seen the newest version in action. After they had climbed over most of the weather and things had settled down a little, he looked over and said, "Okay, David. How long can you keep it going like that?"

"We have battery power for about eight hours," said David. "Once a heart is beating, though, it should continue. After the heart is started, the battery power is really only for the computer, but it can run the pump for a while if I need it to. The heart actually pumps the solution itself, so the pump is a backup. There is sufficient glucose in the solution and the oxygen use is really pretty low. The built-in O_2 bottle should also last at least eight hours. We have an extra tank, a small one, in the duffle if we need it. I think if we can keep it happy, it will be fine 'til we get there."

Carver nodded. "It looks happy now. I just hope you can keep it that way."

They had now gotten above most of the bad weather. David looked out and down behind them and could see the shape of the huge storm. He realized that they had been lucky to get out ahead of it. The pilot turned around to them after they were at a stable altitude and nodded.

"Now that headwind is a quartering tailwind. Right now we're getting an extra forty knots of groundspeed."

"Good," said David, looking up from the heart machine. "What is our ETA?"

"A little less than four hours, about thirteen-thirty," said the pilot. "But the news is not all good."

"What?" asked David, looking over at Carver.

"There may be bad weather in Birmingham when we get there. There's a line of thunderstorms headed that way, and the weather man says they're 'bout three and a half hours out. We may have to find an alternate."

David looked at his watch. It was already two hours and

seventeen minutes since cross-clamp.

"We can't do an alternate," he said grimly. "We have to land at Birmingham... no matter what."

"We'll do the best we can, sir," said the pilot, turning back to the front.

David turned to look at Carver.

"How can we have a hurricane at one end and thunderstorms at the other?" he said, shaking his head. He looked down and rubbed his eyes. "What a couple of days! I can't believe it: two hearts in two days."

Carver nodded, looking over at his colleague. "Are you going to be okay?"

"I think so," said David.

"You should catch a nap if you can."

"I've just got to keep up with this heart now for a while. Should be fine though."

Carver nodded again, stifled a yawn, and then leaned back to get comfortable, trying to catch a few z's himself.

David sat up straight, keeping an eye on the heart machine. He yawned himself.

I'm going to need a perfusionist, he thought, *someone to watch the machine.*

He adjusted his seatback up a little, determined to keep awake.

The heart continued to beat happily, if you could say a beat every six seconds or so was happy. He checked the readout on the machine and then watched the heart beat for a few minutes. Everything was fine so far.

David looked over at Carver, and then back at Perry behind him. Both were already asleep.

He sat up straight again, moving his feet to wake up his legs. His eyelids were getting heavy, but he knew he could not give in to sleep.

How long have I been up now?

He counted back to before DeMarco's transplant. He had maybe an hour of fitful sleep on Wednesday night before the call came in for the heart from Dothan. He had lain down on the couch in his office for about thirty minutes after he had completed DeMarco's case on Thursday afternoon, just a short nap. He had to finish rounds and clinic that day and then get ready to fly to Puerto Rico. Five hours down, he maybe snoozed one, then the issue with the coroner. Then they had the donor and now the flight back. It was Friday already. He looked at his watch, trying to remember.

Three fifteen A.M. Five A.M. Wednesday till three A.M. Friday. How long was that? Five A to five A was twenty-four, plus 5 A. to three A.—twenty-two. Twenty-two plus twenty-four... how much is that?

His mind was cloudy: math usually came easy for him, but not now.

Wait... Twenty-two plus twenty-four equals forty-six.

Forty-six hours with maybe two or three hours of nap.

Not good. And he still had to do Maria's transplant. Tuesday night was his last night of sleep, and that was only four or five hours because of an emergency at the hospital. David bowed his head down, thinking about it, then jerked back up. His eyelids were so heavy.

He looked over at Charles Perry.

Maybe he could watch the heart for a while.

No, Perry hadn't been trained on the pump and besides, it was his responsibility, not Perry's. He knew Perry had plenty to do when they got back as well.

I should have brought a perfusionist for this, he thought.

But the pilot had said they were limited on weight.

I will ask Kardia to put an alarm on the machine, so it would alert me if the heart stops.

He nodded his head. At least that would help next time.

He had to be ready if the heart did stop. There would only be a few minutes to get the cold solution ready and gown and glove and pour it into the cassette. That's what he would have to do if the heart stopped beating. He did not have a defibrillator on the plane.

That's something else to think about including, he thought with a sigh.

So many things were coming up with the actual use of the machine that he should have anticipated.

Well, the heart seemed happy now.

David could hear Carver snoring quietly. He yawned a big

yawn himself, and rubbed his eyes again. His eyelids were really getting heavy.

He had been reading Lindbergh's *Spirit of Saint Louis* recently, about the first solo flight across the Atlantic. Lindbergh had written about fighting sleep on the long flight. He had been up the day and night before he left and was then up over thirty hours on the flight. David remembered one line distinctly, what Lindbergh had thought as he fought sleep, still hours from Europe, out over the vast Atlantic, all by himself.

There is no alternative but death and failure, Lindbergh had said.

No alternative but death and failure, David thought.

David knew how Lindbergh had felt. If he slept and the heart stopped, Maria would probably die. He would never forgive himself. He could see it now. The heart would stop, and it would be no good after just a few minutes. Someone would ask him what happened. "I fell asleep," he would have to say.

There is no alternative but death and failure.

He sat up straight again, watching the heart. Then he slid back and leaned forward, chin in hands. He could see the contraction sequence as it moved through the heart, much more distinct at this slower pace.

But the contraction is still strong. Almost like the heart just waits longer between beats, but still contracts with the same force.

He looked at the perfusion pressure readout. Even though it was not pumping blood through a body, the heart still had to have pressure to function. The perfusion solution pressure was maintained by the machine, giving the heart the solution at a set preload. That is, when the heart expanded, the pressure caused the fluid to enter the atrium, just like blood would in a normal heart. There was also pressure that resisted the heart's thrust, the afterload. David had designed the machine to mimic the body in its natural state. He sat now, enthralled by the amazing organ in front of him, a captive audience, spellbound.

What a wonderful pump.

Is it more than a pump? Is there something else there?

Sally's "cellular memory?"

You certainly couldn't see anything like that, but you

couldn't see brainwaves just by looking at a brain, either.

David shook his head, watching the heart work, still amazed as it continued its steady cadence. He sat there, determined to keep awake. Every few minutes, he would shift positions. He didn't allow himself to get comfortable.

It was still beating happily, almost three hours later.

28

Old Hand

DAVID'S MIND WAS in a fog. He had not slept, but perhaps had closed his eyes a bit, when the pilot's voice came over the intercom.

"We are setting up to land in Birmingham. It may be a little bumpy."

As if it hasn't already been bumpy, David thought.

He sat up straight and cinched up the seat belt tight. He saw Carver and Perry do the same, both now fully awake.

The heart was still pumping slowly and the readout on the machine said that the vitals were still okay. David made sure a seatbelt was around the front of the heart machine as well. After getting situated, he glanced out of the window. The clouds were dark and ragged below, and some of the tops reached up to their altitude. He could just barely see a huge, ominous-looking cloud in front of them, towering up, way above their altitude. The nose had tilted down and they were going down quickly, down into the dark clouds. This was the fastest that he had ever descended in an airplane before. When he looked out again they were in the clouds. Suddenly it started to rain, hard, and the water streamed sideways in the slipstream.

"Hold on tight, Docs. We've got some weather in front of us."

David leaned forward and held down both sides of the heart

cassette.

He had hardly gotten a grip when *WHAM,* the airplane hit an updraft and suddenly shot upward. He was thrust down into the seat, and the heart machine, its weight multiplied by the g-forces, slid sideways.

David increased his grip, leaning over the machine to protect it from movement. At that moment, the airplane slammed downward, just as hard as it had gone up. If he had not had his arms over the pump, it would have flown upward.

David held on as the airplane slammed up, down and sideways as it descended. Though it was dark in the clouds, they were almost constantly lit with lightning, some flashes so bright that he was almost blinded. He could feel the pilot working to keep the aircraft right side up as they plunged downward through the storm. It was a nightmare roller coaster ride, seemingly a never-ending one. The pilot was actually doing a very good job of keeping the airplane on course and on a steady descent.

After a while they were below ten thousand feet and had slowed significantly. It was still bumpy, but now a constant jittery up and down, not nearly as bad as it had been higher.

After a minute, the pilot announced that they were ten minutes out. It was still raining hard, and David was concerned that the pilot could not land in the weather. He clutched the heart machine with his right arm and looked at his watch. Even with the special flight, it was still going to be close on time.

"Gear coming down, we're on the glideslope," the pilot announced over the intercom.

David heard the landing gear as it clunked into place. The airplane was still dancing in the winds, but the descent was steady. David craned his head around to see if he could see the runway, but everything was still gray with rain. He could hear the pilot adjusting the power as the plane bucked up and down in the weather. Then he heard the power come off and felt the nose of the aircraft coming up.

Suddenly out of the corner of his eye he saw a flash of light, and looked sideways. David could see the runway lights, barely. The airplane touched down gently, with a chirp of wet wheels hitting wet asphalt, and the pilot braked lightly, slowing enough to take the first turnoff.

David let out his breath completely for the first time since the descent started. He shook his head as he looked around. He could not see the terminal building or even the tower.

The pilot quickly taxied the jet over to an area that David had never been to before. It was the station and hangars used by the Alabama Air National Guard squadron. David could see a set of open hangars, concrete covered arches designed to protect each of the Guard's F-16s. He could also see a helicopter standing by to meet them. The jet taxied into one of the empty covered hangars, and the copilot started opening the door as the pilot shut down.

"We're here, Doc. Good luck," the pilot said over the intercom.

"Thank you," said David, as he placed the cover over the heart machine.

Perry stepped out with the cooler containing the liver. He was met by an Army corpsman, who started talking to him, gesturing toward the waiting helicopter.

Perry yelled up to them, over the diminishing whine of the jet engines, "I'm going on to the helicopter. He will come back to get you."

David looked up at the pilot. "This flight probably saved a life. Thanks."

"No prob. You take care of that little girl. We will be praying for you. Godspeed, Doc."

The Army corpsman was back at the bottom of the steps and took the heart machine from David. David carried the folded-up cart and Carver carried the other cooler. They heard a sound and turned to watch as a jet attempted a landing, probably a commercial flight. They could hear the engines but didn't see anything in the rain and fog, except maybe a flash of lights just over the runway. Then the engines revved back up and the unseen plane climbed away.

"Missed approach," said the corpsman. "Weather's too low for him to land. You guys were lucky to get in."

He turned toward the helicopter. "Let's go before it gets worse."

David and Carver followed the corpsman and ran through the rain to the chopper. They were both surprised that it was military. They usually flew in the Caraway Lifeflight helicopter.

They buckled in. David sat the covered heart machine between his legs, sliding his feet together to protect it.

"Why the military helicopter?" he asked.

"Weather's too bad for Lifeflight. And, the Governor ordered it." Perry grinned at him.

David looked at the pilot's back, watching him as he readied the helicopter for flight.

He looked back over at Perry. "Weather's too bad? Can this guy land at MCA in this weather?"

"Says he can. Believe me, I asked. He is going to do a GPS approach. He said he's done it seven times before."

The corpsman slammed the door on the helicopter and the turbine started to whine.

David looked up as the rotors began to turn, faster and faster, slicing through the rain. He glanced over and saw that the jet pilots were watching them take off. David saluted, nodding his thanks. Then he felt the aircraft lift slightly. The downwash from the rotor sent sheets of water streaming away on the tarmac below. They turned into the wind, and started to climb into the wet gray sky. The ground disappeared almost instantly as they climbed.

It wasn't far from Birmingham Airport to downtown, maybe even closer to south downtown, where MCA hospital was located. There were no obstacles of any significant height between the airport and MCA, but the area around the hospital was festooned with radio and TV towers. There were also T-cranes, with several buildings going up or being renovated. The pilot would have to be extra careful, particularly in this visibility.

David felt the helicopter climbing as they made the trip over, and it seemed that it climbed higher than usual. He could see nothing but dark gray outside as the helicopter's strobe lights flashed. They flew for a few minutes, the helicopter bouncing in the rough air. Then they almost came to a stop in the air, as it again turned into the wind. David saw the big front floodlight come on, and they started a slow descent, almost in a hover. Thankfully, the winds had calmed, but the rain was still pelting. They could see the big raindrops streaming by in the beam of the spotlight.

They continued to descend, nearly straight down. Neither David nor Carver could see anything but rain and fog for the longest time. They could see the pilot watching his instruments and quickly looking down and left and right as they slowly moved earthward. It was almost like the pilot was feeling his way. At one point, for an instant, David thought he saw a red flashing light over to the side, and remembered a tall crane just west of the hospital, over at Children's Hospital. He could feel his heart in his throat, and almost held his breath, glancing at Perry with a worried look. It was like pea soup around them.

How can he find the hospital in this? Are we going to make it all this way and then crash into the building? David said a prayer again.

Dear Lord, please help us.

Suddenly, as they looked down, just below and to the right, not fifty feet away, they saw the big white H of the landing pad on the roof of the hospital. It was as if the clouds had suddenly lifted, clearing an opening directly below them. The pilot wheeled right slightly and let down almost vertically to the rooftop, slowing as he got close to the roof, the skids finally touching down with a soft *thud*. Everyone on the aircraft seemed to exhale at the same time.

The pilot cut the switches and the turbine started to wind down, the blades slowing and then stopping completely. He turned around and motioned to the corpsman in the back and he reached over to slide the door open. The rain had let up a little.

David nodded to the pilot as he took off his headset.

"Thanks for getting us here so quickly, and safely," he said.

"No problem," said the pilot, smiling back.

"I can't believe that you've landed here seven other times in this kind of weather," David said, as he handed the heart machine to Perry and stepped out of the aircraft.

"This is the first time for real," the pilot said with a grin. "The others were in the simulator."

David was too shocked to think of anything to say. He just glanced at Perry and shook his head. Carver was exiting the aircraft with the liver and turned toward the pilot.

"You're kidding, right?"

"No, sir," said the pilot, still grinning.

David followed Perry through the wide red door of the flight deck and into the hospital. He felt winded, and he hadn't even begun the run through the hospital. The pilot's last comment had really gotten to him.

Thankfully, Perry was pushing the cart and all David had to do was follow. He didn't even know if he could navigate to the OR. The adrenaline that had sustained him for so long was completely depleted and he was at the point that his body was on automatic.

I am so tired, he thought. *I don't know when I've ever been this tired.*

Now they were running, winding through the halls of the University Hospital. It was four floors down the elevator to the corridor to the next building, down a hall, then down two more floors and several corridors before they made it to surgery. David followed, barely keeping up. He felt like a punch-drunk boxer.

When they did reach the OR, the nurse said that Maria was already in the room and was prepped. David nodded to her and then looked at the clock. They were already well over six hours, and he still had to do the transplant. On his best days he might have a heart in and working in an hour and fifteen. This was not going to be one of his best days.

David handed off the heart machine to Todd, his PA.

David went quickly to the surgeon's changing room. He took a minute to use the bathroom, it had been hours since he could, and then quickly washed his hands. He looked in the mirror. His eyes were dark circles and his face sagged. He had to compose himself. He splashed some cool water on his face, and tried to wash some of the sleepiness out of his eyes.

Why did Connor have to pick this week to take off?

"I'm getting too old for this," David said aloud.

Then, he reminded himself that he had been in this position before, and everything had always worked out.

Well, as far as I know it has worked out.

He changed quickly into clean scrubs, and started for the door. There was a little bar area with a coffee pot and snacks just inside the door. He almost stopped for a cup of coffee. He rarely drank coffee, but it would be so good now. No. He couldn't afford the caffeine shakes. He did grab a pack of peanut butter crackers and stuffed two in his mouth, chewing quickly. He had to have some energy if he was going to do this transplant. He ate two more crackers and chugged a glass of orange juice.

Just then the door opened. It was the circulating nurse from the room. "Everything is ready, Dr. Mac. They are waiting for you," she said cheerfully.

David shook his head to clear the cobwebs. He followed the nurse toward the operating room.

"Don't forget your hat and shoe covers, sir," she said. He stopped and quickly donned the required gear. He had almost crossed into the sterile area without them.

Maria was on the table, already prepped and draped for surgery. The anesthesiologist had started to put her to sleep as soon as he knew David was in the unit. The bypass machine and perfusionist were in their place, and the scrub tech had everything set up. Todd was at the back table and was setting everything up for David. The heart was fine, still keeping its slow rhythm on the pump.

"Hello, everyone," David said.

"Hello, Dr. Mac," said Todd. "We're ready when you are." His voice betrayed his concern.

"Just give me a minute to scrub," said David, trying his best to sound commanding, awake and ready to go.

After scrubbing in and donning a sterile gown, David joined the others around the operating table. He took a deep breath, looking down and closing his eyes, calming himself down.

Help me, Lord, he thought.

David took the scalpel and, finding the landmark with his fingers, paused one more moment, feeling Maria's chest rise and fall, and the heavy thump of her oversized heart. Then he placed the sharp blade of the scalpel in the center of the notch. He made a long straight cut with the scalpel, from the notch down to the xiphoid.

He stopped again to get himself ready for the cut through the sternum. This one concerned him. He had noticed when he did the first cut that he was a little shaky, so he lowered his head again to take a breath.

He should not have closed his eyes, but thought just a second would help calm him. When he opened his eyes again, he saw another set of gloves in the field, not Todd's, not the scrub tech's. The gloved hands looked familiar, but in his state of mind he didn't recognize them. Besides, it didn't make sense for there to be another surgeon in the room.

He looked up, into the smiling eyes of Dr. Albert Brighton.

"Hello, David," Brighton said in his characteristic clipped manner.

"May I scrub in and assist?"

David just stared at him in disbelief.

"Umm... absolutely, sir." David was unable to think of anything else to say.

Brighton's eyes were smiling over his surgical mask.

"It's been a few days since I've done one of these."

He looked up into David's eyes.

"Mind if I start?"

"Please do," said David. "Thank you, sir."

"Sternal saw!" commanded Brighton, and the scrub nurse handed him the saw. He checked the saw, then placed it so the blade was just touching the top of the sternum.

"Clear!"

David smiled and leaned in to watch Brighton make the cut.

After Maria's chest was opened and they could see her heart, both David and Brighton shook their heads. Her heart had enlarged almost beyond the size of the cavity. It was gray and listless, hardly moving as it beat. The swollen heart looked sad to David. It was trying its best, but in the shape it was in, it could not do its job.

Brighton looked at him over his magnification loupes.

"What about the donor heart, David?"

"I think it is fine." David nodded toward the heart machine. The heart still beat its slow steady pace. The temp and oxygen level were still good.

Seven hours and thirty minutes since the heart had been started on the machine. There had been less than ten minutes after cross-clamp before the heart had been beating. David knew it would take Brighton another half hour at least to get Maria on bypass and then take the old heart out. Then it would take him nearly an hour to do the transplant.

David looked down at the perfusionist and asked, "It's

plugged in?"

"Yes, sir, since it came in the room."

David looked back up at Brighton. "As long as it is happy on the machine we are okay. If something does start to happen, we will need to go ahead and put it on ice, but should still be okay on time. You don't have to hurry."

Brighton nodded and started the process of readying Maria for heart bypass. David stood in his spot, holding the retractor and suction for Brighton, glad to just watch. He knew that he was in no state to do surgery, but was not going to leave. He still had to ready the donor heart for transplant, and would not go until the case was finished, anyway. He was just relieved that Dr. Brighton was there.

He thought, *How many times have I been in surgery and thought "if something happens to me, there is no one to take over?"*

He remembered a dream he had had, more than once. He was in surgery on a heart case. The patient's chest was open, and he was supposed to do a procedure. As he stood and looked in the chest cavity he could not remember what to do. Could not even remember the names of the vessels attached to the heart. He felt as if he were in that dream right now.

Thank God Brighton is here. I could not have done this case by myself.

It seemed as if time stood still for a while. He was standing there, but only in body. His eyes were open, but his mind was asleep, a strange dreamlike state. He was aware of everything around him, but in a curious, detached way. He even continued to assist with the retractor and with suction, robotically. It was as if his body was on autopilot. Voices were vague, dreamlike. His eyes were open and he found himself watching the heart on the pump.

It fascinated him, its slow pulse seeming to reach out to him, like a beacon. A beacon in the night, flashing, flashing, every six seconds.

Here I am, it said.

David could feel its life. Through the darkness, it was speaking to him.

David was entranced, focusing on the heart, vague voices,

vague shapes around him. He felt numb, but could feel the
energy of the heart.

Everything seemed to stand still.

Suddenly he heard his name.

Startled, he looked up.

It was Brighton, "David... David," he said.

"Yes, sir?" he heard himself say.

"We will be ready for the heart in ten minutes or so."

David looked at him, then down at the field. The bypass
machine was on and Brighton was getting ready to remove the
old heart.

"Yes, sir," David said again, coming alert.

He stood straight. "Just let me change gloves."

He walked around the table and removed the top set of
gloves. The scrub nurse popped a new set on his hands. The
perfusionist turned the heart machine out so he would have
access. David looked down at the perfusionist.

"I will need you to open the top of the cassette in just a
minute."

He looked over at the scrub tech.

"Pick-ups, please."

The heart was still beating, once every six seconds or so.

David watched it for a few beats, then said, "Turn off the
pump."

David watched. The heart continued to beat. Every six
seconds. Steady and sure.

David reached in and clamped the tubing that went into the
heart. It beat its last time on the machine, expelling the last of
the perfusion solution. David quickly removed the heart from
the cannula and then reached in with both hands, brought it
out, and laid it in a basin of cold perfusion solution. Slush was
poured over the heart after it was in the basin. David massaged
it, making sure the solution was evenly distributed, cooling the
whole organ, internally and externally. It still quivered with
life, even in its cold state. He then inspected the heart, assuring
himself that everything looked normal.

He turned to Brighton.

"Heart is ready."

Brighton had just finished removing Maria's old heart. The

scrub nurse held out a basin and Brighton laid the fat old gray heart in it.

David took the new heart over, holding it tight against his chest with both hands. He looked up at Brighton, and then took a quick look in the cavity, assuring himself that it was clear. He handed the heart to Brighton, who examined it as well. Brighton then placed the heart in the cavity, and immediately asked for slush to keep it cool. After the heart was placed in its new home, David watched as Brighton's fingers moved swiftly and precisely, sewing the new heart into its place. McAllister still marveled at the small perfect sutures as the heart was mated to the waiting vessels.

Twenty minutes later, Brighton was ready to unclamp the vessel and let the blood flow into the new heart.

He stood back and looked up at David, his eyes still smiling. "Okay, Dr. McAllister. Go ahead. Let's see if this will work."

David looked up at Brighton, then nodded.

Taking a deep breath, he reached in and unclamped the vessels, allowing the warm blood to flow through the new heart.

In only a few seconds, the heart started to darken in color, back to the look of a healthy heart. It started to warm back up as Maria's warm blood flowed through it.

All conversation in the room had ceased. It was as if the whole room was still, everyone watching, leaning in to see, holding their breath in anticipation.

The heart just sat there.

David's own heart began to sink.

Brighton looked up at him, then glanced over to the scrub tech, cueing her to get the defibrillator ready.

But, as they watched, the heart started to come back alive on its own: first quivering, almost like it was anticipating starting again, and then slowly, very slowly starting to beat.

The monitor mirrored its pulse.

Beep...

Beep...

Beep... Beep...

It was slow and irregular at first.

Then slow but steady.

Brighton looked up at David again, but David nodded.

"I think it's okay. Give it a few minutes."

For a while it settled at a rate of about ten beats per minute, causing David some concern. It was as if it had gotten used to the slow rate. They watched it closely. But, as they watched and waited, over the next several minutes, as it continued to warm, it picked up the pace. When it reached sixty beats a minute, Brighton looked at David, nodded and smiled.

"Good job, David," he said.

David smiled back. Everyone in the room began to talk at once.

David felt a soft hand on his shoulder, and looked around. It was Elsa, her blue eyes smiling. She hugged him from behind. She had been in the room for a while, but David had not known it.

"It works!" she said, looking at the machine, then down at the heart, her smiling eyes beginning to moisten with tears.

David just nodded, his eyes tearing up as well.

Elsa stood beside him and they watched the heart together.

Gradually, the rate climbed to nearly eighty, then it settled down to about seventy beats per minute.

David looked up at the monitor.

Normal sinus rhythm.

29

Best-Kept Secret

DOMINIC DEMARCO WAS not doing well.

It had been six days since his transplant.

For the first couple of days everything had been perfect. The donor heart was good. Dominic, despite his history, was a healthy young man, except for the cardiomyopathy, so his body should have been able to cope better than most. The transplant surgery itself had gone quicker than usual, and the donated heart had been from a young, reasonably healthy person.

Despite his misgivings about the heart going to Dominic, David had been pleased with how well the surgery had gone.

Now, he was worried.

Dominic's labs were getting worse. The heart rate had started to rise, and nothing David had done seemed to help. Dominic had at first become lethargic, and now was barely responding. His oxygen saturation was slowly trending downward.

At first, David and Dr. Burch, the transplant cardiologist, had thought it was a case of acute rejection. This sometimes occurs with transplants: the body immediately recognizes that the organ is foreign and tries to get rid of it. They had done the tests for acute rejection, and were even treating Dominic with an anti-rejection medicine specifically for acute cases. Also, the heart was as close a match to Dominic as possible. Not only had the heart matched by blood type, it also matched by HLA type. They had also done antibody cross-matches before the transplant, at David's insistence. He had really wanted to rule Dominic out for the heart, but all the tests ruled him in, even more than usual.

So, David stood outside of the intensive care room where Dominic was a patient, flipping through the chart, looking at the latest labs, and trying to figure out what was wrong.

He shook his head, and looked over at Shannon, the critical care nurse. "How is his urine output?

"Not too good, Dr. Mac," she said. "It's been running twenty or thirty ccs an hour all day. And he has been running a temp, low-grade. Don't know why, he's been on Ancef. His skin actually seems cool, and you can see that he is pale. Something's going on, just don't know what. Some people didn't think he should have gotten a heart anyway."

David looked at her in surprise. He had never known Shannon to be negative about any patient.

"I'm sorry, Dr. Mac," she said, realizing what she had said. "It's just that my brother died of an overdose. I hate drugs."

David knew Shannon's brother's story.

"I know," he said. "I'm sorry." He continued to flip through the chart.

"You're right. Something's going on here, something different. I just don't know what it is. Maybe it's some kind of sub-clinical rejection."

Wham, it hit him.

He stood straight, shook his head and snorted, thinking...

Some kind of sub-clinical rejection!

Shannon looked at him quizzically.

He remembered vividly his conversation with Sally Debardeleben.

He remembered saying to her "some doctors think it's some kind of sub-clinical rejection."

And then Sally had asked him, "Do you ever have someone that the heart rejects?"

David thought a moment, in a quandary. He had already consulted Carver, asking him if he had any ideas how to help DeMarco. Carver had not been able to help. Now he couldn't get

Sally's question out of his mind.

But what could she do?

He made up his mind.

"Shannon, page Dr. Debardeleben for me."

David stood there, wondering.

What will I do if the heart is rejecting Dominic?

He thought back to what Sally had said about dominant hearts.

Could this be one of those?

David continued to look through the chart. A couple of minutes later the phone rang at the nurses' station.

"Hello Sally, this is David, how are you today?" He turned towards Dominic's room, listening a second or two.

"Would you be available for a consult on a patient of mine? I have an issue that I would like to discuss with you. Umm, really need your insight."

David smiled as he listened. "Some of the things we've talked about. I just want to see what you think."

He nodded.

• • •

David and Sally met in the unit at the appointed time

"Hey, Sally. Thanks for coming over so quickly."

"Let me tell you what is happening. This is a young, otherwise healthy patient, a twenty-year-old male, transplanted last week. The heart is good. There were no problems with the crossmatches, and the surgery went well. He was doing fine at first, but now has some issues, as if he is going into an acute rejection. However, he is not responding to the antirejection meds, and none of the tests are consistent with rejection. I have tested everything I can think of medically, and everything comes back normal. His labs are changing, though, getting worse. His pressure has started to decline slightly, so I have him on meds for that. His heart rate has gotten tachy, but his wedge pressures and CVP are close to normal. I have tried meds, but the heart just doesn't seem to respond. It will settle down a little, but within a few hours it picks back up. He is also beginning to have some changes on the EKG, like a conduction issue, but, again, we can't find the problem. In fact, I can't think of anything that would cause this medically. I called you because I remembered how we talked about rejection, some sort of rejection related to the heart itself, not the body's reaction. Would you be willing to take a look?"

Sally looked at him, almost surprised. "What are you asking me to check on?" she asked.

"Could this be one of those cases that you mentioned?"

"What cases?"

David looked down the hall, making sure the nurses were still down there and could not hear.

"The ones where the heart rejects the patient."

Sally smiled at him. It was obvious that he was not comfortable in asking her to do this.

"It's okay, David," she said with a smile. "I will see if I can help."

"Let's see if we can find out if there were any unusual factors in this case."

Then she said, as if to relieve David's fears, "We'll have to be discreet, as I always try to be, so that there is not a carryover from the donor story to the recipient. Where is his chart?"

David took the chart from the rack, handed it to Sally, and then sat down. Sally sat down as well and started to go through the chart. She looked at the face page. David heard her draw in her breath quickly when she read the name.

"Dominic DeMarco!"

She looked up at David. "Why didn't you tell me?"

"I didn't want there to be carryover," said David with a smile.

Sally just shook her head.

She reviewed DeMarco's history. Then she surprised David by flipping back to the lab page.

"Hmm. He was negative on the toxicology."

"He had been in the hospital several days," said David. "He had another episode of dyspnea, more severe than the last time. But he had to be clean before that. I think the last admission before this scared him sober."

"I saw his shortness of breath was getting more severe," said Sally, "How bad was he?"

"He had to be intubated for a while, placed in the unit. He

was high on the list, right behind Maria. The heart was a direct donation. The donor was also high-risk, but did not test positive for anything. Dominic had to sign a release for the heart because of the high-risk status."

"What do you know about the donor?"

"Not much. Young man, overdose of narcotics, no other pertinent medical history. Had been a psych patient, I think."

"Really?" said Sally. "Local donor?"

"No. He was from down in South Alabama."

"What else do we know about him?"

"That's basically all I know. He was Lisa Kelly's patient. She would know more."

Sally looked over at him.

"Lisa Kelly? I know her. She's a really good coordinator. Very good with families. I've worked with a lot of her families. She does a good job. Let's call the organ center and see if we can get them to call her for us. She may be able to fill in the blanks."

Sally reached over to the phone and dialed the number by memory. When it was answered she talked to the receptionist as if they were old friends. Then she asked if Lisa was on call. When she found out that she was, she asked the receptionist to page Lisa to call them, and gave her the unit number. David looked at her in surprise.

"What?" she said, smiling at him. "I'm here quite a bit. Believe me, I know how to use the phone system."

David just shook his head. He was here quite a bit, too, but didn't know how to do the intercom. He always asked the nurse to make the calls.

Sally continued to go through the chart, asking David about the results of some of the labs. She had taken out a notebook and was writing some of the pertinent facts in it. He showed her how Dominic's vital signs were trending down.

"I just can't find what is causing the problem," he said, shaking his head.

The unit intercom crackled overhead, "Dr. Debardeleben, please pick up on line 2..."

Sally picked up the phone and punched the line button.

"This is Sally Debardeleben." Then, after a pause, "Hi, Lisa, how are you?"

David could hear the sound of Lisa's voice on the phone, but could not make out what was said.

"How are things in South Alabama?" asked Sally.

She and Lisa talked a minute, catching up on each other's lives. Then, Sally switched gears, suddenly becoming serious.

"I have a case I need to talk to you about. A recent donor of yours. This is the twenty-six-year-old male who overdosed. Can you tell me a little about him?"

Sally listened as Lisa discussed the case, interjecting questions occasionally.

David heard her say something about schizophrenia and multiple personalities. Sally was animated in the discussion. It was obvious something interesting had occurred. She wrote furiously in the notebook. She asked questions about the characters, and what sort of personalities they were. A couple of times she glanced at David, shaking her head and smiling. She and Lisa talked several minutes, and then David could sense that the conversation was winding down. Then, Sally asked Lisa if the donor was religious. This started a whole new discussion, with Sally taking notes again. Finally, she wound up the conversation, saying thank you and goodbye to Lisa, but not before securing permission to call back if she thought of anything else or wanted to follow up.

"This is unusual!" Sally said as she hung up the phone.

"What is?" asked David.

"The donor. A very interesting case. Let me fill you in."

David smiled. Sally's dark eyes were filled with excitement.

"You won't believe this," she said, and started to tell David the story that had been relayed to her.

After Sally had told David about the donor, and they discussed the case, he looked at her and asked a question that endeared him to her forever.

"Dr. Debardeleben, what would you recommend as a plan of treatment?"

She looked at him and smiled, pleased that he was consulting her. Then, she reached up and brushed back her hair with her right hand. As her hand came down, it ended up cupped under her chin, and David noticed that she stared to the right, not looking at anything in particular.

"Give me a few minutes to think, how long do we have?"

"I don't know," said David. "He's just not hemodynamically stable. I don't think he is about to die, but his vitals are trending down. I've had patients come out of this, but I've had others who did die, and I just couldn't seem to do anything about it." He shook his head.

"Okay," said Sally. "Give me a little time to work on this. Are you in the hospital all day?"

"I have a short case in surgery at one. Then I can be back over here."

Sally looked at her watch. "Let's say three o'clock, then. Will that be okay?"

"Sure," said David. He got up to walk away. "Thanks, Sally."

"Anytime, David," she said, a twinkle in her dark eyes.

She picked up the chart and went into Dominic's room.

David watched as she entered the room, placed the chart on the table, and then stepped over to the bedside. She stood quietly beside the bed, looking down at Dominic.

David turned and walked out to the unit.

It was actually a little after three before David was able to return to the transplant critical care unit. Surgery had gone longer than he anticipated. As he walked down the corridor to Dominic's room, he could see Sally sitting in a chair beside Dominic's bed. She was sitting very still, and as he got close he noticed that her eyes were closed and that she had Dominic's left hand clasped between both of her hands. McAllister stopped at the door, standing quietly. After a moment, he cleared his throat. Sally looked up at him and smiled.

"Come in, Dr. McAllister," she said.

"Hey, Dr. Debardeleben," he said. He walked over to the bed. "Hey, Dominic, it's Dr. Mac. Can you hear me?"

Dominic moved slightly, but did not say anything.

"He's hardly responding," said Sally, "But I've been talking to him."

She bent over the bed.

"I'll be right back, Dominic. I am going out to talk to Dr. McAllister for a minute."

They both walked out of the room. David looked at her

quizzically.

"Did you find out anything?"

"Several things, David, and I have a treatment plan."

"Good," said David. "Tell me what we can do."

Sally smiled at him.

"David, you're going to have to go with the flow on this one."

"How so?"

"I have asked someone to come in and work with me. Come over and sit down and I will tell you about it."

They went back to the desk where the charts were kept. There were several chairs around where doctors would sit as they reviewed cases. Sally sat down and David rolled a chair over to face her.

"You know how we discussed the donor's story, David, the schizophrenia, the dissociative identity disorder?"

"Yes," David nodded.

"Well, I've been on the phone again with Lisa. Evidently one of the personalities often dominated, and it wasn't the donor's own persona."

"What?"

"The young man's name was Jason. He had other personalities: Rick, Brucey, and Chris."

"What?" said David, again.

Sally smiled, shaking her head. "Did you ever read the book *Sybil*?"

"Yes, and Elsa and I saw the movie."

"Okay. Sort of like that. Jason was the guy, but Brucey, Chris, and Rick showed up at times, according to Jason's family. Lisa is actually trying to get Jason's chart from the psych unit for me, but we can go ahead on what we have until then."

"Okay," said David.

"Well, with dissociative identity disorder sometimes different personalities are in control. In this case if Rick was in control... let's just say things were bad. Rick was not a good guy, supposedly, and had been the cause of a lot of Jason's problems: drugs, alcohol, and so on. Lately, though, Jason had been in rehab and had been doing better. And, get this, Chris was taking lessons from a tai chi instructor and this was helping as well. The family says Jason's life had really changed for the better since Chris was seeing the chi master. He even came to the hospital after Jason died."

"Okay," David said again, shaking his head, trying to keep the names straight.

"I told you this was an interesting case." Sally said with a smile.

"Now this is what is neat. I asked Lisa to look up the tai chi instructor. He is a Mr. Chen." She smiled again. "David, you know how they say that the connection between any two people in America is only through about four people. In other words, you know someone who knows someone who knows someone who knows that other person." Sally used her fingers to denote each connection. "Only four to reach anybody in the U.S."

David nodded. "I've heard that, yes."

"Well, you won't believe this," Sally said.

David looked at her. "Okay, Sally, what?"

"Do you know Bobby Chen, down in I.T.?"

"Sure," said David. "He teaches the docs how to use the electronic medical records."

"That's Mr. Chen's son."

"Mr. Chen, the tai chi instructor?"

Sally nodded. "One and the same."

"Okay, Sally, where are you going with this?"

"Mr. Chen comes up to see his son every other weekend. He is to be in town tomorrow. I have asked him to come by the hospital and work with me. We want to get in touch with Jason's heart. Perhaps we can do it through Chris. If we can, we may be able to settle things down."

David was shaking his head. Sally was losing him.

"This is some kind of witch doctor voodoo."

"No, David. Tai chi is an ancient belief, practiced for hundreds of years. Chi is the energy that animates all things. If we can get in touch with the heart's energy, we may be able to help Dominic."

David was still shaking his head.

Sally looked at him, her dark eyes flashing.

"David, what do you have to lose? You've tried everything else, you said so yourself."

She calmed a little.

"We will be very discreet. If anyone asks I will say that Mr. Chen is a minister and we are praying for Dominic."

David thought a minute. He looked over at Dominic's room and the monitor "Okay, Sally, but you do have to be discreet. I do not want anyone else to know what we are trying. They would laugh me out of the hospital."

30

Dancing Away

IT WAS CUSTOMARY for the transplant program to have a big day of celebration each year in November. The transplant patients from previous years and their families looked forward to these get-togethers, enjoying seeing their doctors and renewing old friendships with other patients. Many had spent weeks or months at MCA waiting for a heart or lung or kidney or liver, and they had made lifelong connections with the staff and with other patients. The organ center also participated in the occasion, with special events for donor families. Most years would see two or three thousand participants. The day started with remembrance ceremonies for donors and their families. There would usually be a speaker, maybe someone famous who had had a transplant. Lunch would be a picnic in the park, with different groups organizing different booths of information and celebration. Things would start to wind down in the afternoon, but there would always be banquets in the evening, usually organized by type of transplant.

David always enjoyed attending the events, and he and Elsa, with Nicholas in tow, would stroll through the picnic and outside venues, catching up with patients and their families. David enjoyed these informal meetings with patients, able to interact in a personal way, far from the clinical setting of the office.

He and Elsa particularly enjoyed the evening banquet, where his patients and their families could have a party together. He loved seeing how they did after their transplants, and loved getting to know them on a personal basis.

The heart transplant banquet was held in a large hall at one of the local hotels, set up and decorated like a reception. There were now several hundred heart transplant recipients from the program, and though not everyone was able to come, when the families were counted, it was a huge group. There would be good food, usually a speaker, and then a band and dancing. The other transplant doctors, the cardiologists, and the nurses from the transplant team were always there.

This year, the group was also celebrating Dr. Brighton's thirtieth year, and his retirement. Brighton had almost completely stopped doing transplants. He had continued his position as professor of surgery in the cardiovascular program, but now that he was approaching seventy, he had decided to slow down even more. He would still serve on hospital boards and have administrative duties, but was giving up his professorship and surgical privileges. There was to be a little roast, with David and some of the other docs participating. Dr. Brighton would then be honored with a presentation. Then the band would start and the party would begin.

As David walked around the room at the beginning, he was surprised to see Dominic DeMarco and his family, all around one large table. Leo DeMarco stood and greeted David, shaking his hand. David forced a smile.

"How are you, Mr. DeMarco?" he asked.

"Please, call me Leo, Dr. McAllister," said DeMarco. "I want to thank you again for what you have done." He motioned over to Dominic, who had stood up as well.

David noticed for the first time that Dominic was holding a small baby. Misty was standing beside him.

"Hey, Dr. Mac," said Dominic.

"I want you to meet someone new."

He turned to hold the baby up for McAllister to see.

"This is David DeMarco." Dominic smiled.

"He's named after you."

McAllister was unable to speak for a moment.

"And I want you to meet someone else."

A man David had not noticed before stood up beside Dominic. David couldn't have been more surprised.

"This is Mr. Wu Chen."

David regained his composure.

"Hello, Mr. Chen. It is good to see you again."

Chen bowed to David and then shook his hand.

David just stood there a second and smiled. He was puzzled. Leo DeMarco broke the silence.

"Dominic has turned his life around since his transplant. He has gotten married to Misty, and we now have a grandchild, as you can see. Dominic is finishing college, but he doesn't want to be a businessman like me. He says counseling or something like that."

Dominic broke in, "I want to work with people who have addictions, like I did. Mr. Chen has helped me focus."

He looked David in the eye. "I have been given a second chance at life. I am not going to waste it."

David looked back at Dominic. He didn't know what to say. He just smiled and shook his head. Then he found his voice.

"That's great, Dominic. I am looking forward to hearing about how things are going. If there is anything I can do to help, let me know."

David shook hands all around again, getting a hug from Mrs. DeMarco. As he walked away, he was still shaking his head, still unable to believe what he had just seen.

He went back to his table. Elsa was sitting there with Kim and Carver, who were now a couple.

David looked down at his colleague.

"What are you doing here, Carver? This is the heart transplant banquet. No kidneys allowed."

"Kim invited me," said Carver, smiling at David.

"The abominable, um, I mean, abdominal guys are too cheap to have a banquet for their patients?" David asked, smiling back.

"Our transplant party was last night. At the art museum. And Jim Nabors was our speaker."

David grinned. "Shazam!"

He chuckled. "Sounds like a nice party."

"Carver, David and I were coming," said Elsa. "But David

had to go into the hospital for a patient."

David shook his head.

"Mr. Brooks died last night."

Carver nodded. "I'm sorry, David."

David shook his head again.

"He was really a neat guy. Just couldn't get a heart soon enough."

Everybody was quiet for a moment.

Then Sally Debardeleben walked up, along with Dr. Albert Brighton.

Brighton was in a black tuxedo, and Sally was dressed to the nines as well, in a long black evening dress.

Everyone stood up.

"Hello," said Brighton, nodding.

"Does everyone know Sally Debardeleben?"

"We do," said David, as he shook Brighton's hand and then gave Sally a hug.

Carver hugged her as well. Brighton hugged Elsa and shook Kim's hand.

"This is Kim Chou," said Carver.

"Oh, Kim and I have worked together before," said Brighton.

Elsa and Kim spoke to Sally as well.

"What a beautiful dress," said Elsa.

"Thank you," said Sally. "It belonged to my mother. I never get to wear it. And when Dr. Brighton asked me to come here, and said he would be in a tux, I couldn't resist."

"I didn't know that you knew Sally, Dr. Brighton," said David.

"I have known Sally a long time, David. We have worked together on several projects."

"Really?" David was intrigued.

"What kind of projects?"

Brighton looked over toward Sally.

"They were about some patients I have had who had an unusual connection to their donor."

Brighton smiled.

"We'll have to discuss it sometime."

He looked at the ladies. "Elsa, you look lovely tonight."

"Thank you," she said.

Brighton glanced at David, then back at Elsa.

"Elsa, do you remember the first time we met David? I believe it was that heart run to Oklahoma City. I think the patient was Vicky Lowe."

"Yes sir, I do," said Elsa, nodding.

"I never thought he would come this far, did you?" Brighton winked.

Everyone laughed.

Brighton suddenly looked up, gazing across the room.

"Excuse me a minute, please," he said, bowing slightly to the ladies.

David looked over to see where he was headed, and saw a tall, elegant lady just walking into the room. It was Ms. Hernandez, coming in with Maria and Jose'.

Sally was standing by him, following his eyes. When she saw Brighton approach Ms. Hernandez and greet her, she glanced over at David, a questioning look in her eyes.

"I think we may have a connection going on there," said David.

"Really?"

Sally turned and smiled at him.

"Well, good for him."

David looked at her.

"Sally. Why didn't you tell me that you had worked with Dr. Brighton?"

"You didn't ask," she said, the familiar sparkle in her eyes.

She sat down by Elsa. "Elsa, tell me about that heart run to Oklahoma," she said.

David just shook his head, thinking back. He listened as Elsa described the night. He could still remember the smell of Elsa's perfume. And the perfect blue of her eyes.

I knew in my heart she was the one, David thought.

At that exact moment, almost in unison with his thought, he heard Elsa say, "I knew in my heart he was the one."

David just looked at her, but his heart swelled with love.

Sally was looking at them both, her eyes still sparkling, and a smile on her face.

Suddenly, the M.C. tapped his mike, saying, "Okay, if everyone would take their seats, it's time to get started."

Brighton left Ms. Hernandez at her table and came back over

to theirs. After everyone was seated, the program got underway.

After they had eaten and the program was finished, and the waiters had taken away the dirty dishes, the band started to warm up. David and Elsa stood up to walk around. As they walked through the center of the room, David heard a voice say,

"Hey, Dr. Mac!"

He looked over and it was Martha Lake. She was there with her family, and he noticed Lisa Kelly was sitting with them.

"Hello, Martha," he said.

"Hey, Alan," he said, shaking Alan's hand.

Martha gave him a hug.

Kristi was sitting beside her mother. David noticed something on her cheek, and as he moved closer he saw it was face paint.

It was a little rainbow.

"Kristi, what's that on your face?"

He drew back a little.

"Do you have the measles?"

Kristi laughed. She was used to David kidding with her.

"No, Dr. Mac, it's a rainbow. They had face painting at the picnic and I got a rainbow. It's not the measles!"

She turned and tilted up her cheek so he could see it better. It was a perfect little rainbow, vivid red to deep violet, shimmering on her cheek. She smiled at him, her cheek dimpling through the colors.

David smiled back, then turned toward the others at the table.

"How are you, Lisa?"

Lisa stood and shook hands with him.

"Good, Dr. McAllister. Good to see you. How are you, Mrs. McAllister?"

"It's Elsa, please. I'm good." They shook hands.

"Dr. Mac, Ms. Elsa," said Martha. "I want you to meet someone."

She motioned to the other couple sitting at the table with them. The man and woman stood up.

"This is Tom and Leslie Raines."

Martha paused a moment.

"My donor's mom and dad."

David looked at them and his eyes started to tear up.

"Rachel's mom and dad?" David asked, reaching out to shake the man's hand. He started to shake the lady's hand, but reached out to hug her instead. He was almost crying now.

Martha and Elsa moved in to be part of the hug. Lisa came over as well.

"You remember her?" asked the girl's mother.

"Of course I do," said David.

They all just stood there quietly for a minute.

"Thank you," David said, reaching back over to pat the man's shoulder.

"You saved Martha's life that night."

"It's what Rachel wanted," said the father, and the mother nodded. "She saved several lives." Then the father shook his head, looking down.

"Thank you," David said, again.

He turned towards Martha, trying to smile.

"Will you save a dance for me?"

Martha brightened.

"I sure will," she said, smiling.

David and Elsa hugged everyone again and turned and walked away.

"That was hard," he said to Elsa quietly.

She just sighed and shook her head.

David rubbed his eyes.

How strong those people are to be here, he thought. *But maybe getting to know the Lakes will ease their pain. I hope so.* He looked up to see someone waving at them. It was Maria.

They walked over to her table. Jose and Ms. Hernandez were there, too.

"Hello, Dr. Mac," said Maria, jumping up to hug him.

Jose stood to shake his hand. David bent and shook Ms. Hernandez's hand as well.

"It's good to see you here, Maria, Jose," he said, "And Ms. Hernandez, such an honor to have you here as well."

"Thank you, Dr. McAllister," said Maria's grandmother, nodding to him.

"Do you all know Elsa, my wife?"

"We do," said Maria.

They smiled at Elsa.

"Maria, you look wonderful," said David.

Maria was dressed in a beautiful green outfit with a short and sassy ruffled skirt. Her dark eyes were full of life and happiness. Her dark skin was healthy, and her white teeth flashed as she smiled back at him.

"The band is about to start, Dr. Mac," she said, tilting her head and cutting her eyes coquettishly at him. "And you have to dance a dance with me."

"What? Me dance? I don't know about that," said David, shaking his head.

"Don't give me that!" Maria said.

"Miss Kim said that you and Ms. Elsa were great dancers. We will do the Rumba. It's my favorite dance!"

Then she glanced at Elsa, adding, "If it's okay with you, Ms. Elsa."

Elsa nodded, smiling at her.

"Okay, Maria." David smiled. "If they play a rumba I will dance with you."

"You promise?"

"I promise," he said, smiling at her.

They turned to go back to their table, smiling at familiar faces and shaking hands as they went. Just before they got back to the table, David noticed Sally, Carver, and Kim standing to the side talking to Mr. Chen. He and Elsa walked over to them. Mr. Chen smiled and bowed slightly, again.

David bowed as well.

"Mr. Chen," he said. "I wanted to thank you for helping with Dominic. I don't know what you and Sally did in that room that day, but it seems to have worked."

Sally smiled. Mr. Chen looked up at him and smiled as well.

"Ahh, Dr. McAllister, you see, chi is here." He placed his hand just below the center of his chest. Then he moved his hand up slightly.

"Doctor, you know life comes from heart, here, close to center. Chi is also in heart."

David nodded.

"Perhaps," said Chen. "Perhaps, when I am up here to see my son we can talk some more. I will teach you tai chi."

David nodded again, glancing at Sally. "I would be honored."

Carver, who had been listening, spoke up.

"I, too, would like to learn tai chi."

"Good," said Chen, nodding once. "I will teach you, also."

Just then, the band started to play. Most people continued to talk, over the music.

Elsa grabbed David by the hand.

"Let's get this party started," she said, heading to the dance floor.

The first dance was a swing, and it wasn't long before there were several couples on the floor, including Carver and Kim. The second song was a little faster, and then the third was a slow dance. David held Elsa close. His heart was beating fast from the fast dancing, and he enjoyed holding Elsa close and letting things slow down. She smiled up at him.

"I love you," he whispered in her ear.

When the dance ended, they headed over to the table to sit down for a minute. The band played a couple of songs while they sat, catching their breath and watching the other dancers. Several people came over and spoke.

Then, the band started to play a Jimmy Buffet tune.

"There's your rumba," said Elsa, with a smile.

David smiled back, nodding.

"I'll be back in a minute," he said. He stood and walked over to Maria's table.

"May I have this dance?" he said to her, holding out his hand.

Maria grinned. "Yes."

She stood and he took her hand in his.

They headed out to the floor, stopping close to the middle. David stood straight, and Maria came to him, lifting her right hand to meet his left. David placed his right hand under her left arm and behind her shoulder, just a little pressure on her scapula. She stood straight, and they waited for the beat to come around.

David said, "Here we go!"

They started dancing. The song was a little fast, and they whirled around in place.

Everything David led, Maria could follow. It was as if they had danced many times before. He was surprised at Maria's ability, and smiled down at her.

"You dance very well," he complimented.

"You lead very well, Dr. Mac," she said, smiling back, the smile taking over her eyes.

David just laughed, looking down at her, thinking how beautiful she was, and how vivacious. Her short skirt swirled as she turned, and he noticed more than one set of eyes in the room watching her. Maria's long, dark hair swirled as well, and she was full of life. David remembered how she had looked just a few short months ago, and then remembered how her old, gray, fat heart had hardly moved when it beat. He could feel joy in his own heart that this beautiful girl was now dancing with him. The joy filled him. She was not even winded by the dance. He twirled her around again, smiling. She was laughing as they whirled around the floor.

When the song was over, and they started to walk off the dance floor, Maria looked up at him.

"Thank you, Dr. Mac," she said, her eyes full of joy.

"Thank you, Maria."

David smiled down at her, holding her under his arm as they walked.

At that moment, the band leader bent over to his mike and said, "Now if anybody likes to salsa, come on out."

Maria stopped him.

"Do you know how to salsa?"

"I don't think so," said David.

"Let's see what it's like," said Maria, cutting her eyes sideways again, smiling at him.

The band started, and they watched as other couples started to dance.

"It looks easy," said Maria.

She grabbed his left hand and they got into dance position again.

"You go forward and I go back, then I go forward and you go back," she said.

"One and two, three and four. We can do it."

David smiled, standing still and holding her. Then he felt her tug him forward with the beat.

"Here we go," she said, as they started to dance. "I know how to do this!"

The boy's heart was happy. It had done this before. It could even feel the music, the strong steady pulse. It could feel the girl's happiness. It could also sense the joy in the other heart that was close. It swelled with joy, matching the beat of the music.

31

My Heart Will Go On

WHEN MARTHA LAKE got home that night after the dance, she was very tired. She had enjoyed the evening out and she had been able to dance a few dances with Alan. She had also danced with Dr. McAllister, and he had even danced one with Kristi. She and Alan had enjoyed spending the evening with the Raines. But the combination of the physical exertion and the emotional energy required from being with her heart donor's family had exhausted her.

After they got home she had got ready for bed and then went to the kitchen to fix herself something to eat. After starting some water heating on the stove she looked in the cabinet. For some reason, lately she had been craving oatmeal. There were several packets, so she took one and opened it into a small bowl. She added a little milk and then some hot water. Next she took out a jar of honey. She liked honey on her oatmeal, but this kind was special. She had gotten it when they were down in Florida. It was called Tupelo honey. It was her favorite. She held the jar up to the light, seeing that there was still some in the bottom. Good. Tomorrow she would have to find a way to get some more. She sat at the kitchen table and ate her oatmeal, savoring the rich sweetness of the honey.

Alan had something to do before he went to sleep, so after

eating and brushing her teeth she lay down by herself.

Martha was still somewhat wound up from the night, and it was hard for her to settle down. It took a while, but the oatmeal and warm milk helped and she slowly began to relax.

She deliberately stilled her body and mind, concentrating on the quietness, the quietness of their room.

Listening in the stillness, she could hear the creaking of the house and the wind rustle in the branches outside. She nestled deeper under the covers, closing her eyes and trying to relax. It was warm and quiet in their bed. Quiet.

In the silence, she became aware of her heartbeat. She could hear it clearly. It was a gentle pounding in her ears. She listened to it a minute.

Her heart seemed faster than usual. Well, this was to be expected, since she was wound up from such a busy day.

She concentrated on the sound, her head down slightly on the pillow. She could clearly hear the *bomp bomp... bomp bomp*. Over and over, strong and steady, never ceasing, it was constant and sure.

She moved her hand to her chest and felt for the beat.

It took her a minute, but she found it, just inside her left breast. She could also feel the edge of the scar on her chest, the scar from her transplant.

Martha counted the beats, watching the seconds flash on the digital clock sitting on the bedside table. First she tried to count the beats and the flashing dots on the clock, but then gave up and just watched until the minute clicked over. She started counting beats again, a full minute this time.

Eighty-two beats before the minute went over again. She remembered Dr. Mac saying that the average was seventy to eighty.

It was as if her heart was talking to her. She puzzled over this for a moment, her mind attuned to her heart.

It was a soothing sound. As if it were saying, "All is well."

The steadiness calmed her. As she listened, her heart rate started to slow perceptibly and she slowed her breathing to keep pace. She kept breathing deep and even breaths, willing herself to relax. She glanced over at the clock, its beats now almost mirroring her heart.

Closing her eyes, she turned and curled into a fetal position, snuggling into the soft mattress and cozy covers of their bed. Gradually, her breathing became deep and regular on its own, and her mind and body calm, serene. But the beat of her heart continued in her ears, still just as strong, but now slower, peaceful.

As she drifted off to sleep, she smiled, comforted by the sound, knowing it would continue. It would always be with her.

She slept the sleep of the innocent, and her dreams were filled with dancing, singing, and rainbows.

Information on organ and tissue donation

Organdonor.gov has information about organ donation as well as links to donation agencies for each state.

Donatelife.net also has information and links.
Individuals can sign up to be a donor by state on these websites.

Many states also allow people to specify 'donor' on the driver's license.

While most states consider a donor designation on a license, signing up on a state site or signing a donor card to be a legal consent, it is also important for families to discuss donation.

Please consider being an organ donor – this is truly a gift of life.

ACKNOWLEDGMENTS

First and foremost, thanks to my wife Deborah for her unfailing love, support, patience, advice, and guidance in this endeavor. Thanks as well to my family for their support, particularly my children Heather, April and Tim. Thanks especially to April for her insight and help during the editing process. Thanks also to the many friends and colleagues who encouraged and supported me in this process, particularly the readers of the early manuscript: Jeanette Nation, Becky Turnham, Nancy Hein, Sandy Lumbatis, and Wilma Van De Perre. I also greatly appreciate John Koehler for giving this book a chance, and Joe Coccaro for his invaluable help in the editing process. Thanks to my colleagues in donation and transplantation for their support, particularly the staff of the Alabama Organ Center. And thanks to Ruby A. Helms, my mother, who passed away last year. A writer and educator herself, she taught me about connections.

CPSIA information can be obtained at www.ICGtesting.com
Printed in the USA
BVOW01s0841080414

350058BV00002B/2/P